SMITTEN WITH THE BEST MAN

PIPER RAYNE

The perfect man for me is a charming, sexy, hot as hell lawyer who knows how to negotiate his way into my panties.
#Pfftwhatever

Been there.
Done that.
Burned the T-shirt.

I didn't swear off all men after my divorce, but I sure as hell swore off anyone remotely like my ex. On the top of that list? Attorneys. Everyone knows they can't be trusted.

Now that I've moved back into my childhood home in Chicago, my focus is my daughter, my mom and me. I haven't given up on finding my happily-ever-after, it's just on hold-indefinitely. Yup, life is in a real upswing.

Then I see Reed Warner again, and I'm reminded of all my mistakes. I push him away, but somehow he weasels his way into every part of my life, not willing to take no for an answer.

In spite of my better judgment I can't stop thinking about the way his designer suits fit his muscular frame, or the way his blue eyes seem to eat me up with every glance.

You know when you're on a diet and even hummus seems

irresistible? Reed is like the equivalent of chocolate éclair and my willpower is fading fast.

The problem? Not only is he a lawyer…
He was the best man at my wedding.

CHICAGO LAW. BOOK ONE

SMITTEN WITH THE BEST MAN

Chapter One

My hand slams down on my alarm, but instead of shutting the bloody thing off, the screaming banshee slides off my nightstand and drops to the floor. I peek out one eye and the immediate sight of the clutter of clothing and boxes in the makeshift bedroom makes me want to squeeze it shut again. The piercing sound of my alarm still rattles inside my head as its cacophony continues from the floor. My palm continually slaps the wood, hoping to make contact with the cord so that I can yank the damn thing up and shut it off.

"Mom?" my daughter Jade calls out to me.

I swivel my head in the direction of her voice and there she stands in her poop emoji pajamas with my alarm poised in her hands like she's offering me a gift.

"Turn it off," I groan and bring the pillow over my head.

Her small feet pad along the hardwood floors, squeaking right at the edge of my bed. The pillow gets plucked from my grasp, and seconds later the overhead light flickers on, blinding me temporarily.

"You're going to be late." My mom's voice adds to the mix from down the hall.

I dream of being woken up by some suave foreign man who doesn't speak a lick of English, while he uses his soft, roaming hands and sprinkles kisses over my flesh to stir me into consciousness. Instead, I get my seven-year-old daughter and my mom to orchestrate my Monday morning trip to Crazyville.

Jade turns off the alarm and sets it down on the nightstand. "It's seven," she says in a completely unalarmed tone.

"What?" I sit up, chip crumbs falling to the rumpled sheets.

"Eating in bed again?" She giggles, and I snatch her up by her waist pulling her onto the bed with me, using my fingers as an instrument to torture her. Torture by tickle.

"Mom, no!" She laughs and squirms.

"It's only six-fifteen."

She wiggles enough to slide away and I release her because I'm later than I usually am, but it's Monday and since I made a deal with Jade that every Sunday is our day, it meant a late night of studying after she went to bed.

"I'll turn on the shower." She walks out of the room and straight into the small bathroom of our three-bedroom bungalow—the house I grew up in. Jade now sleeps in my old bedroom, while I'm shacked up in my mom's old sewing room. She doesn't sew much these days, anyway.

"Thanks, and then—"

"I know. Brush my teeth, get dressed, and comb my hair."

I smile at my independent daughter even though it causes a familiar tug on my heart. She should have had the luxury of having a mom who picks out her clothes and does fancy hairstyles with ribbon and curls before school. A mom who wakes *her* up with the smell of bacon and pancakes and freshly squeezed orange juice. A dad who pulls her mom in close to say goodbye and promises to be at her soccer practice as he kisses the top of her head.

Instead, she's got a dad who didn't blink when I told him we were moving back to Chicago and leaving him in Los Angeles. A mom who gave up her own education only to pursue her degree later in life while she's working a full-time job. A mom who moved her halfway across the country, leaving behind the beach and sunny weather for concrete and dreary rain-filled days.

To her credit, my tough girl never gave me a guilt trip when I sat her down and explained that Grandma needed us. She packed her boxes and hid the tears. I guess people are right when they say she's the spitting image of me.

I get up from the bed, staring at my phone to make sure my new boss, Hannah, hasn't sent me anything urgent. It's not something she expects me to do. But it's been a hard transition from my last boss, Jagger Kale, who expected an answer to any question whenever he asked it. Old habits die hard.

Setting it down, I grab my robe and head out of the cocoon of soft sheets, warm blankets, and quiet space to start my week.

Forty-five minutes later, my heels click on my mom's linoleum kitchen floor.

My to-go cup of coffee is placed next to my purse and my computer bag, while Jade is shoveling Lucky Charms into her mouth, leaving her banana untouched. My mom is still in her pajamas reading the paper mindlessly nodding and agreeing with Jade on the latest second-grade drama at her new school.

"Then Brian told Peter that he liked Valerie and—"

"Whoa," I stop her, sliding my arms into my jacket. "Like? You're talking about friendship, right?"

Jade rolls her eyes and I glance over my shoulder because surely, she's not rolling her eyes at me.

"Mom," she sighs.

My mom curls the corner of the newspaper to eye me over her reading glasses.

"You shouldn't be liking any boys."

"I don't." Jade notices me getting ready, stands, takes her bowl to the sink and grabs her jacket.

I hold out her backpack for her and she slides her arms through it.

"Good because—"

"Boys only detour you from obtaining your dreams. Make your own path for yourself before you allow others to walk beside you," she says in a deadpan voice beyond her years.

"Sorry." I bend down and kiss her cheek. "It's the truth though," I whisper.

Again, the paper peels back, my mom's face showing her displeasure over what I'm teaching her granddaughter.

Jade wraps her arms around my mom's neck, pressing her lips to her cheek. "Love you, Grandma."

My mom pats her arm. "Love you, bug, I'll be outside at school's end." Then she lowers her voice and whispers. I could probably dictate her secret conversation with Jade. She's telling her to open her heart and see the possibilities this wonderful life has to offer.

It's a crock of shit that I used to believe, and it landed me right where I am.

"Thanks, Mom. You sure you're good to meet Jade after school because—"

"I'm good." Her eyes sternly warn me to let the topic go.

My mom might be a softy when it comes to love, but she doesn't allow others to question her ability.

Following Jade's lead, I bend down and kiss my mom's cheek. "Love you. Call me if you need me."

"Uh-huh." She continues to read the paper. "Have a good day."

We grab our stuff and head out the door, so I can walk Jade the three blocks to school. We don't finish walking one block before Jade asks a question that has me wanting to come to an abrupt stop if I weren't already so late.

"What kind of dad is Daddy?"

"Kind?"

Jade jumps from sidewalk square to sidewalk square. "Yeah, like he used to be Weekend Dad because I only saw him on the weekend."

"Where did you hear that expression?" Damn Google. My seven-year-old daughter thinks she's seventeen.

She shakes her head adamantly. "Nowhere."

I shoot her a look with my chin down, eyes wide. Basically, the stern mother look.

"Promise." She holds out her pinky. "Swear."

I pinky swear with her. Knowing my daughter would have crumpled like a cheap suit if she was lying.

"Your dad is just your dad. He'll come and visit, maybe we'll go back and visit him from time-to-time. He might not be able to come every weekend, but that's what's so great about technology."

I say this even though the dipshit has only Skyped with her four times in the past two months. Whatever, I'm being the bigger person here.

"Yeah, but at school, Valerie says her dad is the Date Night Dad. Every Wednesday he picks her up from school and they go to dinner and a movie. He always has a present for her."

"That's nice." My heart clenches over the fact that she doesn't, and likely never will, have that type of relationship with her father.

She says nothing.

I knew this move would be hard on her. Miles away from a dad who never really put her first to begin with, his eye set on making partner at his firm and nothing else.

"Maybe my dad is a Sometime Dad?"

The line of cars on the road ready to drop off their children signals we're nearing the school. The giggles of children mix with the hollering of mom's I love yous. Teachers are ushering kids in through the front doors when we approach, but I stop Jade and bend down to her level.

"Jade," I say, squeezing her shoulder. "Your daddy misses you and I know sometimes he works too much to call, but always know, he's thinking of you. You're his little girl."

She nods. "I get it. He wants to be successful and make a lot of money because Nana and Papa didn't have a lot."

I ignore the spark of anger inside me. Pete needs to watch what he tells her. Money is not everything in life. No one gives a shit what your bank account balance is when you die.

"He just wants to make sure you have everything you want." I tuck a strand of her brown hair behind her ear.

I don't add in that he also wants a new sports car for himself, the condo on the beach, and all the other material things that attract the women whose biggest goal is to score a rich husband.

"He said he sent me a present." Her eyes light up and I really hope she receives it this time around.

"See, he's always thinking of you." I open my arms and she rushes in squeezing my neck.

"Love you, bug," I whisper in her ear.

"Love you, Mommy."

We part ways and she skips ahead of me. "So, Sometime Daddy then?" she asks.

Should've known I couldn't deter her from defining her daddy's role in her life. She's persistent.

"I'd prefer just Daddy, but..."

"Yeah, I'll tell the kids I have a Sometime Daddy."

We reach the steps of St. Patrick Catholic School, the buzz of early morning in full force. Two familiar moms stand at the bottom of the staircase sipping their coffees and having their usual morning chat about every other parent's incompetence in the school.

"Victoria," Darcie coos, pushing her long blonde hair over her shoulder. "Jade," she says my daughter's name like she's been bouncing on the balls of her feet all morning to see her.

"Darcie. Georgia." I bend down and tighten Jade's ponytail, smoothing out the wispy unruly hairs. "Have a great day. Grandma will be here after school."

"Okay. Love you, Mommy." She gives me a looser hug than she did moments ago and before I'm standing upright again, she's with a red-haired girl talking nonstop as the two venture up the stairs.

"Have a great day, ladies." I turn to leave and head to the train station.

"Oh, Vikki," Darcie says. I knew it would be asking too much to sneak away.

I smack on my court smile. The smile I had permanently fixed on my face when my ex and I were going through the divorce. The Stepford creepy-wife one that says I'm content and even-keeled, when really, it's like World War Z in my head.

"Victoria," I clarify for the five-hundredth time since we moved here.

"As you know, the carnival is a month away and since you missed the parent meeting, we signed you up to run an event."

I stare blankly at her. Mostly because I will lose my shit and that will not help Jade with this transition. We need St. Pats. It's the closest school to my house and it's a good one.

"What event would that be?" I ask with the patience I can only assume I honed well while I was working for my old boss, Jagger Kale.

When exactly is this carnival? I don't even know if I'm available. And a carnival? Seriously, get a new idea. It's not the eighties.

"Your choice," queen bee says. "Just make sure there's no food involved. All food has to be inspected before coming in. We don't want anything that could endanger the children. That should be easy for you, right?"

Again, I stare blankly at her, trying to compose myself before I grab her Starbucks cup and squeeze it until it soaks her ridiculous khaki belted jacket.

Hello, if I was a stay-at-home-mom and had all this time on my hands, I'd be sporting the 'I'm on my way to the gym outfit' when in reality I'm going home to lay on my couch And the only reason I'd be wearing yoga pants is because they won't impede the pound of chocolate I'm going to consume. Ladies shouldn't be ashamed of the bonbon stereotype. Everyone knows a mom's real work is from six to eight in the morning and three to nine at night.

"Great, I'll arrange something," I say with a smile and a nod, then turn to step away before I tell her what I really think of her signing me up for something without my consent.

Like a flash of lightning in the sky, the sight of the smiling man leading a little boy up toward the school stuns me. I stop and stare, my mind blank.

I don't think about the Sometime Daddy dilemma, or getting to work on time, or the carnival event I have to plan. Instead, I try to figure out how many years it's been since I last saw Reed Warner.

Chapter Two

"Who is that?" Georgia whispers to Darcie behind me.

I turn and face them again. I'm surprised because I figured these two knew everyone at this school.

They already knew my name and Jade's on our first day. *Scary as shit, let me tell you.*

"I have no idea, but I need to find out." She sips her drink.

If I were among friends, I'd have made some smart-ass joke about their teenage behavior, but I'm just as enamored by this man.

His blue suit jacket is stretched across his broad shoulders with the front open, so I can see his taut waist with a crisp white linen shirt tucked in and a polka dot tie laying around his neck undone. The tips of his dark strands look damp and to top it off, a scruffy beard adorns his chiseled jawline. He's not completely put together, as though he was running late and had to rush out the door.

He stops at the top of the stairs, says something to Principal Weddle that makes him laugh, gives the boy a hug, and then a fist bump. The boy smiles from ear to ear and heads inside.

Weekend Dad.

"Is he Henry's dad?" Darcie poises it more like a question. "I thought..."

She's cut short when he approaches us. I'm a good five steps away, but his blue-eyed gaze meets mine first before moving to Darcie and Georgia.

"Hi, I'm Reed. Can one of you lovely ladies let me know what time school is finished?"

Again, his intense gaze finds me. Does he remember me, too?

"Um." I swallow down the extra coating of saliva in my mouth.

"Three-o-five," Darcie says, tilting her head as though she's trying to figure him out. "Tell me—"

"Thanks a lot. See you, ladies." He tips his head to them. "Victoria, nice to see you again. I'm late, but we should catch up." He doesn't wait for a reply and climbs back into the Uber waiting by the curb.

Funny, but no staff member is screaming at him to get out of the way.

"Did he really just leave when I was mid-sentence?" Darcie asks Georgia.

"That he did," she confirms, hiding a smirk I bet is begging to show itself.

I step away, not bothering to say good-bye because well, my thoughts are elsewhere.

It all comes back to me in a cyclone of competing thoughts. *Reed Warner.* The best man at my wedding. Jesus, who put him in a *Weird Science* machine and popped out Chicago's most beautiful man?

"He must be the dad. One of those weekend dads."

Darcie's phrase makes me stop for a second at the edge of the sidewalk.

Reed is a dad? To a kid Jade's age? Then again, I don't think he and Pete kept in touch for long after we moved to Los Angeles. A million scenarios bounce around in my head. Is the boy a result of a one-night stand? Is he married? Does he split custody with the boy's mother?

The questions keep coming the entire train ride into downtown. I try not to think about him, but he's on my mind more than the strawberry rhubarb pie I passed over at the grocery store yesterday. And just like the pie, indulging might feel good in the moment, but afterward, I'd only feel regret.

OPENING the glass door to my newest place of employment, I rush over to the ringing phone, removing my jacket as I sit down and answer it at the same time.

"Good morning, thank you for calling the RISE Foundation, this is Victoria, how can I help you?"

"For starters, you can get your ass on a plane back to Los Angeles."

Jagger Kale—my old boss.

I smile. "You got me this job," I say, leaning back in my chair and glancing at the clock. "Honeymoon over already?"

"First off, I got you that job because I'm awesome. Second, how do you know I didn't just nail Quinn and now she's passed out next to me in post-cunnilingus bliss?"

I don't encourage his crass mouth with a laugh, even if I'm smiling.

"Thank you again," I say with genuine gratitude.

For Jagger to hook me up with Hannah when I was

leaving his company in Los Angeles shows what a good guy he is. Yes, he can be arrogant and egotistical and probably too self-involved, but there's just something about him that makes it difficult not to like him anyway.

"How's the new assistant?" I ask.

"He sucks. He gives me attitude."

"I gave you attitude."

"Not the same thing."

I miss him, too, though I'd never admit it. We had a good thing going in Los Angeles. Jagger was my first boss post-divorce and I teetered on that line where he had good reason to fire me more than once at the beginning. I was cynical and hated all men. Until he got his shit together and reunited with Quinn, he was the epitome of everything I hated. I knew he'd prove the stereotype wrong.

"I'm just staring out at the ocean from my deck. How's Chicago? I sent you a stock of Vitamin D." He chuckles.

There's some noise behind him and his hand muffles the receiver. I swear there are kissing noises.

"Victoria," he says matter of factly.

"Leave the woman alone. Hi, Victoria." Quinn's singsong voice tells me she's living her real-life fairy tale.

"Hey, Quinn."

"Hold up, I'm putting you on speaker," Jagger says.

A second later, the sound of crashing waves is the backdrop to our conversation. I miss the ocean. The warm weather, sand between my toes and the sun made me a happier version of myself.

"How is Jade doing?" Quinn asks. "Adjusting?"

Plates and cups clatter in the background and I'm guessing they're putting out breakfast on the deck.

"She is." I turn on my computer because Hannah could come through the door at any moment. "So, you're not sick of your new husband yet?" I ask in jest.

Quinn giggles and then I hear her squeal followed by kissing noises once again.

Stab me in the heart, why don't you? Between school and work and Jade and my mom, the most tongue action I've gotten lately is from my mom's cat, Moe.

"Well, I hate to interrupt, oh that's right, you called me."

"Sorry," Quinn says with a soft chuckle. "We're still in that can't keep our hands off each other phase."

"No apologies necessary. I'll just go back to daydreaming about your latest hero and wishing someone like him enters my life."

She laughs. "You liked Van, huh?"

Quinn's a romance novelist and I'm lucky enough to get all her books pre-release.

"How could anyone not?" My stomach clenches remembering the hot moment when he cornered her against the wall, the urgent kisses and sultry lovemaking.

"Is he based on me, too?" Jagger asks.

I laugh.

"No, babe," Quinn says.

"You're imagining what other guys would do to you?"

Quinn laughs now. "I'm not the heroine. It's fiction, babe. You know…*not* real."

"Even so, tell me what Van does, I bet I rock your world tenfold," Jagger says with his usual cocky arrogance.

"Good luck with that." I type in my password on the computer and click open my email.

"Right here on this table." Jagger's voice is faint like he's walked away from the phone, signaling my cue to hang up.

"Okay you two, thanks for calling to check up on me. Gotta go. Talk soon."

I press end as Quinn tries to say goodbye and based on

her giggling I'm guessing that Jagger's probably undressing her.

The silence of the office still feels strange to me having gone from a company of hundreds to an office with three to five people in it, depending on the day.

Jagger's friend, Hannah Crowley, a multi-millionaire in her own right, decided to start a foundation to empower young girls. Knowing I had to relocate due to my mom's declining health, Jagger scored me an office assistant position with her charity. It is less responsibility than I'm used to having, but I work daily with two amazing women and at this point in my life I couldn't ask for a better place to be.

I'm responding to a few emails when the glass door swings open and the louder of my two co-workers rushes over and collapses in the chair across from me.

"Holy hell, did you hear what happened last night?" Chelsea asks.

Chapter Three

$\mathcal{C}$helsea is gorgeous. A few years younger than me with shoulder-length blonde hair that's straight as pin one day, curly the next and who has the fashion sense of a New York City high end designer. Her nails are always painted, her makeup flawless, and her clothes wrinkle-free.

Kind of like me pre-Jade.

I'm not complaining. I'll take my stained Target clothes, smeared makeup self any day as long as Jade's there when I get home.

"Happened last night to whom?" I remove my hands from the keyboard and give her my full attention.

She throws her bag on the other chair and crosses her legs. "Hannah. And her son of a bitch ex."

"What?" I lean closer, my elbows propped up, a pen between my hands.

"That slimy fucker slid in under Hannah's nose at the venue we were going to have the gala at and stole our spot for some hospital fundraiser. She called me last night and said we have to start our search all over."

"Now we have nowhere to hold the gala?" I shake my head.

"I looked up a bunch of places and I'm thinking we head north of the city." Chelsea's leg bounces up and down while she speaks.

"Will people travel that far?"

I'm not sure if it's Hannah's own money that's keeping RISE afloat right now, but she's putting together a huge black-tie event with a silent auction to be held at the end of summer to raise money for the various smaller charities that our foundation supports. We had the venue secured, or so we thought.

"I think so. Half of them live on the north shore anyway. That's where the money's at."

I nod, she's right. Chelsea and I both come from the city, but Hannah, she grew up in the north burbs until she relocated downtown.

"It's a little farther north, but it's right on the lake and there's a hotel. I called this morning and we may have to change the date, but they have some availability." Chelsea stands and grabs her bag.

"Where do you find the time?" I follow her, turning on the copier and heading to our small kitchen area to start the coffee. We all seem to support the economy and grab our own cups on the way in, but we have guests in the office on occasion.

"Let's see. I'm not going to school, I don't have a seven-year-old or a mother who needs help." She raises her eyebrows and I laugh.

"Be jealous." I spin the opposite way into the kitchen as Chelsea goes to her office. "Be very jealous," I call out.

"I did have a date though," she announces, and I leave the coffee for later, exiting the kitchen and making my way over to Chelsea's office. Hannah didn't mention anyone coming in first thing today anyway.

"A date?"

Chelsea's dating is much like someone put her in a reality show with the most unwanted men in America and made it her quest to find something good about them. Spoiler alert—she never does.

"He took me to a poetry reading."

I rest my shoulder on the doorframe. She moves around through her office, a woman on a mission, plugging her laptop in, setting out her notepads. The woman is meticulous.

"Sounds romantic."

"It was open mic night." Her tone is dry as she boots up her computer.

"Fun."

I'm guessing from her unenthused blank stare it wasn't.

"He recited a poem."

"About you?" I smile.

"Yeah, Vic, in the hour he knew me he wrote me a poem." She rolls her eyes.

"It could happen and that would mean something."

"Don't tell me you believe in signs?" She takes a seat at her desk. "I thought we were in this whole 'single forever' thing together?"

Chelsea's divorced, too. I don't know much as far as who, what, when or why, but divorce is divorce. The stigma hasn't faded. People still give you that look like your dog got run over when you tell them you've been divorced. The assumptions of cheating spouses, addiction problems, money problems, secrets and lies. It's like someone opened the door to your soul and peers in to see all the ugliness you tried to hide. Her one saving grace is that she never had kids with the bastard.

"You're telling me he wouldn't have wooed you if he'd written a poem about how beautiful you were on a whim?" I cross my arms in front of me and give her a disbelieving look.

"No. However, I probably would've nailed him in the taxi on the ride home, but we wouldn't be picking out china patterns." She shakes her head.

I thought I was cynical until I met Chelsea. But she seems to work at it like it's part of her job description.

"Still, he's creative. That's a good sign. Most bad boys aren't creative."

"He cried on stage." She looks at me over drawn brows. "He read a poem he wrote about his breakup with another girl."

"You're kidding, right?"

I try to stop myself, but I laugh anyway. This is Chelsea's life. Someone could write a book about it, I swear. Maybe I should introduce her to Quinn.

"Wish I was. Another dud and I couldn't even kiss him goodnight. I mean...rule number one is don't talk about your ex on a first date and this guy goes and cries over her while reading a poem he wrote for her."

"Ouch." I cringe.

"Yeah, smack me with a Band-Aid on my bruised ego. I'm taking a break from men." She throws both of her hands up in front of her.

I roll my eyes. "Uh-huh."

"Watch me. Bye, bye. It was a shame though, he had that cool hipster vibe going on."

Her attention shifts to her computer as she types in her password.

"Hipster?"

She laughs and points at me. "Don't even say it. I told myself I'd try all flavors of men."

I raise my hands in a placating gesture. "Hey, I'm not laughing. I can't even remember the last time I had any flavor at all."

Then we both laugh. Tears leak from the side of my eyes and Chelsea sounds like she's hyperventilating she's laughing so hard. "He had dark-rimmed glasses and a beanie and dressed like he grabbed his clothes off his bedroom floor."

The door opens, and Hannah stops in her tracks, staring over at me bent over and clutching my stomach.

"You started the Monday morning divorcee dating recap without me?" she whines, tossing her bag on the chair in front of my desk, her hands cupping her coffee as she hurries over to Chelsea's office.

I grin inside. She's *so* different than Jagger. He'd be barking orders at me before he even finished passing by my desk.

She squeezes by me, plopping down, well, Hannah doesn't plop anywhere. She slides into the chair with elegance and grace. Her tight dress and contrasting high heels will probably be the biggest trend next month. She's one of those women who oozes class and is always a step ahead on fashion.

"Give it to me. I need a laugh," she says and takes a sip.

"Chels went on a date this weekend," I say, and Hannah's smile tips up from ear to ear.

I told you, Chelsea's dates are like finding little chunks of gold in a sea of crap.

"YAY!" she raises one arm in a little cheer. "How bad was it?"

"Not too bad," I remark and the phone rings, so I run over to my desk, letting Chelsea fill Hannah in on the details.

"Good morning, thank you for calling the RISE Foundation, Victoria speaking, how can I help you?"

"Is Hannah in?" the man on the line asks.

"Can I ask who's speaking?"

"Mr. Bennett. She's expecting my call."

"Sure thing. Hold please." I place him on hold and head to Chelsea's office where Hannah is laughing, slapping the edge of Chelsea's desk.

"I'll pay you to go on another date with him. Maybe he'll write a poem about you."

Chelsea flips Hannah off.

"Hey, I'm your boss." Hannah can barely spit out the words without laughing.

"Then go and keep this place afloat. I'm obviously never going to meet a man who can handle me *and* take care of me." Chelsea types something on her keyboard.

"Hannah, there's a Mr. Bennett on hold for you," I say.

Her eyes light up and her head tips back. "Yes, I need to talk to him. Forward him to my desk." She stands and rounds the doorway of Chelsea's office.

"Hey, Vic," Chelsea stops me before I follow Hannah. She looks like she's seen a ghost. Her face suddenly pale and her features drawn. "Who's Mr. Bennett?"

I shrug.

"Tax attorney," Hannah hollers from down the hall.

"Oh, okay." Relief streaks across her face. "Never in a million years," she mumbles more to herself than me I think.

"Is everything okay?" I ask.

"Peachy," she says, but I'm not sure I totally believe her.

"Maybe you need a guy like a tax attorney," I joke hoping to lighten her mood again.

"No, *you* need a man like that. Boring and responsible. I need a bad boy with a heart of gold."

"Pretty sure those two things are mutually exclusive, Chels."

"They're like unicorns. Rare."

"But magical." I smile brightly.

She crumples up a piece of paper and throws it at me. "Go."

I run the small distance to my desk and pick up my phone.

"I'm transferring you now, Mr. Bennett."

"Thank you."

I press the button and after I hear Hannah pick up, I stand and go over to shut her door.

"He had a sexy voice," I singsong, passing by Chelsea's office on the way to take another stab at making the coffee.

"A sexy tax attorney would be like discovering a real-life unicorn." She follows me into the kitchen.

Monday mornings are laxer around here than I'm used to, but we all work hard and get done what needs doing.

I move about preparing the coffee pot and turning it on. "What happened to you experiencing all the flavors?"

She shrugs. "Let's talk about you. Maybe someone like this Mr. Bennett is the one for you. You said he had a nice voice." She crosses her arms, bringing her Starbucks cup to her lips.

"I'm anti-men, and honestly, who's going to sign up for this train ride?"

"I would," she says, her perfectly straight white teeth sparkling. "Seriously, though, you're hot and gorgeous. A total MILF. Jade is easy-peasy. Your ex is thousands of miles away."

"Sometimes there's more baggage hidden than exposed." I lean against the counter.

"I get wanting to take time to get settled, but don't underestimate yourself. Any man would be lucky to have you."

Chelsea is rarely serious, so I smile and accept her compliment.

"I saw the best man from my wedding this morning."

Her eyes widen. "Details." She pulls out a chair, sets her cup on the small table, and props her chin in her hands.

"At first I didn't recognize him. The last time I saw him was so long ago. He's grown up a lot."

She purses her lips. "Grown up how?"

"Chelsea," I sigh.

She giggles. "What are you hiding? A hidden affair? A secret kiss?"

"No."

"Come on. You're blushing, and you keep fidgeting. What am I missing?" She narrows her eyes. "Was he an a-hole? My ex's best man was a piece of shit."

I shrug. "No, Reed was always respectful and nice."

"Oh, gotcha. Booorrriinnnggg," she draws it out and I can't help but laugh.

"No, I mean he would joke around, was friendly, but I didn't know him that well. Him and Pete had been good friends since they were younger. Went to college and then to law school together. When Pete and I were with him, it was like Pete only wanted to talk to him. Reed was always the one asking me questions trying to include me while I was trying to grab a little bit of Pete's attention."

"Is Pete gay? Is that why you divorced?" she deadpans.

"No," I answer. "He's heterosexual, just not monogamous."

She nods. "Gotcha."

I turn around to toss out the coffee filter now that it's

done brewing, busying myself to try not to think about my old life and all the feelings that get churned up when I do.

After a moment I still and release a loud sigh. "I thought I was over it," I admit.

A chair slides along the floor behind me and I turn to face her. "You are."

"Then why do I want to hammer Reed with a million questions and ask if he ever saw Pete cheat on me? What did Pete say about it? About Jade?"

She wraps her arm around my shoulders. "That's just normal curiosity and if you ask me you're more worried about what he thinks about you."

My head snaps in her direction. "No, I'm not. The last thing I'd ever do is insert myself into someone's life who knows Pete. Especially the man who witnessed me make the worse decision of my entire life when I said I do."

"Hmm..."

"Hmm... nothing. It was awkward, he acknowledged me and then hopped in the car before I could say anything."

"Is he hot?"

I roll my eyes.

"I'll take that as a yes. Did you get that feeling?"

"What feeling?" I want to deny that I know what she's talking about, but I do, and I haven't experienced that in so long.

Her eyes flutter closed, and she inhales a deep breath. "Where you're floating, and it's like little fairies are hovering around his head."

I laugh. "More like my stomach flipping and flopping and my mouth salivating like a Doberman in front of a steak."

"Ugh, I'm jelly. I'm in a drought. Chicago has lost all

its attractive men." She walks over to the chair again and falls back into it.

"Come to school with me tomorrow and see for yourself," I joke.

"I might have to take you up on that."

"Okay, ladies, back to work." Hannah knocks on the doorframe. "Chelsea come tell me about this new place we can hold the gala."

Chelsea follows but turns around at the door. "Talk to him tomorrow."

"No."

She tilts her head. "I dare you." Her nose crinkles like she's testing to see if I'm in fourth grade and don't want to look like a loser.

I shake my head.

"Didn't think so. I think I need to see Jade soon." A conniving smile tilts her mouth and she heads down the hall before I can say anything.

I don't underestimate Chelsea. She's the swinging single version of Darcie from St. Pats.

Chapter Four

I didn't see Reed the rest of the week. He never showed up again during drop-off at St. Pats. So, it was probably like I figured—Weekend Dad.

I didn't dare ask my mom if she remembered him from my wedding and had seen him during pick-up. Jade never talked about the little boy, Henry. Darcie and Georgia never said another word about him.

Monday morning rolls around again and as usual, I'm a complete shit show on the walk to school. I haven't had time to get a coffee and Jade is eating a granola bar with a sippy cup full of milk. It was a bad morning for my mom, so we're on our own today.

"Grandma okay?" Jade asks, slowing her skipping.

My mom was diagnosed with multiple sclerosis and though her illness isn't to the point that she requires daily care and someone to live with her full time, it made me realize that there's no longer any reason for me to be so far away. I wanted to be here to help her when she needed it.

"She's just tired. We had a long day yesterday." My mom and I took Jade down to the lakefront for a picnic and to see the fountain. Twenty minutes into our journey my mom looked exhausted.

"Will she pick me up today?" Jade asked.

"Maybe. If not, I'll be here."

"Can I come to your office?" Her eyes light up. She's the only girl I know who's excited about the prospect of sitting in an office and coloring. Then again, Chelsea sneaks her candy and Hannah lets her play on her computer. They spoil her more than her dad. Sad but true.

"We'll see."

I'm at the edge of the tree-lined sidewalk when I spot the little boy climb out of an Uber car. A tingling sensation rushes through my body, as anticipation swirls with dread over seeing him again. My feelings are somewhat conflicted, to say the least.

The door on the other side of the car opens and my eyes refuse to look in any other direction. The dark strands of his hair are gelled in place this morning. His tie is knotted and laying over his light blue shirt, and his teeth hold a silver tie clip as he adjusts the tie and puts it in just the right spot before taking it from his mouth and clipping it on.

"Mommy." Jade pulls on my hand and I stumble forward until I catch my footing.

"Sorry," I mumble, my gaze still on him as he smiles and nods to the moms and dads coming back down the stairs after dropping off their children.

"Henry!" Jade screams next to me and Reed turns in our direction.

Shit. I'm frozen in place as if I was touched in a game of freeze tag.

The little boy waves and Jade waves back. Reed's lips tip up and if I hadn't sworn off men for the time being, I'd melt into a pile on the sidewalk.

"You know that boy?" I ask.

"Yeah, that's Henry. He's kind of quiet but really nice."

"Is that his dad?"

Her face scrunches. "Henry doesn't have a dad."

Boyfriend?

Jade skips and stops where we usually say our good-byes. "Please take me to your office after school." She clasps her hands together and her voice holds the whine she's used to get her way most of her life.

"If not today, then Friday, okay?"

She seems halfway appeased and wraps her arms around my middle. I kiss the top of her head. "Have a good day. Love you."

"Love you."

Then she's gone, trampling up the steps talking to anyone and everyone who will talk with her. I'm so fixated on her I don't notice Reed approaching me.

Soon the new rain smell of a spring morning in Chicago is replaced with his scent—musky and manly. All my other senses fall to the sidelines while my sense of smell hijacks all others. For a brief millisecond, the entire world blurs like the backdrop of Jade's school photos.

"Do you remember me?" Reed's deep voice draws me from my revelry and switches my auditory sense back on.

"You hung on my wall for years."

I place my hand in his outstretched one. His hand is soft but callused and swallows my smaller one. Something happens when our skin connects. Something I'd only ever read about in books. Something I didn't think was real.

But I can't deny the electric feeling that surges up my arm or the feeling of connection we share when our gazes lock.

I swallow hard, hoping I'm not too obvious, urging my brain to help my body get a clue.

This guy is the enemy.

He chuckles, but there's nothing egotistical or condescending about it. "Past tense?"

"Don't act like you don't know," I say wryly.

He looks chagrined and bows his head slightly. "I was sorry to hear about you and Pete."

He seems genuine and I suppose I shouldn't judge him yet, but it's hard given my history. He hasn't been a part of Pete's life as far as I know for quite a long time.

"So, Jade knows Henry?" he asks, moving off the subject of Pete and me.

How on Earth does he remember her name?

"It appears that way."

His smile grows. Did I just see a sparkle glimmer off his teeth?

"Henry has a hard time making friends. It says a lot about you that Jade is so welcoming to him."

"Me?" I rock back on my flats, trying not to make direct eye contact with him so I'm not sucked into the vortex again.

"Don't you think that in this day and age a child's behavior is a direct reflection of their parents? Maybe not when they're teenagers or older, but at this age?"

If anything, I'm snarky to people. Which he already knows.

"I don't know about all that. I'm not that pleasant to be around, but Jade makes friends with everyone. She has her father's charm. The difference is, she's sincere."

"I don't think that's true." He slides his hands into his pockets and tilts his head to the side, studying me.

"I tend to push people away. Keep only a handful close. I'm sure Pete must've complained about it."

Take the bait, Reed.

"I haven't talked to Pete in years...we had a bit of a

falling out." Before I can latch onto that he continues, "I remember you being pretty accommodating."

"Just what every woman wants to hear—that she's accommodating." My sarcastic tone only makes his smile wider and his eyes sparkle more. *Damn it.*

"Well, you'd have to be to deal with Pete." His gaze moves up and down my body until he locks eyes with me. "Let's catch up. Coffee?"

My mind is telling me to run. I'm not as accommodating as I used to be, Mr. Reed Warner.

"I have to get to work."

He chuckles and sucks in his bottom lip, biting the corner.

Okay, that was a direct hit to the center of my thighs.

"Tomorrow?" he asks.

"How about I'll call you?"

"You don't have my number." His eyebrows lift.

"I have a busy life."

He says nothing. Just stands there and waits. Totally infuriating.

"What?" I snip.

"Just waiting to see how many excuses you have at the ready." A shit-eating grin tips the corners of his lips up and I'm not sure whether I want to kiss it or smack it off his face.

"Don't you have a girl—"

"Excuse me!" Darcie's annoying voice interrupts me. "You." She points to Reed.

He turns in her direction and points his thumb at himself. "Is she really talking to me like that?"

"Yep. Have fun with her." I pat his arm, ignoring the bulge of his hard bicep and race down the sidewalk to catch my train.

Look at that, Darcie's going to do my dirty work

because she'll probably bother him so badly he won't come back to St. Pats' drop-off again. At least I can hope.

My phone rings just as I step onto the train. "Hello?"

"Victoria." Darcie barks my name like she's the head nun at a Catholic high school and I'm showing cleavage.

"How did you get this number?"

"I have my connections," she says, and I already know from her tone that she's about to ruin my day.

"What's up, Darcie?" I try to hide the irritation from my voice, but I'm not sure I'm entirely successful.

"I just found you a partner to help with the carnival event."

I blow out a breath and find a seat in the back of the train. "I don't need a partner."

"Well, he would only help out if it meant that he could work with you."

A million swear words set off like a round of fireworks in my head.

"You're kidding me?"

She laughs. "I wish I was." I detect a bite of jealousy in her tone. "If I was single…anyway, he requested you and we so rarely get fathers or father figures so in this case, I have to let him have what he wants. And for some reason, that's you."

I watch the city skyline getting closer out the window. "Who is he to Henry?" I ask.

She laughs and then I hear chatter behind her. I wish I was in front of her, so I could shake her shoulders and get her to focus on me.

"Oh, you'll find out."

"Henry's mom's boyfriend?" I ask.

"Nope. Ask for yourself. Gotta go. Oh, and I'm sending him your phone number right now."

Click.

The line dies. Mother fucking hell. Am I trapped in some *Mean Girls* reunion movie?

I haven't even tucked my phone back into my purse before it dings with a text. I'd ignore it if I wasn't worried that it could be my mom needing me.

Unknown: *Hey, it's Reed. The stunning guy you just reacquainted yourself with twenty minutes ago. How about a nightcap tonight to brainstorm ideas for the carnival?*

I add his contact information into my phone, so I don't mistakenly answer again.

Me: *Don't you have a son to watch at night?*
Reed: *Nope.*
Me: *I don't think your girlfriend would appreciate your invite. We can talk details over a morning coffee and that's it.*
Reed: *???*
Reed: *Not even dinner?*

I don't respond.

REED: *Lunch? Even business associates have lunch together.*

I shake my head and try to tamp down my temper.

Reed: *Fine. But mornings are hard for me.*

I'm being difficult for the sake of being difficult now. I can't very well ask Hannah to come in late to plan some stupid carnival booth anyway.

Me: *Saturday?*

Reed: *My place.*

The three dots appear but I respond before he can.

Me: *McDonald's on Peterson. The kids can play, and we'll talk. Noon.*
Reed: *You run a hard bargain and I make a lot of deals.*

What the hell does that mean?

Reed: *I take it that's the end of our conversation?*

I don't reply because there's nothing else to say.

Reed: *Message received. Have a great day, Victoria.*

I tuck my phone back into my purse with a giddy feeling inside. Damn it. I wish my stomach would get the message my brain is trying to send it.

Chapter Five

"So, you and the steak are meeting at Micky D's?" Chelsea asks. "Kinky. You going to make out in the tunnel slide?" Chelsea takes a bite of her turkey sandwich.

We're at a deli on the main floor of the building we work in. The Sandwich Place is our go-to for lunch if we're all in the office. It's owned by an Italian family who, get this, have one son who's a police officer, one who's a paramedic and one who's a firefighter. I haven't met them, but Chelsea knows them—the girl knows everyone, I swear—and if the rumors are true, I may have to fake faint in front of them for some mouth to mouth action.

"Steak?" Hannah asks, the spoon from her soup hovering right in front of her matte red lipsticked lips.

"Yeah. Vic is the Doberman drooling over the steak," Chelsea says as if that explains things.

"I'm missing something." Hannah takes a graceful sip of her soup.

I'd love to set a meatball grinder with extra sauce and

provolone in front of Hannah and see how delicately she can eat it.

"Let's take a poll," Chelsea says, setting her sandwich down. "Hannah, would you date the best man from your wedding?"

Hannah chokes, soup dribbling down her chin. I guess I don't need to do the meatball grinder experiment. I grab a napkin from the black holder in the middle of the table and pass it to her. She dabs at her chin, leaning over the table so she doesn't stain her dress. I'd be worried too. It probably costs more than Jade's tuition for the year at St. Pats.

"No."

"See." I shoot Chelsea an I-told-you-so look.

"Why not?" she asks.

"For one, the best man at my wedding was my brother."

"That's completely different. The steak isn't related to her or her ex." Chelsea leans back like she just gave the best closing argument, and everyone is having an ah-ha moment.

"Okay, who is the steak? Is this some riddle?" Hannah's confused, and she looks at me to clear things up.

"The steak is my ex's friend who stood up as his best man at our wedding. The steak is the guy who I ran into at Jade's school last week. The steak manipulated the system, so we'd have to work on a carnival booth together at the school fundraiser." I sip my soda once I'm done.

"The steak wants you to eat him." Hannah grins.

"Exactly," Chelsea says.

"No. The steak probably heard some bullshit from Pete about me in bed."

"So, I'm right. I totally pegged you for the kinky kind."

Both Hannah and my heads whip in Chelsea's direction. She holds up her hands, laughing. "Well?"

"No. I mean...just no," I sputter.

"We'll let you plead the fifth on that one." Hannah's perfectly manicured hand graces my leg with a pat. "But don't be ashamed. It's bullshit how men can brag or downright lie about their performance, but we're supposed to act like we're laying there with our legs open and have the ability to come with a soft whisper. I'm a screamer and I'm not ashamed." She smiles, and I can't tell if she's entirely serious or not.

"I'm a cowgirl. I ride," Chelsea adds.

"That doesn't surprise me." I take a bite of my sandwich.

God, this is good.

"Come on Vic, we all shared. Tell us something." Chelsea leans forward on the table and even Hannah's eyes are set on me.

I feel the flush heat my cheeks. Having Jade so young I forget it wasn't just my education I left behind when I married Pete. I left friends who cared more about going out Thursday through Saturday than waking a sleeping baby for her feeding. It's been a long time since I've had close girlfriends to confide in.

"I don't know." I shrug. The meat on my sandwich is looking really intriguing right now.

"Don't make her say anything she doesn't want to." Hannah picks up her spoon and goes back to her soup.

"I'm a biter." I rush the words out super fast like it will somehow make them less embarrassing.

"Hah!" Chelsea's hand smacks the table and a few people look over. "I knew it," she says in a quieter voice.

I roll my eyes.

"Nice. You have to be pretty damn good at what you're

doing to make me a biter." Hannah brings the spoon to her mouth and takes a small sip. "Few have been successful in that department."

Chelsea seems to be deep in thought for a second and I guarantee she's committed everyone's sexual preference to memory.

"Anyway, back to the steak." Hannah's gaze shoots my way.

"The steak will remain untouched." I sip my drink.

Chelsea scoffs. "Please, I guarantee you're gonna to have that meat in your mouth at some point."

I almost spit my drink all over the table I laugh so hard.

"Does the steak have a name?" Hannah asks after we've settled ourselves.

"Reed."

"Is he still close to your ex?" she asks in response.

"He says no. I haven't seen him since we moved out of Chicago to Los Angeles, so he's probably telling the truth."

"Then go for it. If anything, it might get to your ex." Hannah waggles her eyebrows and grins.

I never knew she could be so spiteful, but from what I gather, her divorce was really nasty.

She has a point though. Anything that would annoy Pete has its benefits.

"I have too much on my plate right now to worry about getting back at my ex. This will have to be platonic."

"Let me take Jade for a weekend. Have a weekend full of hot sex, leave your love bites on him, and get it out of your system." Chelsea finds her voice once again with advice I *won't* be taking.

"With how he's inserted himself in my life already, I'm thinking he might want to put a ring on it if I sleep with him."

The girls laugh, and we go back to our lunch. I'm

hoping the topic of Reed will be tossed into the garbage along with our trash.

We're almost finished eating when a gorgeous guy with olive skin, perfect dark scruff on his chiseled jaw and the darkest brown eyes I've ever seen walks in. Chelsea's smile turns up to full wattage.

"Luca!" she says, standing and embracing the prime rib in front of us.

Hannah knocks her knee to mine and we share a look.

"This is my co-worker, Victoria and my boss, Hannah." She swivels him toward the table. His chocolate gaze lands on us and I take in his paramedic uniform. "This is Luca."

"Hi." He puts out his hand to shake both of ours. "Chelsea told me your office is just upstairs."

"If by upstairs you mean twenty floors, yes." I smile, and he does, too.

He's handsome, but the grin on his face says he's Chelsea's match in the partying arena.

He turns his attention back to Chelsea. "I meant to ask you, I saw on Instagram that your cousin is getting married."

"Are you still stalking her fiancé?" Chelsea jokes and his shrug and his smile says he's got no shame.

He turns to the table again. "Do you know that Chelsea's cousin is a Winter Classics skier and she's marrying a Classics snowboarder?"

Chelsea shrugs, but her proud smile says she's not embarrassed by it.

"Really? Who? I was glued to the screen this Winter Classics," Hannah says.

"Skylar Walsh is my cousin," Chelsea says.

They share the same last name, so we should've guessed.

"That's awesome. Do you think she'd be willing to speak at the gala?" Hannah asks, ever the opportunist if she sees something she thinks will help raise money for the charity.

"She knows all of them. Mia Salter, Demi Harrison." Luca nudges his shoulder to hers like 'why didn't you share that you know all these famous athletes.'

That's not Chelsea's style and even I know that.

"You're holding out on me girl," Hannah says.

Chelsea eyes Luca. "I'll make some calls. See what I can do."

"Oh, it's too late to get something together for winter and have them do a day on the slopes, but it's something to think about for next year."

The older woman who called out our numbers walks around the back counter and over to our little group where she hits Luca over the head with a menu.

Hannah and I stare on wide-eyed.

"Ouch. Mama." He holds out his hands.

She shakes her head, her eyes piercing into him. "Don't give the phone number out again."

Chelsea laughs, obviously understanding whatever it is that's going on here. "Still?" she asks him, and he shoots her a smirk as if to say, can you blame me?

"It was nice meeting you." He swings his arm around his mama's shoulders and the two of them walk away, speaking Italian.

"Cute," Hannah says. "Too young for me, but you two should think about it."

"You couldn't be more than five or six years older than him," I say.

"Doesn't matter how old he is, that's a big N-O from me," Chelsea says.

"A paramedic with a body and face like his? I imagine

there's a lot of competition and he probably likes it that way," I say.

Chelsea points at me. "You have good intuition, Vic. His mom is mad at him because he gives all the women he meets at bars the deli phone number."

Hannah wipes her mouth. "Never mind then. He's not the one for either of you."

We all stand and dispose of our trash. Chelsea runs over and gives Luca a quick hug goodbye. He raises his hand in a wave to us and we each smile with a wave back as we're exiting the door. I turn and run smack dab into a man wearing a suit and my heart halts for a moment before I realize it's not Reed. Why would it be?

"Excuse me," I say, sliding by the man.

"No, excuse me." His eyes flit over my body like I'm on the menu.

"Is that the steak?" Chelsea jokingly asks as we walk by, ignoring the guy.

"Yeah, baby. King cut T-bone. Want a bite?"

Hannah and I stand there with our mouths ajar. Seriously, a little kid just walked by.

"I'd have to douse it in A1 sauce before I could even stomach looking at it." Chelsea lets the glass door shut behind her and we rush to the entrance of our building laughing uncontrollably.

It really is good to have girlfriends again. Just another reason to stay single. I let a man distract me from growing new friendships before. Never again.

Chapter Six

*E*leven-fifty-five Saturday at the McDonald's on Peterson, Jade and I walk in, hand in hand. I glance around, not seeing Reed or Henry, so I order a happy meal for Jade and a meal for myself.

We sit down with our food in a booth that Jade picks out. So far everything's going great. Until the door opens behind me and Jade's eyes widen, a huge smile overtaking her small face.

"Henry!" she exclaims, her hand up in the air.

Like the other day, I smell him before I see him. That musky and citrus mix that's like a heat-seeking missile right between my legs.

"I would have bought you lunch," he says, arriving at the edge of the table.

Henry and Jade talk about the play area and I take him in. Faded jeans, a black pullover jacket, and a pair of soccer sneakers. A memory of going to one of his soccer games at a park once flashes through my mind. It was like a rec league or something. I thought he was jaw-dropping in a suit but his casual look makes me want to nuzzle into him on a Sunday afternoon all day.

"Don't you know yet, Mr. Warner, I'm the independent type." Jade glances over to me with a strange look on her face.

A smile creases the edges of his eyes and an embarrassed flush, runs through my body. How stupid did I just sound?

"I do know that Ms. Keebler."

"Clarke now."

He rocks back on his heels, a look on his face to suggest he had wondered.

"So, you're not the cookie maker anymore?" he chuckles, and I eye Jade because the poor girl still holds her father's name. "Who doesn't want to be associated with E.L. Fudge? He's the best."

Jade smiles and then goes back to her conversation with Henry.

"Usual, Henry?" he asks the little boy.

He nods at Reed and I really need to finalize who he is to him.

"Great, I'll be right back." He taps the table with his knuckles and then heads around the row of tables to the front.

"Can we play?" Jade asks.

"After you eat. Come over here, Jade." I slide closer to the wall, waiting for her.

Her face loses the excitement. "I'll sit with Henry." She situates herself and I wonder how the fact that she picked out a booth did not set off any alarm in my mind.

"Um, no Jade, just while we eat." I pat the spot next to me. Henry looks at me like I have three heads and what's the big deal if he sits next to Jade.

The kid will understand one day it's not Jade sitting

next to him I'm worried about, it's the fact that--

"Perfect." Reed slides in next to me, his strong thigh pressing against mine. "Couldn't have set this up any better if I'd tried." He winks, and I slide until my entire left side of my body is pressed to the wall.

Jade slides down into her seat across from me, focusing on her meal again. Henry sits down next to her and Reed hands him his meal. He doesn't open the sauces, doesn't put the straw in his cup, which I believe might be soda and he lets the kid set everything up himself. My eyes glance to Jade's spot. Her nugget box is opened with the fries in the lid, sweet and sour sauce open and sitting next to her ketchup. I added the straw to her milk and have a napkin there for her to clean up after. The toy is tucked into my purse until she eats.

"Looks like a car." Reed tosses Henry the toy and the little boy catches it.

"Have it." Henry shrugs and sets it between him and Jade.

"What did I get?" Jade sets her eyes on me.

I shoot her my non-verbal 'you know the rules' look.

"Henry got his. Can I have mine?"

My eyes look over to Henry and Reed, both looking between us. Not judging, just intrigued.

"Eat some nuggets." I nod my head to her uneaten food.

"Come on. I want to know what I got," she whines, and I close my eyes because the last thing I want is for this to become a whole thing over a McDonald's cheap toy.

"Jade," I give her my warning tone, but I can already tell it's not going to work today. "Eat." I'm a little more curt this time around.

Reed gets the hint. "Henry, eat your meal."

Henry's eyebrows crinkle at Reed's authoritative voice.

I'm sensing whoever Reed is to Henry, he's not an authority figure.

Henry does take a bite of his hamburger.

Meanwhile, Jade crosses her arms over her chest in defiance.

"If you don't eat, you don't play."

A small sound escapes Reed, but thankfully Jade didn't hear it because her eyes are set on challenging me. I play her game, not really caring what Reed thinks. I want to drive him away anyway. Maybe I should hold the toy hostage longer, so she throws a tantrum and then he'll realize he doesn't want a ride on our crazy train.

Jade slides forward, picks up a nugget and then nibbles it.

Once she's finally eating, I look at my plate no longer interested in eating with Reed right next to me. I pick up a fry and eat it, then take a sip of my soda. This is not a first date. This is nothing. After repeating that a few times, I finally pick up my chicken sandwich and take a bite. When the tomato and lettuce slide out of the sandwich because of the abundance of mayonnaise and it lands in my lap, I repeat to myself that this is a good sign. After all, we want Reed to run far far away.

"Shit." Reed's hand moves over to pick up the vegetables out of my lap.

"You said a bad word," Jade scolds him.

His head flicks her way at the same time my hand grabs his wrist to stop him from plucking something out of my crotch. An electric current shudders through my body.

"Sorry."

"He says that all the time," Henry says and him, and Jade talks about parents swearing. "My grandpa is the worst. He says the f word." He lowers his voice once he gets to f.

Jade's jaw opens although I'd bet the house in Vegas her dad uses that language around her.

"Once my dad put up the finger at someone in the car next to us. Then the guy rolled down his window and if I'd collected money for a swear jar, we'd be going out for ice cream after this."

Reed chuckles lightly to himself and excuses himself.

"My grandpa yells at his neighbors, saying get the potatoes out of your damn ears."

Jade laughs uncontrollably, rolling all around the booth. "I don't have a grandpa." She doesn't say it in a mean way,, she says it like it is the way it is. "I have a grandma though."

"Does she say funny stuff?"

Reed returns with some napkins and water. "Here."

"Thank you. It's not too bad actually." I focus on the stain on my jeans which thankfully, should be fine once they dry.

Jade continues telling Henry things my mom says. Reed is soaking in their conversation with a few looks my way.

"My grandma says it's a good thing my mom left my dad because a rotten apple spoils the whole barrel." Jade shrugs not understanding exactly what it means.

"Your parents are divorced?" Henry asks as though we're not sitting right across from them.

"Come on you guys, eat up." Reed encourages them, now willing to set some rules.

The two take a bite of their meals, but I know my daughter. "Yeah." She looks at Henry. "Yours?"

Henry looks over to Reed, not for permission, but something else. I just can't put my finger on the way he looks at him.

"My parents died."

Chapter Seven

ade's eyes find mine and I honestly have no idea what to say.

"I'm sorry, Henry." I find my voice, wishing I had something more comforting to offer.

Reed just smiles at Henry almost proud that he said it.

"Who is he?" Jade asks, nodding toward Reed.

Thankfully, I don't have to do it. The boyfriend of the mom is out of the question.

"He's my big brother."

I nod, it all clicking together now. He took custody of his sister or brother's child. Another check mark under good guy.

"He's old."

"Jade!" I widen my eyes at her.

"Sorry," she mumbles, her eyes peeking up at Reed.

"It's okay, I suppose I am to you." Reed takes it all in stride, balling up the wrapper of his sandwich and then laying his arm along the back of the booth behind my head.

"He's not my actual big brother." Henry shakes his head like she's crazy to believe him.

I guess I'm just as naive as Jade.

Reed says nothing, letting Henry tell us everything and I admire that in him. He lets him dictate what he divulges to us.

"I don't get it?" Jade's eyebrows crinkle.

"I live with my grandparents, so they signed me up with a program and I got Reed, he teaches me how to be a man."

I spit out my drink and little droplets of Diet Coke splash on the table.

"Dirty mind," Reed whispers, blotting up my mess with a napkin.

"Oh, I want one to teach me how to be a woman," Jade says, and I close my eyes.

"Why don't you guys go play and if you get hungry, come back."

The two forget the conversation they were just having and run over to the play zone.

I fall back to the booth. "I feel like I just went through therapy."

Reed laughs but doesn't move from his spot.

"You can slide on over to the other side." I point, but he just smiles.

"Would that make you more comfortable?" He waits for the answer. His arm still stretched behind me, his fingers dangerously close to my skin.

"Yes."

"One day, you'll want me here." With his promise, he throws away his finished containers and slides into the other side of the booth.

"You're part of the Big Brother Foundation?" I ask just to clarify I caught on while Henry was talking.

"Yeah."

"Admirable." So admirable it might give him two check marks next to good guy.

He shrugs. "Well, if you knew how I started you might not think so since my intentions were purely selfish to begin with."

I wait for him to tell me more.

He blows out a breath. "In high school, my parents wanted something good on my school applications, so I signed up for the mentor program at sixteen. At first, I felt so out of place and thought I had nothing to offer these kids. I mean, a rich kid from Winnetka who got everything they wanted? The more I did it, the more I enjoyed it. Once I turned eighteen, I decided to become a Big Brother and I've done it ever since."

"Jeez, I'm kind of blown away right now."

"Well, it shot my parents in the foot."

"Why? You're a lawyer. What kind of parents aren't happy with a son becoming a lawyer?" I sip my drink.

"Victoria, Victoria, Victoria." He shakes his head. "In my parents' minds, I'm not a lawyer, I'm just an assistant district attorney on the government's payroll."

Shit, I didn't even know that. I figured he was like Pete, a defense attorney.

Another check mark for Reed. But he *is* still a lawyer so that's an X. Maybe the two cancel each other out.

"Point?"

"Families like the Warner's don't go into public law, we should be in the private sector making lots of money with which to rule the world." He says it with a tone of arrogance he clearly doesn't possess.

"Well, sorry to offend." I use the same accent and he laughs.

"You'd fit right in."

"Well, I didn't know any of that. I didn't even know you were Reed from the Warners of Winnetka." He points, clearly enjoying the fact that I'm playing along.

"Get with it, Victoria." He pretends to stand the collar up on his pullover, but it flops back down. "See, even my clothes rebel."

I glance over to the play zone and watch for a minute as Jade and Henry chase one another around. "How long have you been Henry's big brother?"

He follows my line of vision. "Two years. His grandparents raise him now. That's why I drop him off on Mondays at school. Ned and Helen usually meet their friends for coffee Monday mornings."

"How did his parents die?" I ask, turning to face Reed again.

It's none of my business and if he wants to tell me to buzz off, I won't be offended.

"Car accident." The corner of his lips turn down.

My heart breaks for the small boy and I look over to him again. You'd never guess he's been through so much, except for his quietness.

"Ned is kind of old school—doesn't want Henry running and jumping in the house. I think that's why he's quiet. But once you get to know him, you'd be surprised." He stares over at him with such love and affection that I can practically feel my pupils morphing into cartoon hearts.

I pinch the skin on my arm. Ouch, that damn well hurt, but at least I'm not looking at him all googly-eyed now.

"Well." I straighten in my seat, grab my notebook and pen from my purse and lay them out in front of me.

"We're back to business I assume." His gaze flicks to my notebook.

"Well, that's why we're here." I poise my pen over the paper.

"I wondered how long you'd let the casual conversation continue." The smirk on his face says he's not surprised that I'm not acting like I'm all sorts of impressed after learning all the admirable things he does for Henry and this city.

"I don't want to hear it from Darcie, so we need to get going on this. If you don't have any ideas, I have one."

He stands up, unzips the small zipper at the top of his pullover, grabs the hem of the jacket and pulls it over his head. His shirt rises, giving me the pleasure of seeing his love arrow in all its glory. His groin cleavage and happy trail are an arrow pointing south and everything in me wants to see where the road leads. Preferably with my tongue leading the way.

The shirt falls down, covering my sneak peek, leaving only Reed's amused expression on display.

"So..." I swallow a large gulp and attempt to focus on the sheet of paper.

His large frame slides back into the booth, where he clasps both hands in front of him on the table, waiting for me to continue. Thankfully, he makes no sly comment about catching me ogling his body.

"I was thinking we do something different. Who's paying for the tickets?"

"Darcie said it was the parents," he says.

"Okay, I have an idea. We get a car from a junkyard, remove the fluids, and anything else that's dangerous. Then we sell tickets to let someone have at it for a few minutes to release all their pent-up aggression."

His smile grows as he leans back in the bench seat. "I like it. I think a few of the moms—Darcie included—could unleash a shitload of sexual frustration. Will she approve it though?"

"I didn't plan on telling her. I was going to make it a surprise." I look over at him with my most serene, full-of-shit smile.

"Man, I knew I always liked you."

I roll my eyes and a second later a fry hits my forehead. "Did you just throw a fry at my head?"

He glances over his shoulder and points to the elderly woman in the next booth.

The smile won't stop teasing my lips as I look at him. He's so easy. Too easy. There *has* to be something wrong with him.

Duh, my subconscious chimes in—he was the best man at your wedding *and* he's a lawyer. Double whammy!

Chapter Eight

On Monday, despite myself, I'm giddy knowing I'll see Reed again. The fact that I bought a new outfit yesterday and dragged myself out of bed early this morning to do my hair and makeup is because I want to feel good about myself, not because I care whether Reed Warner notices me or not at school drop-off.

Jade and I are trying to avoid the cracks on the sidewalk as we make our way to St. Pats, playing that old school 'step on a crack break your mother's back game.' When we're only a block away, a car slows down next to us.

"Jade!" Henry screams out the window and Reed raises his hand in hello and then returns to the task of tying his tie, the clip between his teeth once again.

And there goes my stomach on the new rollercoaster ride it seems to be finding so much enjoyment on. Yes, he's in the back of an Uber, but it's an intimate portrait of the man as he readies himself for the day. Every man is different. Pete used to have to stand in front of the mirror to do his tie up in the morning and it was always a studious process. I miss that part of being a couple—knowing the intimate details no one else does.

"Hi Henry!" Jade's voice draws me from my thoughts. She runs down the street trying to keep up with the car. "I'm gonna beat you!"

"Hit the gas!" Henry yells at the driver.

"Jade," I warn, stepping up my pace, but she ignores me. It's not that she's so far ahead I can't see her, but there are so many cars coming and going at this time of day that I worry someone won't see her when they're leaving the parking lot to our right.

A short sprint later and I've caught up with her. I'm sure all my efforts at appearing put together were wasted after the impromptu morning jog Henry and Jade forced on me. Not Reed though, the man strolls from the car like he's a half hour early to an appointment and doesn't have a care in the world, looking completely put together in his grey three-piece suit. He slides his wallet into the front pocket of his suit and rounds the back of the car.

"Did you hear what happened?" Georgia asks Darcie to my left.

Not really feeling like getting into the St. Pats' gossip mill this early on a Monday morning, I set my gaze on Jade who's now talking to a group of kids at the bottom of the stairs.

"Morning Sunshine," Reed says when he reaches me, his voice smooth and sultry.

"Hi." I smile nicely and then tap Jade on the shoulder.

She turns, holds up her finger and then continues telling her friends how she and Henry went to McDonald's on the weekend. Henry offers a smile but adds nothing to the conversation. She says something about the toys and all the kids laugh. Then I see why Jade is such a perfect friend for Henry. The other kids initiate conversation with

Henry about what happened and Jade steps back, letting Henry take all the credit for whatever they all find so amusing.

I choke back tears realizing that the divorce, the move, the less than involved father hasn't screwed her up too badly because she knows how to be kind and compassionate to someone who needs it.

She turns to face me and must see some of the emotion on my face because she gives me a funny look for a second. "Bye, Mom." Jade wraps her small arms around my neck and squeezes.

"Have a great day, okay?"

"I will." She leaves me without another look. "Let's go, Henry."

Henry says goodbye to Reed with a fist bump and then the two of us stand in the middle of the concrete walk-up watching the two of them enter the school with a crowd of other kids.

"Want a ride?" Reed's voice has me turning slowly in his direction.

"No, thank you." I sip my coffee and step toward the sidewalk.

"So, I guess dinner is out of the question?" he asks, and I stop.

He doesn't fidget, his cheeks don't flush. In fact, his hands are in his pockets and he's rocking back on his heels. You'd never guess that he just put himself out there and asked me on a date. I'm sure he must know the answer before I even say anything, yet, he's not too intimidated to ask me anyway.

"I'm not into dating right now but thank you for the offer."

He clasps his heart dramatically, his head falling back while he groans.

"Don't even act like I just ruined your life." I shake my head with a smile.

He stands upright. "You can deny me, but don't do it so politely. Tell me the real reason you won't go to dinner with me."

I glance to the side finding Darcie and Georgia watching on with narrowed eyes. What do they care? They each have diamond rings on their fingers worth more than my annual salary.

"You're a smart guy, Reed. I'm sure you can figure out why this won't work." I motion with my finger between us.

"I'm not friends with Pete anymore. Maybe an acquaintance, but—"

"It's not just Pete. I mean that's a huge part, yes. You have two strikes against you though. You're a lawyer like my ex *and* you were the best man at my wedding."

A deep intake of breath followed by a murmur has me glancing across the small courtyard.

The MM's—Mean Moms—are gathered together, Georgia's mouth ajar.

"Now we're the scuttlebutt."

He follows my gaze and then steps forward.

"I'm nothing like Pete." His voice is lowered so we can't be overheard. When I don't answer, he lets out a sigh and says, "Come on, let me give you a ride. I'm due in court this morning and it's right near your building."

"How do you know where I work?" I cross my arms over my chest.

"I'm the ADA for the county, I know almost everything."

I stare at him and he finally smirks.

"I may have Google'd."

My heart does a leap in my chest that it shouldn't. What I *should* be thinking is that his behavior is borderline stalkerish, but instead I'm finding it worthy of a TV rom com.

"I'm just getting on my feet again after our move. Trust me when I say that I have so much shit you don't need to deal with."

He nods to the waiting Uber. "It's just a ride to work, Victoria."

"I'm sorry. I can't." I place my hand on his arm and he looks down at it. Is he feeling the surge of energy between us, too? I quickly retract my hand and turn away to head to the train station.

I don't have the guts to turn around. Instead, I keep my eyes forward and thankfully my cell phone rings in my purse. Happy for the distraction from the magnetic pull drawing me back to him, I answer on the first ring.

"Hi, Hannah."

"Victoria, how far away are you from the office?"

I can tell from her voice that she's flustered.

I glance in front of me at the houses on either side of the road as I walk. "I'm just about to hit the train station," I fib.

"This new dog I got has gone into heat and I have to drop her off at the veterinarian. I told myself not to book an appointment for a Monday morning. NO!" she screeches. "My new Persian rug. God, how much blood can come out of one dog?"

"I'll get there, Hannah, you take care of Lucy."

"Thanks. Can you pick up a pastry plate or something? My meeting is at ten and I was going to stop, but now..."

"Yep. I'll handle everything." I sling the strap of my purse further up on my shoulder and quicken my pace.

"Come on," she pleas, to the dog I assume. "The dog won't walk on a leash. How do you get a dog to walk on a damn leash?"

I stifle a laugh. "I have no idea. I'm a cat person."

"I should be a cat person. Thanks, Victoria, you're a lifesaver."

Click, the line dies and I'm about to climb the stairs to the L train when I realize there are people standing everywhere. It's even more crowded than usual and taxis are arriving in droves and driving away just as fast.

"What's going on?" I ask a woman who is about to climb into a taxi.

"Not sure, but it's delayed by like an hour I heard."

I cringe. "Seriously? Can I share the taxi with you?"

She smiles. "Where are you going?"

"City. Downtown."

That smile turns down immediately. "Sorry, I'm not going that way. I'm going Southside and if I go through downtown, I'll be late." The woman honestly looks like she feels bad and I'm not about to make someone else late.

"Go," I wave her off. "I'll grab another one."

She slides into the back seat. "Good luck."

The taxi pulls away and you'd think the world is about to end the way people are cutting in front of one another for the taxis.

I walk a block down figuring if I can get away from here, I'll be able to catch one before it reaches the station. I'm only walking for a few moments when I notice a car double-park a few cars up from me. A window rolls down and before I hear his voice, I already know who it is.

"Care for that ride now?" Reed's smug face appears like he knew the entire time catching the train today was going to be impossible.

"Am I going to have to take out a restraining order?"

He opens the door, steps out and motions for me to join him in the car. A few taxis behind him honk, but it doesn't faze him as he waits patiently.

"I guess I know what you need before you do." He winks. On any other guy, it would come off cheesy as hell, but somehow on Reed, it's charming.

I step forward and stop just outside the door. If I stepped any closer our chests would touch. "One ride and I need to stop for Danishes on the way."

He chuckles. "So, I get breakfast, too. Sounds like a date."

I slide into the car and scoot over to the far side, giving the driver a small smile of thanks. Reed slides in next to me and takes up the majority of the space, his knees hitting the back of the passenger seat.

"It's not a date," I say once I'm settled.

"Yet."

"Never."

"If you say so."

He shrugs, and though he may sound like he's in agreement, the cocky smirk splashed across his face says differently.

Chapter Nine

Wednesday night when I arrive home from my evening class, Jade's laughter echoes from behind the door and I smile to myself. Inserting the key into the lock of my childhood home, my body craves the serene comfort of my daughter and our new life.

I don't mind going to school. I actually enjoy it more than I did eight years ago when I was only a year away from earning my degree. I could strangle myself every time I think of the bad decision I made, knowing full well at the time that that's exactly what it was. No, it wasn't the fact Pete and I didn't use protection and ended up pregnant with Jade. It wasn't marrying him quickly so that his family didn't have the shame of an unplanned pregnancy to their name. I loved Pete and when I walked down that aisle, I truly thought he was my forever. The mistake I made was letting him convince me to leave college with one year left so I could follow him to Los Angeles.

I knew it wouldn't be easy—raising a baby and finishing my degree—but I naively thought Pete signed up to stand beside me, not in front of me.

Pete had other plans though. Maybe it was because it's all he knew growing up. Who knows? He had a stay-at-home mom while I had two working parents. To me having it all meant a family *and* a career. Pete felt differently.

He envisioned coming home to a home-cooked meal, a perfect wife who brought him a drink at the end of the day and wore lingerie to bed every night. I didn't miss the disgust in his eyes when I swapped out my satin for flannel. But I'm not naive enough to believe that our bedroom problems were the only reason he strayed.

Pete was someone who was never fulfilled with what he had. He's still that way.

I hate the memory of the weakness that lived inside of me while we were married. I was trying to make something of us while losing myself in the process. When I signed those divorce papers, I made a promise to myself. I'd never let a man run my life again.

"Mommy!" Jade screams when I walk through the door, getting up and running toward me dressed in her rainbow emoji pajamas.

My mom glances over from the chair, a curious look in her eyes. "How was school?"

I hug Jade tight against my body. "Good, but I'm glad to be home."

Jade runs back to the couch to watch some game show on the television. "Grandma is so smart. She's getting every answer right."

My mom smiles and pats Jade's head as she gets up from her chair and walks by her. "I saved you some dinner."

I drop my book bag on the entryway bench and follow my mom into the kitchen.

"Thanks." I slide into a breakfast bar chair and my head falls into my hand.

The caregiver my mom is, she sets the plate in front of me before heading over to the silverware drawer. "Drink? Wine?" She sets the cutlery beside my plate.

"Sure." I pick up the knife and fork, cutting into the chicken. "Thanks, Mom. I'm not sure what I would do without you."

She sets a glass down in front of me and pours the white wine she keeps in the fridge for me into my glass. "I feel the same."

We share a look expressing how grateful we are to have each other. Two scorned women who want their independence but find refuge in one another. The hardest decision my mom ever had to make was probably asking me to move back to Chicago.

Technically, she didn't ask. She didn't have to. I'd never put her in the position of feeling like she had to beg me to return.

When she called me and told me that all the issues she'd been having had been diagnosed as multiple sclerosis, I was handing in my resignation to Jagger the next day. You can imagine how that conversation went until I trusted him enough to be honest about my reasons for leaving.

Jade can still see her dad. He has the money he so desperately wanted, so he can fly here whenever he wants to see her. Even when we lived in the same city, he barely made time for her. Now that we're back, his family only lives thirty miles from us, not that they'll go out of their way to see her.

"So." She slides into the stool on the other side of me. "Jade was talking about a boy named Henry today."

From her tone I know exactly where this conversation is going.

"Her friend, yes."

"Apparently he's some man named Reed's little brother." Her eyebrows shoot up.

I roll my eyes. "Not biologically." I chew the chicken.

"What?" Her forehead creases in confusion.

"He's part of the Big Brother/Big Sister program. Henry's parents died when he was young, and his grandparents raise him."

"Oh." Her hand covers her heart. "That's so thoughtful of him."

I nod, continuing to devour the home cooked meal that tastes better than anything I've ever made.

"She told me that Reed is really nice, and he makes you laugh." This is my mom's M.O., dig, dig, dig, but never ask directly. I'm not nine anymore, and the fact she knows all this information says she did to Jade hours earlier what she's doing to me now.

"Just ask, Mother." I set my knife and fork down.

She giggles, standing up and grabbing her water from next to the sink. "Are you dating him?"

"No."

"Do you want to?" Staying on the other side of the kitchen island she leans forward so her face is right in front of mine.

"No."

"Have I ever told you how much I love it when your cheeks turn pink like that?"

I wad up my napkin and toss it at her. "Mom, you know I'm not ready. He's nice, but this Reed is Reed Warner. Pete's best man when we were married."

Her eyes widen and she's quiet for a moment, thinking, assessing. She holds the crumpled napkin in her hand, reaches over, and grabs me another one from the holder.

"I never understood that friendship, but I thought

maybe Reed was one of those Eddie Haskell types. You know, polite to the adults and different behind closed doors."

"When did you even talk to him?" I ask.

She scoffs. "What is the term, cougars?"

"Mom!"

She laughs, throwing the napkin back at me. "I talked to him at the rehearsal. He was a nice kid. Wish I would have swapped them out at the altar."

"Yeah, I wouldn't have noticed at all." I spear a piece of chicken with my fork and continue eating.

"Well, it would've been the best thing I ever did." She turns around to the sink.

"You don't even know Reed." I lift the wine glass to my lips.

She swivels around, drying her hands on the dishtowel, then flexes them a few times before setting the towel back down. "I know people and my gut doesn't lie. I knew Pete was bad news."

"How do you explain Dad then?"

Her lips turn down. "I was young. My gut sense hadn't fully matured yet. Then I had a family and back then..."

She doesn't finish, and she doesn't have to because she stayed with my dad because she had nowhere to go.

"May he rest in peace," I say.

"Or in hell," she mumbles, but I catch it.

I don't even hold it against her. My dad put her through more than Pete did me and I loathe him like the devil.

"Enough about your father. Let's talk about Reed." Her eyelids flutter. "Why don't you want to go on a date? The divorce was final two years ago."

"It's not the time for all that, Mom. Besides, he's a lawyer."

She cringes.

"Second of all, he was the best man at my wedding." I say it in a voice that implies you'd be crazy not to understand the obvious problem with that.

"It seems to me Pete kept his friends like he did his wife —not happy and not close. You haven't seen him since what, after Jade was born?"

"Once we left Chicago, I never saw him again. I'm not sure about Pete. It's not like I was in the know about everything he did while we were married." My mom nods in understanding while I walk over to the sink and rinse off my plate.

Her hand runs up and down my arm. "Give it another shot. One date isn't going to hurt anyone. Not every guy out there is a Pete."

"Says the woman who has been alone since Dad left, what? Nine years ago?"

"It was different with me. You're young and..." she glances to the archway into the family room. "You have Jade. Pete's as good of a dad as he was a husband—lousy. You should've seen Jade's eyes when she was talking about Reed. She said he went into the play area and chased them around?"

I giggle thinking about it. "Until the teenage manager kicked him out."

"See." She points to my face.

"What?" I straighten my lips.

"You might be able to control those lips, but your eyes are transparent. Always were. And there's life coming back into them." She pats my shoulder. "Just think about it, Dove."

She tries to soften me by using the nickname she used to call me when I was Jade's age. I place my plate and silverware in the dishwasher, grab my wine glass and head to the family room.

I sit down and Jade slides over on the couch to join me. I snuggle her into me as she laughs at the gameshow on TV.

Just as I'm finally relaxing, my phone dings from my coat pocket. Jade jumps up and races over to the hook where it hangs.

"No, Jade." I'm not dealing with anything tonight.

"It might be Daddy," she exclaims, not listening to me. She digs into my pocket, pulls out my cell phone and her lips dip down for a second.

Of course, it's not him. There's probably a big case or a tight, twenty-something pussy that needs his attention.

"It's Reed," she says, her eyes scanning the text message.

"Jade, give it to me." I reach forward, able to pull her back by the sleeve of her jammies. She falls into my lap and I grab the phone out of her grasp. "You're not allowed to read my texts."

She giggles and squirms until she's sitting next to me. Leaning over the side of the couch, she tries to whisper to my mom. "He got tickets to a movie."

"Oh really?" my mom asks, and I don't dignify either one of them with an annoyed look.

Reed: *I mistakenly bought 4 tickets instead of 2 for the Imax this Saturday.*

Me: *Sucks to be you.*

Reed: *Henry misses Jade.*

Me: *He'll see her tomorrow.*

Reed: *I miss you?*

Reed: *Too soon?*

Reed: *Yeah, too soon. Thought so.*

Me: *You saw me two days ago.*
Reed: *Come on. Are you really going to make me beg here?*
Me: *We went over this on Monday.*
Reed: *I'm not asking for a date. It's a playdate for the kids. Yoga pants optional.*

I laugh and glance up to see Jade and my mom staring at me.

"Are we going?" Jade asks, trying to peek over my shoulder.

"I have school work."

My phone buzzes in my hand and I look down again.

Reed: *We don't have to sit next to each other.*
Reed: *I'll let you pay.*
Me: *In that case...*

"Please, Mom," Jade begs next to me.

"One movie isn't going to hurt," my mom says while Jade looks on, pleading with her hands in a prayer pose in front of her.

Reed: *I guess I'll find someone else. Maybe Darcie's available.*
Me: *Not going to work.*
Reed: *It was worth a try though.*
Me: *You're very persistent.*
Reed: *My persistence got you to work on time with the best platter of danishes in the city.*

He has a point but giving me a ride to work and going on a date with him are two different things.

Me: *Fine. We'll go. As a PLAYDATE. And only if I pay for lunch.*

Reed: *You sure you aren't the lawyer?*

The reminder of him being a lawyer makes my stomach clench.

Me: *We'll meet you at Navy Pier.*
Reed: *I'll let you have that one. Movie starts at eleven thirty.*
Me: *See you then.*
Reed: *Not if I see you first.*

He better not have anything else planned. I rest my phone on the seat cushion next to me.

"Are we going?" Jade asks.

I nod.

"YAY!" She jumps around the room.

"Time for bed. Say goodnight to Grandma," I say, rising from the couch.

My mom looks at me over Jade's shoulder, and her expression reminds me of when I graduated high school. The pride there pierces my heart because I know it's undeserved. Even if I agreed to see Reed on the weekend, I can't do what she wants me to do. I can't open my still-withered heart to Reed.

Chapter Ten

"How's the steak?" Chelsea throws herself down into the seat in front of me.

"Stop it with the steak analogy. I'm trying to imagine him more like liver." I finish typing an email to the company doing our favors for the gala and give her my attention.

"Maybe just gouge your eyes out so you don't have to see him anymore?"

"I'll have to try that. Thanks for the suggestion." I dismiss her by looking back at my computer screen.

"Jeez, I was about to tell you about a date I went on last night."

Now she has my attention.

"Mid-week?" She nods, and I wonder what kind of guy was worth her time during the week. Chelsea is fanatical about her schedule during the week. Every day after work, she goes to work out, heads home, makes dinner and then binge watches Netflix while she probably color codes her panty drawer.

"Yeah, but sadly I totally missed the signs." She digs

into her bag and retrieves her phone, pulling up a picture and shoving the phone in my face. "Check out his profile."

"Whoa. Talk about steak dinner. He's aged to perfection."

"Yeah and he's a model."

"Jeez, Chels, a model?" I enlarge the picture. "His abs look like they were drawn on." I take in the fine specimen for another second. "Don't you find it weird that he's not wearing a shirt?"

She grabs the phone from my clasp. "He was supposed to be on a beach."

"Still, why would you choose that picture?"

"Vic, the lack of shirt isn't the problem."

I wait for her to fill me in.

"It's the fact that when I showed up at the restaurant, *this* was him." She shoves the phone back in my face where a picture of an average looking guy is on the screen, not nearly as well groomed as the previous man. I'm thankful that he's chosen to wear a shirt to cover up his beer gut.

I purse my lips to try to stop my smile that's tugging at the corners of my mouth. "Oh, man."

"Yeah. He told me he thought I knew the picture was a joke because the guy is some famous model."

"Who?"

"I Google image searched the picture and it's a model for a sunscreen company. It's not like we're talking Gandy or Tyson here. How was I supposed to know?" She stares at the photo again.

"How did you handle it?" I cringe, wondering how harsh Chelsea got.

"At first, I just left, but once I got outside, I composed myself and decided that after I went to all the trouble of getting ready and taking a cab there, this guy is going to pay for me to eat at Alinea."

"Alinea says something positive about him, don't you think?" You're not getting out of there for less than a few hundred dollars a plate.

She nods. "I guess. He might not have washboard abs, but he can swim in a pool of hundreds."

"So?"

"So, nothing." She shrugs. "He was a nice guy. Polite, listened to me ramble on about my cousin's upcoming wedding. I even broke the cardinal rule and talked about my ex. Which was probably good because he didn't even try to kiss me after." She looks as confused as she sounds. "It was a weird night but I'm thinking that's what I need."

"To catfish someone?" I chuckle.

"No! I need to date only nice guys. Exclusively nice guys who aren't all about themselves and how much pussy they can get."

"You're going to narrow it down to one flavor?"

"Yes, vanilla. But there are still variations within vanilla. You can have homemade vanilla, natural vanilla, French vanilla, vanilla bean..."

I smile while she tucks her phone back into her purse. "Don't. You know me. I'll probably go on two vanilla dates before I crave that chocolate covered ganache bad boy again." She stands up. "Come on. Hannah said the car is pulling up in a few minutes."

Just then the office phone chimes and I recognize Hannah's cell.

I pick up the phone. "On our way down."

Chelsea waits at the door while I pack up my stuff quickly and lock up behind us. A few minutes later, we climb into a limo to make our way up north to try and secure the gala location.

THREE HOURS later the contract is signed and we're on our way back to the city.

Hannah lays her head against the back of the seat. "Thank goodness that's over."

"Yeah, and your ex can shove it up his ass because this venue is so much better." Leave it to Chelsea to bring up a touchy subject.

Hannah nods but doesn't say anything. After a few minutes, she sits up and presses the button on the partition. "Jacob, can you drop us off at the corner of State and Madison?"

"Yes, Ma'am." He nods, and Hannah leaves the partition down.

"Victoria, is your mom okay to watch Jade tonight?"

"Yeah, I wasn't sure when we'd get back, so I already made arrangements."

"Great. Girls, we're going out for happy hour tonight." She toes out of her heels and rubs her perfectly manicured toes against one another. No surprise since she wears fuck me pumps all day every day. Those things must hurt like a bitch.

"Don't worry, Hannah, I'm free."

Hannah glances to her side at Chelsea with a smile teasing her lips. "We both know you have your weeknight ritual and you didn't already have plans. Besides, there will be guys where we're going, and they'll be rich."

Chelsea pretends to rub her hands together and then drops them unexpectedly. "Rich doesn't always mean hot."

"Rich guys are their own breed of bad but not in the way you like them." Hannah winks at her with a smile. "I want girl's time anyway. We need to unwind. We've never been out together socially before."

The idea is great, I love both the ladies I work with and a little adult time with the girls sounds perfect.

A while later the limo pulls up to the curb, stops and we step out. There's no bar in sight.

Once the limo pulls away, Hannah slides in between us and links both her arms through ours and we walk in the opposite direction like Laverne and Shirley with a sidekick. A few seconds later she leads us down an alley.

"Not really in the mood to get mugged tonight." Chelsea slows her steps which makes all of us slow down.

"There are cameras watching the alley and there's always someone's watching those cameras." She pulls us farther down the alleyway. "This is the safest alley you've ever been down."

When we reach a plain looking, worn black door she unhooks herself from us and knocks four times. I wait for the small window section to slide across, so someone can peer down at us and ask us the password, but disappointedly, that doesn't happen. Movies make everything look so cool.

Instead, a large man with a barrel chest opens the door from the other side. "Ms. Crowley," he says to Hannah.

"How are you doing tonight, Sam?"

He nods. "Haven't seen you awhile. I was worried."

Hannah shakes her head like she understands his line of thinking. "Uh uh. Never. I got this in the divorce." She winks.

He tips his head and smiles.

"These are my two friends." she turns and gestures to where we stand behind her. "Victoria and Chelsea."

He nods. "Pleasure ladies. And I have to tell you this… don't go telling anyone about this place, otherwise you'll see this face on the other side of your door at home."

"Point taken," I say, wondering what kind of place Hannah's bringing us to.

"Oh, and you can't get in here without her." He points to Hannah.

Chelsea slaps him on the shoulder. "No worries big guy."

Sam looks over to Hannah and she giggles. Only Chelsea would do that to someone as physically imposing as this man. We enter and step through another door. The sound of clinking of glasses and chatter makes me more comfortable about our surroundings. At least I know Hannah didn't draw us to this place to have us murdered.

We enter the bar area and are met with dark wood-paneled walls with a matching bar. The far wall is lined with red velvet booths while small pedestal tables are strategically placed around the room with fabric backed chairs.

"Did we just warp back to the forties?" Chelsea asks.

"I love it," I say.

Hannah swings her arm through mine. "This place is called Torrios Table because Torrio—"

"Was the one who got Capone into the mob," I finish for her.

"Yep. See how smart you are? Once you get that degree you're going to leave me." She pretends to pout, and I smile in return. I've never seen this fun side of her before.

"Let me get my degree first then we can worry about what I'm doing. As it is I'm the oldest person ever enrolled in college."

She leads us to one of the booths and slides herself in until she's in the middle, so Chelsea and I take a spot on either side of her.

"No, you're not, and just think of all the younger men you have at your disposal this time around." She grins.

"You want her to go cub hunting?" Chelsea picks up and glances over a small menu on the table.

"I'm not old enough to be a cougar." I lower my voice. "The thought of dating a younger guy who knows nothing about women, does nothing for me. He wouldn't even know his way around a woman's vagina, let alone how to get me off."

Chelsea raises her hand in the air as if to signal 'victory!'

"I knew you were just being nice."

"What's that supposed to mean?" I lean forward and smack one of her hands down from across the table.

"It means…I knew there was a smart-ass hidden in there."

Hannah smiles. "I agree with Victoria. Next go around I want a man who can take care of my needs. That knows his way around a woman's body as well as he does the sports channels on television."

We all nod in agreement.

"And I don't care how many partners he's had because I say the more women, the more skills he learned from them. As long as he can be faithful, we'd be good." Hannah raises her hand to get the waiter's attention although I'm certain he noticed her when she came in. Hannah is hard not to notice.

"Ms. Crowley, so nice to see you again." He bows down. "Good evening, ladies. May I suggest a bottle of Chardonnay?"

Hannah shoots him a tight smile. "Not tonight." She looks from one side of the table at Chelsea to the other at me. "Three Vespers."

He tries not to act surprised, but I see the emotion register on his features for a split second. "I'll be right back."

As we wait for the waiter to fetch our drinks, I soak up the rich atmosphere. The room is filled with mostly men, men in suits. Men like Reed. Probably lawyers or some other equally untrustworthy profession where they take advantage and rip people off. Married men probably come here to unwind, leaving their wives alone. Whoa, Earth to Victoria.

The waiter brings over our Vespers and we're each a vision of poised sophistication as we slowly bring the glass to our lips and swallow a small sip, when what I really want is to pour it down my throat I'm so thirsty. Not to mention the buzz will help tremendously to push away all thoughts of He-who-shall-not-be-named.

"You know I have to ask. How did you get in here?" Chelsea leans forward.

"Family. My dad's been a member since he was of age and his father before him. It's changed hands a few times, but what doesn't change is that money speaks."

One thing I admire about Hannah is that for all her class and grace, she doesn't come off like she thinks she's better than you and doesn't look down on people who aren't in her tax bracket, but at the same time she keeps it real. I wonder if she was always that way or if her divorce changed her? Divorces have a way of changing everyone.

"Nice. Man, to be you." Chelsea brings her glass to her lips with a small shake of her head.

Hannah doesn't say anything and sometimes I think Chelsea needs reality glasses because she believes she wants things without truly knowing what that will bring her in her life. She wants a bad boy with a heart of gold, but hearts of gold don't mean they'll respect her. She wants Hannah's life, but I'm fairly sure Hannah went through hell in her divorce. My mom welcomed me with open arms after my divorce, but I'm not sure her family did.

Hannah's hand suddenly comes down between Chelsea and I on the table with a hard smack. I grab my glass before it tips over. "I can't believe they're letting that piece of shit in here."

Chelsea and I follow her gaze to a table in the front-right corner. A man in a sharp suit fit to perfection and salt and pepper hair sits with two other men. He seems to be doing the majority of the talking in their threesome, the other two men nodding their heads like he's their professor lecturing.

"Which one?" Chelsea asks. "The gray-haired one?"

"I'm not sure I'd call it gray," I say. "It's more that sexy, distinguished shade."

I'm not sure what Chelsea sees but if Hannah's looking for a guy who can map out a woman's erogenous zones, that's him. He stands, still talking to the men. They laugh and it's clear it's not forced, that whatever he said was truly funny. Turning around he walks to the bar, slides his empty glass to the bartender and orders another one.

Our eyes remain glued to him with varying degrees of emotion. I'm intrigued because I'm not sure I'd ever consider a guy with salt and pepper hair at my age, but I'm sure he'd teach me a thing or two with five minutes in the stall of the women's room. A quick glance across the table and I see that Chelsea's eyes are narrowed like she's trying to figure something out. Hannah's are on fire, as if she could incinerate him on the spot.

He taps his fingers on the bar to the rhythm of the soft music coming through the speakers. The expensive silver watch adorned on his wrist jiggles lightly with the movement. Just as I'm about to examine the rest of him, his head turns in our direction and his gaze sweeps over us and then doubles back. The guy cocks an arrogant smile and strolls around the bar to our table.

"Shit, we've been spotted," Chelsea murmurs. We both put our heads in our drinks while Hannah, well, Hannah keeps her punishing eyes on him.

"He's coming over," I whisper like I'm thirteen and the hot mystery guy at the mall is approaching.

The scent of his expensive cologne hits my nose as he reaches the end of our table. "I must not have done a good enough job if you can still afford this place." He's speaking directly to Hannah, looking straight ahead at her as if Chelsea and I don't exist.

"I thought they had standards at this place." Hannah slowly looks him over and I give her credit, she doesn't pause or stutter, and manages to keep a look of disgust on her face.

He rocks back on a laugh, his tongue slowly sliding over his lips. "It's nice to see you again, *Ms*. Crowley. Snarky as always." There's an air to his tone. Playful and flirtatious and it makes it hard not to stare up at him in adoration. This man isn't just a panty melter he's a panty incinerator.

"Sorry, I can't say the same." Hannah brings the glass to her lips, sipping it and letting her fingers run up and down the stem.

My gaze shifts across the table to Chelsea who seems just as enthralled in their banter as I am.

"Oh, come on. I had a job to do, surely you under-stand that."

Her fingers continually slide up and down the glass stem, her eyes fixated on him. "If I wasn't with my employees I'd have a few choice words for you."

"Don't let us stop you," Chelsea spits out and then instantly looks chagrined. "I didn't mean to say that out loud," she whispers to me.

"Listen to the girl. Don't hold back. That is, as long as

you can handle the same in return." Without invitation, he sits next to Chelsea and her blue eyes widen in my direction as she slides closer to Hannah at the back of the booth. We're like two scared kids whose parents are going at it.

My phone rings in my purse and all heads turn my way.

"I'm sorry." I fumble to find the phone.

Meanwhile, Hannah leans forward and unleashes a string of curse words and name calling but I could never put them all together. By the time I silence my phone, seeing it's my jackass of an ex, Hannah's leaned back in her seat, legs crossed, sipping her drink as though everything is normal.

My gaze shoots to the man who's still wearing the cocky smirk he's had on since he arrived at the table. "Let me buy you ladies the next round. After all, I get paid pretty well when I win." He winks at Hannah and she narrows her eyes to slits but says nothing.

He stands and saunters away as if he wasn't just told to stuff it in a room full of people.

"Go after him and give him a piece of your mind," Chelsea says. "What an asshole."

Hannah's gaze stays on him at the bar. We watch him point to us, the bartender's attention turning our way.

"He's not worth it," Hannah says, back to her collected self.

"From the heat that just filled this entire booth, I'm not sure about that," I say. "Who is he?"

Hannah's eyes don't leave his. "Roarke Baldwin. My ex's divorce attorney."

Chapter Eleven

"There they are!" Jade jumps up and down in front of Navy Pier when Reed steps out of the Uber.

He must have stock in Uber. Has he never heard of public transportation?

Jade makes the first move and runs over to Henry, talking a mile a minute about the movie we're going to see, while Reed waits patiently, his gaze flickering my way every other second or so. He fist bumps Jade and ushers the kids away from the side of the road toward the entrance.

"Happy Saturday," he says, tucking his hands in his jacket pockets to show he's not stepping over any boundaries. He looks good in his casual wear—a white Henley with a jacket over top and worn jeans.

"Hey," I say. "Cute."

He chuckles his usual amusement that ignites my stomach flipping. "I thought so."

"Let's go." Jade tugs at my arm. "I don't want to be late."

"I think she's spoken." He nods to the glass doors that lead into Navy Pier.

Trying to keep the kids to the Imax theater without getting distracted is more of a struggle than I'd anticipated. I drag Jade away from a colored sand booth and Reed steers Henry away from a place selling fidget spinners. We usher them past popcorn stands and ice cream parlors, though both of those sound good right now. My stomach rumbles from the multitude of scents wafting out of the different restaurants as we make our way down the long pier.

"I think we should go on the Ferris wheel after the movie," Reed says as we pass a picture of it.

"Yeah!" Jade exclaims, eyeing me to see if she'll be allowed.

I hate that look. Usually, I don't say no when we're places like this. We do everything and anything because she's young and I know the deal, soon she won't want me anywhere near her. I've had a boulder in my stomach ever since this morning when she asked me if I was really okay with going and if I didn't want to be with Reed, then we didn't have to go. She's so intuitive. Break my heart, why don't you.

"Sounds fun." I smile down at my daughter and remember that she only got one call this week from her dad. One. She deserves some fun.

"Really?" Reed says. "I thought I'd have to work a little harder for it."

"We're here, aren't we? Might as well make the most of it."

I know he's staring at me as we continue the walk to the theater, but I force myself not to look back at him.

We arrive at the theater and Reed handles the tickets, after which we head to the concession stand to order our popcorn, candy, and drinks. We each hand our cards to the young girl behind the register at the same time and she looks uncertain as her eyes flicker from his credit card to mine.

"Take mine. I'm the man," Reed says, and the girl's shoulder rises in agreement, plucking it from his grip.

"Um, you being the man does not mean you pay."

"It does when I tricked you into coming." He winks and that, as well as the word *coming* rolling off his tongue, makes it feel as if hot lava has replaced the blood in my veins. If it weren't for that, I would've had a snappy comeback.

Was I blind at my wedding eight years ago? Did I ignore the pull between us, or was I so hung up on Pete I didn't notice other men?

He signs the receipt, shoves his wallet in his back pocket and we catch up to the kids who are going over the movie posters along the wall.

"Icees?" Jade's eyes light up. She takes the cup Reed's offering her and then hugs me.

"Tell me you're not one of those moms?" Reed asks, handing me my own cup.

"What kind of mom is that?" I fill up my cup with diet soda because I'm a hypocrite of a mother.

"The kind who prohibits their kids from eating foods with red dye or at Halloween says you can have one piece of candy and then the rest we give away." He fills his own cup and I hand him a straw.

"No."

"Good."

"I let her have five pieces."

He looks over to find me smiling. Being a Big Brother doesn't really grant him access to judge. I'd like to see him get a small child to bed after an unlimited amount of candy on Halloween and then tell me his stance on the subject. I might not stop Jade from consuming Red 40, but I had acquaintances in L.A. who did, and it's scary how differently they behave.

"You probably make her brush her teeth and floss before bed."

"I truly am a monster of a mother. I mean, saving her from cavities and hyperactivity? Someone arrest me."

He laughs, and we follow the two little ones to the theater. "Where do you stand on vegetables?"

"Every meal and I duct tape her to the chair until she finishes every broccoli floret."

"Jeez, I won't even ask about desserts," he jokes.

His chest presses on my back as he leans forward to pull the door open for all of us.

"Row E, seats thirteen through sixteen." His attention is on the kids, while mine is on him. For the first time, I can't help but imagine if he was mine. Is this what it would be like? When we were alone could I press my lips to his soft pink ones? The thought has an ache building between my thighs.

The kids rush in through the second door, but I'm frozen in place and he seems to be too, his eyes losing their usual carefree sparkle. Now, his eyelids are hooded and he's so close to me I can see the darker blue flecks in his irises. I lick my lips.

"Excuse me," a man's voice says behind us.

I blink and the moment between us disappears. "So sorry," I say and bow my head, walking through the doorway.

We don't speak as I walk up the stairs to the row where Henry and Jade are already putting all their snacks out and taking off their shoes on the recliners.

"This isn't home," I tell Jade, but she just smiles, tucking her shoes under the flip out leg part of the chair.

They're sitting in the far two seats. They look so comfortable and the last thing I want is to uproot all Henry's snacks, just so I don't have to sit by Reed.

"I'll have to thank Henry later," Reed mumbles, sitting down next to me.

"Armrest stays down."

He holds the popcorn bowl in his teeth as he holds up both hands.

"You do know teeth aren't tools, right?"

After his jacket is off, he holds the popcorn in his lap. "Thanks, Mom."

I pretend to narrow my eyes even though I'm really telling him that because every time he holds something with his teeth, I imagine my panties between those same teeth as he drags them down my legs.

The lights darken.

"It's about to start," Jade coos and her and Henry slide back in their seats and quiet down.

"I've never wanted to punch a guy in the face before as much as I did that man for interrupting us," he whispers into my ear.

A jolt of arousal hits its mark in my core. I turn my head and his glittering eyes hold mine in the darkness. Those sparkling blues light up with the same lust coursing through my body as the screen flickers from light to dark.

One kiss, Victoria. It won't hurt anyone. Just one.

"Mom," Jade tugs on my sleeve.

I swivel my head her way and she's got half the bowl of popcorn emptied onto her lap.

I help her pick up as much as we can but by the time she's once again ready to watch the movie, I don't have the nerve to look back at Reed.

For the rest of the movie, I'm hyper-aware of the energy Reed's emitting to my right. He's alive and oh so tempting next to me. From the corner of my eye, I notice his hands. How he only picks up each kernel with three fingers. How his strong thighs flex under his dark jeans when he shifts in his seat. Though my body would love to pull up that armrest and nuzzle into his strong chest, I force myself to lean on the armrest closer to Jade.

Reed Warner might have the sex appeal of Magic Mike, but he doesn't know what he'd be getting himself into. Besides, I refuse to listen to my heart or my sex drive anymore.

Chapter Twelve

"I forgot to tell you. I scored a car for the carnival at the kids' school." Reed and I walk along Navy Pier after the movie, Jade and Henry in front of us, pointing and gawking at all the big boats.

I cringe. "You did? How much was it?"

"It's covered."

I shake my head. "No way. Let me pay. It was my idea."

"Not necessary. I know a guy."

"You know a guy?" I look over at him with an eyebrow raised.

He shrugs, but his eyes tell me he's full of shit. We reach the end of the pier and the kids stare out at the boats on Lake Michigan.

"I get everything else then. The eye protection, the sledgehammers—"

A soft chuckle escapes his lips. "You're going to buy the sledgehammers by yourself?"

"Why wouldn't I?" I turn to face him.

"Because they weigh a shit-ton."

"I'm stronger than I look," I say with mock confidence. Inside I'm wondering exactly how much sledgehammers really do weigh.

Reed nods, though I'm not sure he's really buying it, and pulls his phone out of his coat pocket.

Pictures.

"Jade and Henry, look over here." He snaps a few pics of their smiling faces. "Go stand by the kids," he says to me, still holding the phone out in front of him.

I cross my arms over my chest. "Nope."

His arms drop a few inches. "You don't want me to have a photo of you?"

I shake my head. "No, that's not it."

That's totally it though.

He shrugs and stuffs the phone back in his pocket. "We need to go down to the county to get approval plus we should talk to the principal at St. Pats. I figure we should do it together."

"You already did all that research?" I step over to a nearby bench facing the lake and take a seat. The cold metal on my backside and the cool breeze coming off the lake remind me that summer is still a ways away.

Reed follows me over and sits down beside me with only a few inches separating us. "Well..."

"You paid someone," I finish for him.

He doesn't look over at me. "I have assistants. They like to take care of things."

I shake my head in mock disappointment, though I guess I'm not really surprised. I'm sure he's a busy guy. "Are you going to have your assistants order your future wife flowers for your anniversary?" My joke doesn't hold the humor I thought it would when it leaves my lips.

He shifts to face me on the bench, no amusement to be

found in his perfect features. "Never. Is that what Pete did to you?"

"No. Pete didn't buy me flowers." My gaze finds the pigeons flying around, I feign interest—anything to let me break the connection with Reed. I'm ruining a beautiful day with my baggage, slicing it to pieces with the knife still lodged in my back from my ex-husband's betrayal.

He doesn't comment and I'm certain that's because he knows it to be true.

Jade and Henry keep themselves busy and the silence between Reed and myself seems to grow heavier and heavier, like a weighted fog surrounding us until he finally speaks.

"I like you, Victoria," he murmurs his confession.

"Gee Billy, I think you're swell too. Want to share a milkshake?"

He glances over at me. Fear grips my heart. He's going to call me out on my bullshit, force me to confront things I don't want to. Instead, he says wryly, "I think that's my line."

"What?"

"The milkshake, back when Billy and Jane were sharing milkshakes, a girl never would've asked."

I can't help but laugh.

His shoulders rise and fall. "It's the truth."

"Good thing I wasn't a teenage girl in that decade."

"I'm not sure. If you were then, maybe you'd be more amenable and agree to go out with me." His tone is light and teasing, but it's clear he wants to know why I keep denying him.

I face him ready to explain myself. Time for me to just lay it out there for him. All the complications that are my life.

"Listen."

Hearing Jade and Henry talking about a dead fish that's floating in the water, I know they're fine, so I give Reed my complete attention.

"It's not that I don't like you."

He covers his heart and pretends to faint. "Did you just admit you like me? Has hell frozen over?"

My eyes bore a hole into his head and he raises his hands in defense. "Sorry," he murmurs.

"What's not to like? Though you're a *lawyer*," I spit the word out like it's a curse. "You're the assistant district attorney, you volunteer for Big Brothers and go above and beyond in that regard. You bought us tickets today, bought the snacks. Already have the car for our fundraiser..."

I break eye contact by glancing over at the kids under the guise of making sure they're still okay, anything to grab every ounce of willpower to say no to this man.

"Reed?" A woman's voice rings out through the early spring air and everything in me tells me not to turn in her direction, but I do anyway.

Reed's gaze leaves me for her, but the full wattage smile that's usually reserved for me doesn't grace his face.

"Give me a minute." He gets up, not bothering to wave the woman over, he heads over to her as though willing her not to get any closer.

"I saw those kids and that woman you're with and thought to myself, that can't be Reed." Her giggle is fake and forces the same reaction in me as a fork against a plate does.

"It's Henry and his friend from school," he says to her.

I refuse to feel slighted that he didn't mention me.

"Oh, Henry." She coos. "Henry!"

I keep my eyes forward, but Henry and Jade look past me to the woman yelling.

"Who's that?" Jade asks Henry, her gaze not leaving the woman.

Henry doesn't smile at first, but he raises his hand to waist level like a teenager does to a parent at school.

"Olive," the boy says.

"Who is she?"

I love Jade's persistence. She's going to do my dirty work without even knowing it.

"Reed's friend. I think they were boyfriend and girlfriend."

All my muscles grow rigid and my back straightens.

"They dated?" Jade's face is contorted in complete disgust.

Despite myself, I feel the same as my daughter.

"I saw them kiss a few times." Henry shakes his head like he's eating an insect and tastes something foul.

"Ew," Jade says.

"Come here, Henry, look how big you've gotten!" Olive says.

Henry glances their way again but doesn't go to Olive.

"Henry!" Reed's tone of voice is that of a fathers who expects his child to do as he's told.

The impulse to wrap my arms around the little boy and say 'he's mine' is strong. And not just Henry.

"I'll be back," he says with the enthusiasm of a child who's been told to turn off the video game because it's time to get to school.

Henry mopes past me and Jade comes over to sit next to me on the bench, her feet dangling. The smell of her watermelon shampoo reminds me she's what's most impor-tant and the fact that she seems a little upset by the present situation tells me she's invested, and I haven't even gone on an official date with him yet. In her mind, she's probably thinking that we'll all move in together into some happy, cozy home. Such is the mind of a seven-year-old.

"Are you having fun?" I ask her, wrapping my arm around her shoulders and laying the side of my head on the top of hers.

"Yeah. The movie was good. I can't wait to go on the Ferris wheel."

The Ferris wheel. I almost forgot.

Henry finishes with his hellos and comes back over and sits next to Jade.

"Do you guys want to go on the Ferris wheel?" I ask. "We'll let Reed finish talking to his friend."

"Yeah!" they both exclaim at the same time.

"Okay, Henry go whisper to Reed that we'll meet him over there when he's done."

Yes, I'm sending the boy to do my dirty work. Don't judge.

"I'll go with you." Jade stands and the two of them round the bench. I rise and step far enough away to make a quick getaway. After they tell Reed, we can just head in that direction without him having to introduce me.

"Hold up," Reed says to the kids with his pointer finger raised, when he sees they're trying to get his attention.

Olive is rambling on about some mutual acquaintances, divorces, and why anyone in this day in age anyone would commit without a prenup.

"I mean, she had to go to Target to buy her panties and bras." Olive hasn't taken a breath let alone give anyone else a chance to speak. She looks over at the kids as they wait patiently. "Sorry, kids. This is adult stuff. Give us a minute?"

Her hair is long and blonde. It's not a natural shade, but she's spent a fortune to try to make it look that way. Her eyes are light, but I'm not close enough to tell if they're blue or green and she's dressed more for brunch than a walk along the pier with her expensive handbag resting on her forearm.

"My mom is taking us to the Ferris wheel, so meet us over there once you're done," Jade interjects, and I fight the proud smile that wants to reveal itself.

"What?" Reed looks over to the bench and then over to where I'm standing. "Give me one second." He holds out his arm, waving me over.

Olive is still talking as though no one has said a word and for the first time, I wonder who she's here with. I look farther down the pier and spot a group of uppity looking people asking passersby to take their picture, which they promptly examine and then ask for it to be reshot.

I glance back at Reed who continues to wave me over. "No," I mouth at him.

He continues on, insistent that I make my way over. I roll my eyes but do as he asks. I approach, and he draws me into their circle with his hand on my back.

"Olive," he says. When she doesn't stop talking, he tries again. "Olive," he says louder and finally she snaps out of her rambling.

"Oh hi, I'm Olive Ashbury." She holds out her hand and her gaze flicks to Reed's arm behind my back. "Are you two?" she motions between us with her outstretched hand.

The kids have left by this point, playing tag around our little huddle, using each one of us as shields.

"Not yet, but I'm working on it."

I stare over at him in disbelief.

"Oh," Olive says, surprise in all her features.

"I'm Victoria by the way." I finally hold out my hand and she extends hers back out for me to shake, handing me the tips of her fingers instead of her entire hand. How very royal of her.

"And you're that one's mom?" she asks, pointing to Jade who has a hand on either side of Reed and is ducking and weaving from one side to the next, trying to see where Henry is.

"Yep," I answer, purposely not using yes. Improper and proud.

"You're so young," she comments.

"Well, it was great seeing you, Olive. We have to get going." Reed claps his hands for the kids' attention and they stop messing around and walk back up the pier.

"Wait," I call out and they halt.

"Well, kisses." She presses her cheek to Reeds and kisses the air on either side. Then does the same to me, pausing for a moment to speak low into my ear. "Good luck with him. I thought I snagged a diamond, but I found out he was a cubic zirconia, if you catch my drift."

She pulls away from me as though she just said a casual goodbye and we watch her for a moment while she strolls back over to her friends.

"You dated her?" I ask.

"Moment of weakness." He turns me around by my shoulders. "Ferris wheel!" he yells and points.

The two kids cheer and jump.

Her words haunt me as we make our way over to the ride, because I thought I found a diamond once, too.

Chapter Thirteen

The line to wait to get on the Ferris wheel is painfully slow. I guess everyone in Chicago decided to venture out the moment spring set in, desperate to get out of hibernation after a long winter. Jade and I only experienced a few short months of the blustery cold. I'm not sure she'll be loving the snow as much next year as she did this year. She might have her roots in Chicago, but she's a Cali girl at heart.

"Want to talk about Olive?" I ask, happy to steer the conversation clear of me and onto some of the baggage it seems Reed has been hiding.

He stares down at me, the sun lighting one side of his handsome face as it peeks out from behind a cloud. "No."

The kids are in front of us, debating which Ice Age movie is better, paying us no attention.

I knock him with my shoulder. "You know my dirty past, give me some of yours."

"I don't know your past."

"Sure, you do." I look over at him like he's crazy.

He shakes his head, the sun playing peekaboo with his

face again. "I know you were married. I know you had Jade. I know you got divorced."

I shrug. "That's all there is to know."

He leans forward, his eyes on the kids the entire time. "Bullshit," he whispers and the hairs on my arms stand straight up.

"You know Pete. I'm sure you probably knew all the reasons we should've never gotten married before I stepped foot in that church." I keep my voice low, so Jade won't overhear.

The sun hides behind another cloud and it not only brings a chill to the air, but to Reed's face.

He says nothing.

"I'll take your silence as a yes."

Not really into finding out exactly how much he knows, I focus my attention back on the kids, pointing and talking about how much we're going to see. Reed stays behind us, lost in his own thoughts, not living in the moment like he usually is.

An eternity later our turn arrives, and we step into the Ferris wheel car. I drag Jade to my side by her sleeve and wrap my arm around her.

"I was going to sit with Henry," she whines.

"This way you can both see out the same window." She stares at Henry across from her and they smile at each other like I'm a genius.

I point out landmark buildings for them and they ask questions like how many people live in Chicago, what happens when you live above the clouds. It's then I realize that in all the sightseeing we've done, I've never taken Jade to the Sears Tower.

Yeah, yeah, Willis Tower now, but never to a true Chicagoan.

"Can we go today?" Her eyes light up.

"Next weekend." Her lips dip and she glances at Henry, the two of them sharing a look like parents are lame.

Reed's busy on his phone, not even enjoying the ride or taking in the sights. Whatever, he's not spoiling my day with Jade.

"It's open, we can shoot over there after this," Reed says without glancing up from his phone. I guess that's what he was checking on his phone. Yet another way to hold me hostage.

"Yay!" Jade high fives Henry.

"Then you'll miss all those other rides." I point to the swing ride and few others down below us.

"They'll be time after," Reed says innocently. Too innocently.

I glare over at a smiling Reed again.

The kids swap seats with us, so they can see the lake and the boats. We talk about the lighthouse and what a lighthouse keeper does. I have to Google a few facts because I'm not the encyclopedia they believe me to be.

Finally, our time comes to a close and the ride stops so we climb out.

"The swings!" Henry says.

I hand them each their tickets and they run over to the ride. Stepping forward to join them in the waiting area, Reed tugs on the sleeve of my jacket.

"Hold up."

I slow my walk.

"I'm sorry. It's just...you're right." He runs his hand across the back of his neck, looking everywhere but at me.

My stomach bottoms out. What must he think of me?

"I figured."

"I'm not proud of the fact I knew Pete wasn't the man for you, but it's not what you think."

With my attention fixated on Jade and Henry, I stop at a stand to buy some water. "What is it then?"

Images of a naked stripper laying across a table and Pete plowing into her in the middle of his bachelor party come to my imagination. The embarrassment and shame of being cheated on might be the worst thing to come out of my divorce.

"I never saw him cheat," Reed says emphatically.

I roll my eyes.

"Swear." He pulls out his pinky finger.

My eyebrows shoot up. "I do the pinky swear thing with Jade, Reed. I'll believe you if you say so. Not like it really matters anyway."

The lie is that it does matter to me for some reason.

Seeming appeased, he hands a twenty over to the cashier and stuffs his hands in his pockets.

"I'll get it," I say, grabbing my wallet out of my purse.

"I already did." He smiles that panty melting one that ignites every nerve in my body.

"So, you never saw him, but…"

He pushes the change into his pocket and we walk forward, I unscrew the cap to the water and down a sip.

"There was a night I had to tell him not to put me in a bad position."

"He was flirting?" I guess.

I'm not surprised by it. I saw Pete flirt with my own eyes more than once. You'd think he thought I was blind.

"Yeah, but that doesn't mean it was anything more. They could have just been talking."

"Pete interested in a woman's thoughts on things?" I widen my eyes and a smile tips his lips. "Not likely."

"You've got me there." He pauses, and we watch the kids get on their swings, the attendant double checking their harnesses. "Henry looks like he's going to throw up."

Reed's right. He's pale and his eyes are darting between Jade and us as if he's contemplating escape.

"Maybe he feels pressure to go on the ride because Jade wanted to?"

Reed hangs over the metal guardrail. Cupping his hands over his mouth, he yells, "You okay, bud?"

Henry nods, but there's nothing convincing about it.

Reed steps off the rail and the swings moves back to me. "I'd watch out for flying vomit, just in case," he says to me.

We sit down on a concrete stoop and watch the kids as the ride gains speed, waving when they pass by us.

"Victoria, there's more than that." Reed's voice doesn't hold its usual confidence.

I swivel in his direction.

"I didn't understand what you saw in Pete. I wasn't willing to kill the bro code, but if he would've crossed that line in front of me, I would have…but not because I'm a noble person." He holds my gaze for a second before continuing. "I would've done it because I was being selfish."

"Reed." I place my hand on his knee. "Do not feel guilty for not telling me your suspicions. It's not like the two of us were friends. I understand where your loyalties were."

"Are you listening to me?" He runs a hand through his hair and I get the sense that he's frustrated by me, which gets my back up.

"Spit out whatever you're trying to say."

Instead of growing more frustrated with my attitude, a smile teases the corners of his lips. "I liked you then and I like you now."

My stomach flutters with his admission. I don't know if he means he liked me as a person in the past or *liked liked* me, but it doesn't matter. I wish I could wrap my arms around his neck and kiss him like I've wanted to for weeks, but things aren't that simple. I'm not that simple.

"Reed. I like you, too."

"Then what's the problem?"

I eye him for a long time willing myself the courage to put it all out there. He sits patiently and waits until I finally take a deep breath and speak.

"I come with a lot of baggage and they aren't filled with makeup, sexy heels, and lingerie. They're overflowing with doubt, trust issues, and low self-esteem. I come with a carry-on in the form of a seven-year-old little girl who, yes, seems adorable and sweet for the few hours you've seen her, but there's a more difficult side. I won't even mention the oversized bag in the cargo hold that is my ex-husband.

"I don't come with that new love glow. I don't possess the belief that we kiss and live in bliss, happily ever after. I come jaded. My corners aren't round and smooth, they're sharp and jagged. So, as much as I like you, and believe me I *am* attracted to you, this thing between us can't happen. I'm sorry."

I turn my attention away from him and unscrew the cap of water, gulping down the cold liquid like it will help push down all the raw emotion rising within me.

We sit in silence for a few moments and I can't believe he hasn't fought me on this. Not that I want him to, but I expected some sort of comeback.

"You're right, I dated Olive. It was off and on. Never really that serious. Her family is friends with my family."

Not what I was expecting.

"We went to the same expensive private school. We hung around with the same entitled crowd. We each got an insanely expensive car when we turned sixteen. Both of our educations were off-the-charts expensive and paid in full when we graduated. We shopped at the same designer stores. Flew to the same vacation destinations. I thought she was what I wanted…or maybe I convinced myself I was what she wanted. I don't know."

His hands knot together and in all the times I've been around Reed, he's never looked this intense, this nervous.

"She tried to stop me from being a Big Brother. Told me my time was too valuable to spend it playing house with someone else's kid. I know her type. Even though we weren't serious, she had our big mansion in North Shore picked out. Had our kid's names decided and a Pinterest board of decorated bedrooms for them. She tried to mold me into someone I wasn't. Someone I never wanted to be."

The swings slows down, and I spot Jade, her hair wind-blown and chaotic. Henry's actually smiling.

I could take a lesson from the kid. Some things are always scary starting out, but worth it in the end.

"I'm not going to convince you how wrong you are about everything you just said. I'm not going to sit here and counter each argument one-by-one—which for the record, the prosecutor in me very much wants to do."

I chuckle, then stand, brushing the dirt off my ass. "Thank you."

"What I'm going to do is prove it to you. See, Victoria"—he corners me between the cement wall and the metal gate while the kids wait patiently on the other side of the ride for the attendee to let them out— "I want a woman with goals. You want to get your degree. I'm behind you. You want a career and a family. I'm your equal in parenting responsibilities. You want to have a loving and supportive boyfriend. I'm him. This thing between us isn't my imagination. There's chemistry and energy bursting between us every time we're together. But I refuse to push myself on you because I want you to come willingly, and I guarantee you will."

"Mommy!" Jade's loud voice has Reed stepping back, but his cocky smile says he means every word of what he said.

It's all I can do to lock my knees and stay standing. "Did you have fun?" I ask when she jumps into my arms.

"So much fun! I'm starving."

"Let's go eat then." Reed high fives Henry. "I'm so proud of you, bud. You conquered a fear."

Henry beams but stays silent, per usual.

I watch Henry's hand find its way into Reed's, he glances over his shoulder to make sure Jade and I are following. A small pit forms in my stomach.

I can't be wrong. In my experience, if it seems too good to be true—it is.

Chapter Fourteen

"MOM!" Jade screams from the front door.

"Coming." I hop along, sliding my foot into my right heel then walking through to the kitchen.

She's standing there, her hair in a haphazard ponytail, her spring coat unzipped. But can I really complain? She's dressed, her backpack is on, her lunch is in hand.

I glance over at my mom who is sitting at the kitchen table, reading the paper.

"I can take her if you like," she says.

Most days I would be grateful for my mom's offer. I'd say yes thank you and give Jade a kiss on the cheek before dashing out the door. But today isn't Tuesday or Wednesday or Thursday or Friday—it's Monday. And as much as I hate myself for it, I'm not skipping a Monday morning drop-off.

I might not be able to have Reed as my own, but he's like that late-night snack you know you should stay away from. You regret it after it's in your stomach, but while you're consuming your craving, you're in bliss.

It's a love-hate thing with Reed. I love to see him. I love to interact with him. I hate myself afterward.

"Nah, I got her." I slide my arms through my coat and grab my bag. "Thanks for the coffee." I raise my to-go cup at her.

"Make sure you eat breakfast," she says, straightening her paper.

"Love you." I blow her a kiss because the three steps out of my way seems more like a mile after an activity-filled weekend and a late night studying.

"You, too. See you after class tonight."

"Finally." Jade throws the door open. "Bye, Grandma, love you."

"Love you, bug."

Jade heads down the walkway to the sidewalk while I shove my phone into my bag, double checking that I have everything.

"Henry?" Jade's confused voice triggers a reaction in my body—equal parts panic and excitement.

My heart thumps harder in my chest and a light sweat forms along my hairline because where Henry goes, Reed follows. At least on Mondays. I might not want to want him, but he pulls the giddy school girl side out of me anyway.

I lock the door behind me and then circle back to the street to find Reed outside his usual Uber car with Henry and Jade already in the backseat.

"It's only three blocks," I say.

My heels click on the concrete and I don't miss the way Reed's heated gaze takes me in, igniting the familiar pull between us. It must be that look I'm addicted to. The one that makes me wear sexy undergarments even though no one will see them. The one where I *want* to do my hair and makeup.

"Well, in those heels, I bet it'd feel longer." It's only his gaze raking up my legs, but it feels so much like a caress that I have to fight to keep my eyes open.

"I can handle it."

"Of course, you can, but you're riding into work with me today." He nods to the car.

"Excuse me?" I pretend I'm annoyed by his proclamation, but in truth, the idea of Reed bossing me around has my nipples peaking. In the bedroom. In all other areas of my life, I prefer my independence.

He opens the door where a smiling Jade and Henry are waiting for me.

"It's pointless when we're basically going to the same place and I've decided that it's more convenient this way. I have court tomorrow and I tend to get uptight the day before when I'm prepping. You help with my anxiety. Besides, why would you want to take a train when you can enjoy the pleasure of my company?"

I can't even control my lips. A full-on smile gives away how much this guy has already won me over.

"I guess since you have it all figured out, I should be thanking you."

"No thank you necessary."

I slide into the car and he shuts the door, folding himself into the front passenger seat. I double check Jade's seatbelt but of course she's already buckled in.

Three stop signs later, the car pulls up to the curb and Reed gets out first, opening my door before I can.

"Not so manic this Monday, huh?" I eye his already done up tie and tie clip then step out, ignoring the prying eyes of Darcie and Georgia.

"I was so excited to see you, I woke up early." He winks.

I roll my eyes, not wanting to give away how much I love the way he wears his feelings on his sleeve.

"Have a great day, Jade." I hug her to me, but she's already trying to wiggle away from me.

"See you, bud." Reed fist bumps Henry.

We watch them walk into the school and wave to the principal.

"Get in." Reed ushers me back in the car, sliding in behind me and shutting the door. "Go, Abe, go!"

The Uber driver looks at Reed much like I am, confused. Where's the fire?

Knock, knock.

"I'm late, Darcie," Reed speaks through the glass.

Not a fire exactly but it's possible she breathes fire because dragon lady is an apt description.

I tighten my lips trying to hold in my laugh and avoid looking at her.

"Reed, I need to talk to Vicki."

"I'm really sorry, Darcie, there's no Vicki here." How he can say it with such a straight face, I have no idea.

"Reed." Her eyes narrow and the laugh leaves me like an overinflated balloon.

"I need to get to the office. Gotta go." He faces Abe again. "Just go."

"Vicki!" she yells, but I just wave my fingers in her direction as the car pulls away.

"It feels good now but come tomorrow she's going to make my punishment that much worse." I pull out my phone with the hopes that we'll each do business on the way in.

"I'll be your bodyguard."

"You don't take Henry to school on Tuesdays."

He shrugs, his phone buzzing and I watch him pull it from the inside pocket of his suit and read the text. His warm smile disappears and for the first time, I wonder what he's like in court.

His fingers move over the screen and I turn forward, only to find Abe's eyes on mine. He smiles, and I smile back, staring out the window as he winds through the streets of the city toward downtown.

I inch forward. "Hi, Abe, I'm Victoria."

He smiles at me in the mirror again. "Not Vicki?" he asks, amusement creasing the wrinkles around his eyes.

"Definitely not."

"It's nice to meet you."

"Are you on call for this guy?" I thumb in the direction of Reed, who's still off in lawyer land.

"Every morning. He's on his own at night."

"Maybe he's cheating on you with a Lyft driver?"

Abe chuckles, turning right. "Not Reed." He winks. "Any music or morning show you prefer to listen to?" His fingers are poised over the controls on his dash.

"No. I'll just work. Thank you though."

I slide back in my seat and he turns on a talk radio station.

"This is the best. Turn it up, Abe." Reed's bubbly personality is back, and his phone is tucked away. "It's the Second Date Update."

Abe ups the volume and the radio personalities are talking to a girl about a date she went on and now she's complaining that the guy won't return her phone calls.

"This show will call the guy or girl to see why they're not returning the phone call," Reed whispers to fill me in. "You gotta hear some of this crap."

We listen to a woman explain how she was left at a cooking class. Her date excused himself to go to the bathroom, and never came back.

"See. I'm already looking good," Reed says, waggling his eyebrows.

"Because you've never left me at a cooking class? We've never even been on a date."

"Yet."

"Never."

"Listen." He taps his ear.

Hitting some traffic, Abe slows down.

The radio announcers call the guy to get his side of the story.

"I'm not sure what the argument could be for him leaving her at a couple's cooking class," I mumble, and Reed's hand stretches out, squeezing my knee.

Skin to skin contact. All the air leaves my lungs in a rush.

"There's always a reason," he says.

Abe nods his head in agreement.

The man answers the call and at first, he's pissed that they're calling him, then after a minute, he doesn't want to share the reason why because he doesn't want to embarrass the girl.

"He doesn't want to embarrass a girl who just called a radio station on him? I think this is set up," I say, my usual skeptical self.

"Either way, it's hilarious. The perfect way to start your morning." Reed elbows me gently.

Abe nods his head in agreement. Of course, he's not going to offend the guy who's footing the bill.

We continue to listen and the guy explains that the girl told him she slept with some other guy in the class. And then she proceeded to go on and on about how good the guy was in bed.

Reed shoots me a look that says, 'See? I told you this was the best morning show ever.' It was funny, especially when the girl said that her date missed out because she's never had an upset customer.

"Customer?" Reed roars and Abe looks at us through the mirror, his own amusement lighting up his face.

"See how many crazy women are out there? Save me." He clutches his heart and his head falls to my shoulder.

I push him back up by his forehead. "I think you'll do just fine out there."

"I'd do better with you."

"Stop it. Otherwise this co-commuting stops."

He holds up his hands. "You can't tell me you don't prefer a ride in on an Uber that gets you to work faster while enjoying the company of me and Abe over a jam-packed train."

I say nothing because what can I say? He has a point and for some reason, I have no snappy comeback for him, so instead I take a sip of my coffee.

When the big architectural high-rises swallow us up as we hit downtown, my body calms knowing my close prox-imity to Reed is coming to an end. A girl only has so much willpower this early on a Monday morning.

"Abe, my building is right above The Sandwich Place on Washington," I say.

He nods and smiles through the mirror.

"Have you been? To The Sandwich Place?" Reed asks.

"Yeah, we go a few times a week."

"I guess I'll have to frequent there more often." His teasing grin goes on display.

"I'm usually with my boss." Hopefully that will keep his stalking tendencies to a minimum.

"I'm as good with bosses as I am with parents." My stomach flips when he winks.

"Abe, how much longer?" I ask.

Reed chuckles beside me.

"Three minutes," Abe says.

Luckily, Reed's phone rings and a scowl appears when he looks at the screen. "I have to take this, hold up."

"Reed Warner," he answers with authority. My mind shoots to me secured to a bed with his ties and him using that same stern voice as he explores my body. "No, that's not the deal."

The car slows even though there's plenty of space between the car ahead of us and our bumper. Abe couldn't make it any more obvious that he's trying to make sure Reed finishes his phone call before I hop out of the car. We're inching forward at a snail's pace and he's purposely stopping behind the buses now.

"I can get out here," I lean forward and whisper to Abe.

"Wait until I stop," he says.

Reed's hand lands on my knee again and then he holds up one finger. I've been here before. When one minute turns into five, turns into one more phone call. I used to sit there next to Pete as everything got pushed ahead of me. Well, my time is important, too.

"I gotta call you back," Reed says, his eyes on me the entire time. "No, Bill, I don't give a shit. I'm asking for five minutes, not a lifetime which is exactly what your client is going to get if this goes to jury because you keep me from saying goodbye to my girlfriend." He doesn't wait for a reply and clicks the phone off.

"I'm not your girlfriend."

"Yet."

"Never."

"I got it from here. See you tomorrow morning, Abe. Thank you." He opens his door and steps out of the car.

"Thank you, Abe." I slide toward the open door.

"See you next Monday," he answers.

"Oh, no. This was a one and done."

I accept Reed's hand but before I clear the interior of the car Abe speaks. "Whatever you say. But I'll see you Monday."

I shake my head. Even this Uber driver thinks Reed will get what he wants. Well, I've dealt with lawyers before and I don't fall for their case winning, persuasive closing arguments—anymore. It's all bullshit sprinkled with a few big words.

"You must be the steak."

My hand's not out of Reed's when his gaze shoots from the woman he doesn't know back to me. I close my eyes wishing I would've fled the car moments earlier because Chelsea will not make this easy on me.

Chapter Fifteen

"Steak?" Reed asks, his eyes lighting up because I'm sure he's figured out it's not a bad thing to be compared to.

"Chelsea." My tone is curt and displeased.

She straightens her computer bag over her shoulder, her gaze taking in every inch of Reed. He's looking exceptionally attractive today. A gray suit instead of his usual blue. His jacket hangs open displaying a buttoned-up vest underneath which his tie is tucked into. His usual mop of hair is gelled to perfection and a satin-mustard handkerchief that matches his tie peeks out of his front pocket.

"Who dresses you? A Nordstrom's personal shopper?" Chelsea asks the question I was just wondering.

Reed chuckles, holding his hand out for Chelsea. "Reed Warner, and I take pride in the fact that I'm a big boy now and can dress myself." He gives her a playful wink.

She accepts his hand, her eyes still roaming over him like he's too much for her to take in all at once. "Definitely a steak."

110

"Chelsea, I think you have an early morning call, right?" I say and nod toward the building.

Her gaze flickers to mine. She could say anything at this moment and that scares me more than Reed's close proximity.

"Yeah, I'll leave you two alone. Very nice to meet you, Reed Warner."

"You too…Chelsea?" he questions since I never properly introduced them.

The sidewalk is filling in with everyone rushing off to work before the start of the day.

"Sorry. Chelsea Walsh," I point to her. "Reed Warner."

"Nice to meet a friend of Victoria's," Reed says. "Tell me, what's the secret to getting her to accept a date with me?"

My cheeks heat as Chelsea pretends to think about it. "She's a tough one for sure." She taps her lips with a newly manicured nail. "Bribery is probably your best option."

"Bribery?" Reed questions and glances over at me.

"You just need to figure out what it is she wants most." She gives me a meaningful look and then looks back at Reed.

"I am a lawyer, so that should be somewhat easy." The smug grin on his face says he's playing.

"I better get upstairs before the boss comes in. See you up there, Victoria. I hope to see you again, Reed." She nods in his direction.

"You'll see me again. I'm relentless when I want something."

"That's for sure," I mumble.

"Refreshing to see a man who doesn't give up on what he wants."

I clear my throat and they both look over at me. "Bye, Chelsea."

She waves her fingers in the air. "Bye." She turns on her heels, running right into a man. He grips both her arms to allow her to find her footing again.

He's wearing jeans, a t-shirt and a black leather jacket, his hair mussed in multiple directions. Not in an I-don't-care way, but in a sexy, I-just-got-fucked kind of way.

"Hello, there." Chelsea's voice oozes seduction. "Care to escort me to my building?"

The man laughs, staring down at her with a promise of reckless, casual sex that will surely leave her legs wobbly. Huh. Maybe I get the bad boy obsession a little bit after all.

"Didn't I see you in the courtroom just last week?" Reed says next to me.

"Huh?" The bad boy stares over at Reed and it's clear the moment he recognizes him.

Chelsea turns, the guy still holding her up. "You're a criminal?" she asks him, half with disgust, half with what sounds like intrigue.

The man nods.

Chelsea stands back.

"What are we talking? Murder? Robbery? Armed robbery?" I'm not sure if Chelsea is hoping he was there for a misdemeanor or a felony.

"You should move it along."

Reed's stern voice has him taking the suggestion and he winks, his brown eyes almost promising Chelsea that they'll have fun another time. Then he crosses the street to the sound of brakes slamming and horns honking at him.

"Did you see that chiseled jaw?" Chelsea's head circles around like she's about to pass out.

"I saw that he's unfamiliar with a crosswalk," I deadpan.

Reed raises his eyebrows at me. "I better get going so I can stay on schedule this morning." His warm body stays close to me.

"Thank you for the ride." I smile politely.

"You're welcome."

His teeth bite down on his bottom lip and I wait for whatever else he wants to say.

"Standing date next Monday," he says.

"Not a date."

He's smiling before he even says the word I know is coming next. "Yet."

"Never," I singsong like the joke is getting old and roll my eyes.

He glances down the road to the courthouse and then back to me. "Tell Chelsea that guy isn't the guy for her. Remember I'm the ADA. It's my job to be able to tell the good from the bad."

"I haven't forgotten." It's one of the reasons I'm keeping him at arm's length.

"I know you haven't." He frowns for a brief moment. "Have a great day, Victoria." He runs his hand down my arm, a path of goose bumps chasing behind his touch.

"Bye." The word comes out needy and breathier than I intended.

He grins then steps off the corner, raising his hand as he continues to look down the one-way street and reaches the other side without one squeal of brakes or honk of a horn. Stopping on the other side, he circles around and a case-winning smile crosses his face when he sees that I'm still watching him.

"Lovesick puppy!" Chelsea calls out from the entrance of the building. "I thought you were playing hard to get!"

I swivel on my heels and dodge the people walking

along the sidewalk like I'm in a game of Frogger until I reach Chelsea.

"I'm not playing hard to get." We step through the doors and I press the up button on the elevator.

"Sure, you are."

We get on the elevator, and I'm thankful no one else joins us. Chelsea isn't good at keeping her mouth shut in front of others.

"I am not. I just don't want a relationship," I say as I press the button for our floor.

Her face morphs to a stone-cold serious expression. "The man I just met practically has a sticker on his forehead that says, 'I'm excellent in bed. Use me, abuse me, and toss me aside.'"

Diagnosis confirmed—Chelsea is nuts.

"No, he doesn't. He has a 'I'd be a devoted husband, fun dad and love you forever' sticker."

The corners of her lips tilt up until she notices I'm watching her and then she tempers her reaction. "Just sleep with the guy and get it over with."

"He's not that type of guy, plus—"

She rolls her eyes. "Every guy is that type of guy, Vic. What is it really?"

The bell dings, and the doors slide open, leaving us in the **RISE** foyer in front of the glass doors. We step off the elevator and I turn to face her.

"I haven't dated anyone since the divorce. You think I don't see what a wonderful guy he is? I do, and that's why he can't be my rebound guy."

I walk through the glass doors and into my work area, Chelsea following behind.

"Whoa, whoa, whoa. I thought we weren't going out with him because he's a lawyer and was the best man at your wedding? Now you're bringing in a third reason?" Chelsea sits down in the chair across from me as I boot up my computer.

"There's a host of reasons. Lawyers lie, yes, but technically he works for the public interest to put the bad guys behind bars, a noble profession. The best man thing is bound to cause trouble, but it really would be a great fuck you to Pete if I did sleep with his best man. Not that I would because of that."

She leans forward in her seat and points to me. "He deserves it."

"I'm not against ever getting married again, or dating, or living with someone, but right now I need to finish school. I need to make it, so my mom lives with me, not the other way around. I want to show Jade how to live your own life and let the man join your life, not become your life. Reed's the type of guy who will gladly add us onto his shoulders—he'll house us, feed us, clothe us, and love us." My voice quivers despite my best effort to stop it from doing so.

"Vic," Chelsea sighs. "You can have all that *and* get your degree *and* have a career."

I shake my head. "Maybe, and Reed might be the person to allow me that, but what if he's a rebound and I lose him because I'm not mentally able to move on yet? There's a reason I haven't dated in so long."

Chelsea leans back with a forlorn expression on her face and I wish I was capable of reading her mind right now.

"I understand." She stands and leans forward to squeeze my hand before walking down the hallway. "But at least screw him." The echo of her laugh trails along with her as she heads into her office.

The office door opens and Hannah races in, her heels clicking faster than I've ever seen before. "Just the person I need to beg." She points to me and doesn't stop, but heads right into her office.

What now?

Chapter Sixteen

"*B*eg?" I ask following Hannah into her office.

Her space is like walking into a Pottery Barn office catalog if there was such a thing for office furniture. White desk with a green fabric chair tucked underneath. A leather couch and a flower-patterned chair are arranged in the corner with some knick-knacks with empowering sayings by women strewn throughout the space. Don't get me wrong, it's all beautifully done. She had a decorator, but the vision was hers. It screams femininity and I love that she didn't cave to the typical dreary brown and gray office furniture.

"I need a lawyer."

I tilt my head. "A divorce lawyer?"

"No. I'm already divorced." She holds up her left hand where her ring finger remains empty. "Someone to look over some contracts. There's a similar foundation out there that's coming after us saying that our name and slogan is too similar."

"Oh no. Okay, I can look someone up. I'm sure it won't be a problem." I jot it down on my pad of paper. "What about that tax attorney who called the office a few weeks back?"

She's already shaking her head. "He's great with numbers, but I need someone who knows lawsuits and contracts. Not to mention, I already tried him. He's on vacation or something. His secretary said he couldn't be reached. Where does someone go that a cell phone can't be answered or an email sent?"

She scrunches her face up as if the thought is really beyond her understanding. The man's probably on an anniversary trip with his wife or a family trip and doesn't want to be disturbed.

"I'll find someone." I turn around to head to my computer thinking this will be an easy task.

"Victoria?"

I circle back around. She's sitting down in her chair and plugging in her laptop now.

"What about that steak guy? Isn't he a lawyer?"

I wave her off. "He's the assistant district attorney. We should probably find a specialist for this."

She types in her password, and then leans back in her chair, her fingernails tapping on her desk. "Could you give him a call? He's what, just down the street, right?" She glances out the window as if she can see his office from here. Which she probably can since we're high enough in the building.

"Um… I'm sure he's busy. I guarantee I can find someone else." I step backward.

"Maybe he can just take a quick look on his lunch break?"

Why is she pressing this issue?

"Um…"

"You're not comfortable with it." She waves me off. "I

would never put you in an uncomfortable position. Never mind."

All the tension leaves my body.

"It's just this company is threatening to file later today and I'm desperate for someone to make sense of this," she continues. "There are terms I just don't understand. This will affect the programs we're already implementing with the girls and I'd hate for them to stop. Losing traction would be detrimental to our efforts." She pauses for a second. "Once you find someone, try to get them here today. I'll pay double."

I nod, stepping out of the room.

Shit, shit, shit. She's not even a mother and she can guilt trip almost as well as my own. Fuck.

I sit down at my desk. Finding the right lawyer is easy, getting him or her here today even with double pay, will not be. And what if we end up with one of those ambulance chasers because we don't have time to vet the right person? And then there are the girls. Girls my daughter's age.

With a mental curse, I pull my cell phone out of my purse.

Holding it in my lap, I stare down at it for a few seconds. This is a business transaction. I'll offer to pay him. Yes, brilliant. If he's getting paid, then it's not a favor.

Convinced I've come up with the best possible plan given the circumstances, I pull up his name.

Me: *Do you have lunch plans?*

Three dots appear immediately, and I wonder if there's ever a time he doesn't have his cell phone close at hand.

Reed: *Is this Victoria?*

Me: *Do a lot of women text you asking about your lunch plans?*
Reed: *Well…I am a catch. Just ask your friend Chelsea.*
Me: *Try to get a hold of your ego for a second. This is business related.*
Reed: *Business? Did you commit a crime in the last half hour?*
Me: *My boss wondered if you'd look over some legal contracts for her?*

I go on to explain the situation and his response is immediate and exactly what I was expecting.

Reed: *What do I get for my trouble?*
Me: *Double pay.*
Reed: *Double pay?*
Me: *Yes, we'll pay double your normal fee.*
Reed: *I don't do favors for money. That's called prostitution. ;)*

I ignore the innuendo and text him back.

Me: *It's not a favor, she'll pay you.*
Reed: *I work for the state, I can't take her money.*
Me: *But you can do it as a favor?*
Reed: *Have I asked for anything in return?*
Me: *No, but you will.*
Reed: *You wound me! Why do you insist on thinking so poorly of me?*
Me: *In my experience lawyers rarely do something for nothing.*
Reed: *You just haven't experienced the right ones. ;) See you at noon.*
Me: *What do you want in return?*

Me in a bed naked with chocolate sauce dripping off my nipples? I can take one for the team.

Reed: *Nothing. See you then.*

Me: *Thank you.*

The three dots appear, disappear, appear again but another text never comes through and I worry that I may have actually pissed him off this time.

"He'll be here at noon, Hannah," I call out.

"Thank you, Vic, you're a lifesaver."

Funny, I feel like a little bit of an ungrateful bitch at the moment.

WHEN THE DOOR opens at noon, my breathing picks up pace expecting to see Reed. Instead, a woman dressed in an expensive looking pant suit walks in with a briefcase clutched in one hand. Her hair is dark and shiny, cut right to her jawline which accentuates her beauty. She laughs, glancing behind her, and I see Reed stroll in behind her with his perfected swagger and million-dollar smile on display.

No wonder he didn't want anything in return, he had a lunch date already.

He shuts the door behind him and leads the woman to the edge of my desk.

"Good afternoon, Victoria," he says, all business, like all I really am to him is the receptionist.

"Good afternoon." I tap my pen on the desk in an effort to relieve some of my irritation.

"This is Raegan Gilroy and she's an intellectual property attorney. She's probably the best one to look over your contracts."

Raegan places her hand out in front and I stand, shaking it. "Pleasure to meet you. If you want to have a seat, I'll tell Hannah you're here."

"Thank you." She smiles, a perfect row of straight teeth unveiled from between her plump red lipsticked lips.

Reed winks and follows her to the couches in our waiting area.

I lift the phone at the exact same time Chelsea steps out of her office. She glances to her right and then to me and back to her right again.

Reed waves. "Afternoon, Chelsea."

He can take his good afternoon and shove it up his ass.

"Hey," she says and then clears her throat. "What are…"

"Chelsea," I call out and she walks over to me rather than standing there awestruck.

Raegan Gilroy whispers something to Reed and he smiles, whispering back, shaking his head.

"Can you please grab me a photocopy of this while I let Hannah know her appointment is here?" I shove a stack of papers at Chelsea and for once in her life, she does what she's asked without arguing.

Once she's heading down the hall, I pick up my receiver and buzz Hannah's office to let her know her appointment is here.

"Send him in and can you sit in and take notes?" Hannah asks.

"Sure, but he is a she. Reed brought an intellectual property attorney with him to look over the contract."

"Really? Perfect. Send her in."

I hang up, stand, straightening my own skirt. My outfit looks like I got it from the thrift store in comparison to Raegan's.

"Ms. Gilroy, Hannah is ready."

Raegan stands, again whispers something to Reed. He shakes his head and she says nothing more, smiling at me as she meets me right outside Hannah's office.

I open the door, following Raegan in. "Ms. Gilroy, this is Ms. Crowley." I introduce the two of them and take a seat on the couch by the window, notepad in hand.

They shake hands and I see the stack of contracts sitting on the corner of Hannah's desk. She picks them up and rounds her desk.

"Thank you so much for doing this on such short notice. Oh, Victoria, on second thought we're good. I don't need notes but thank you." She smiles and then signals toward the couch to Raegan, effectively dismissing me. "Can we get you anything?"

"No, I'm good." Raegan looks at me because yes, I am the beverage go-getter. Isn't she a smart one.

"Let me know if you change your mind." I leave the room, closing the door behind me. When I return to my desk I find Reed in the chair situated in front of my desk, his ankle propped up on his knee, revealing black socks with lines on them, his black shoes shined with no sign of wear.

"Thank you. That was nice of you to set us up with an IP attorney." I sit down at my desk, sliding my chair in.

"I'm nice like that." He winks, and I want to glue his eyelids open, so he can't repeat that sexy move.

"There's that ego again. I enjoyed its short vacation."

He raises his hands in the air. "I'm not going to stop thinking I'm the best person for you. I told you I'd prove it."

"How long until you think you'll give up?" I shift some papers around my desk that don't really need shifting.

He shakes his head, his foot drops to the floor and he leans forward. "Never. I told you I like you, Victoria. I want you and I'm not easily sidetracked when I'm this sure about something."

"Am I really supposed to expect that you're just pining away for me, remaining celibate until I say yes?"

He grabs his phone from his pocket and tosses it on my desk, followed by his keys.

"Here."

"What?"

"The password to my phone is 624507. The round key is for the front door of my building. The square one gets you into my condo and that small one, that will get you into my safe." He leans back in his chair like it's case closed.

"I don't want any of this. I trust you."

"You clearly don't. I could tell you thought Raegan was a lunch date I brought here with me. Why would I bring a woman here when I'm trying my damnedest to get with you?"

I pick up his phone and keys, placing them on the edge of my desk. "Believe me, I don't *want* to worry about that stuff. I don't *want* to think the worst, but that seed was planted in me a long time ago and the roots grew too deep. At this point, I don't know how to kill it."

He stands up, circling my desk and leaning against the edge. His fingers graze along my forehead down my face until he's cupping my cheek with his hand. And it feels good. So good. And comforting. And scarier than all of that, it makes me feel safe.

"I'll help you. I know I'm asking you to make a giant leap, so let's start small. A dinner. A meal and I'll drive you home right after. We won't even have dessert. If you want to take a taxi home, fine. I just want to spend time with you."

I swallow down the anxiety threatening to make me bolt. The idea of giving someone else a chance to hurt me again has me wanting to push him away. But in his eyes, I see only adoration and decide that this will be the time I give him what he wants.

"One dinner," I whisper, barely believing the words coming out of my mouth.

"One dinner."

"Nothing more."

"Not yet."

"Okay."

His eyes widen with my agreement. "I'll pick you up Friday at seven."

"Okay."

"You're being way too agreeable now. What's the catch?"

I giggle softly and close my eyes as his thumb runs along my skin. "No catch."

"Keep the password to my phone. Check it any time." He slides down, crouching down in front of me, his hands wrapped tightly around mine. "I have nothing to hide."

I nod.

"The offer is never off the table. One day you'll learn to trust me. I promise."

He guides me up by my hands, takes his phone and keys, stuffing them into his jacket pocket.

"Where are you taking me?"

"Lunch."

"You're pushing your luck."

"This is business. St. Pats' business." He winks.

He never lets go of my hand and as much as it scares me, I don't want him to.

Chapter Seventeen

It's nine o'clock at night when I finally drag myself up the walkway toward my childhood bungalow, hoping Jade is asleep because every limb in my body is more exhausted than it felt when she was a newborn. Working out with Chelsea before my class was not the best decision.

My phone rings as I step through the door. Jade runs over, hugs me and then steals the phone out of my jacket pocket.

"Jade," I sigh.

My mom is laying on the couch, her eyes closed, the television on some Disney show I'm sure is teaching my daughter how to be sassier than already comes naturally to her.

"Daddy!" she screams so loud, my mom's eyes pop open.

"Oh, I'm sorry. I must have dozed off." She moves to sit up.

"Mom, go to bed, I'll take care of her tonight. Thank you."

I really can't expect her to manage Jade for much longer. It's not her job to raise a child all over again. We came here to help her, not the other way around.

"No. I've got my second wind now." She half smiles.

Jade skips around the house with my phone pressed to her ear. "School's good," she says, her voice holding the excitement only her daddy receives. Each call like an unexpected surprise.

"The bastard?" my mom asks in a near whisper, pulling the blanket off her legs.

"Yeah."

She rolls her eyes and stands up, collecting Jade's dishes.

"No, Mom, I got it." I take them from her hands and head to the kitchen where Jade is rounding the center island like it's a racetrack.

Once I've set the dishes in the sink, I place my hands on her shoulders to stop her and point to the table. She frowns but sits down.

"Can we FaceTime?" I hear her ask.

Pete must accept because she hangs up and then dials him right back with FaceTime. I glance over, and his face is displayed on my phone, his backdrop the usual one—his office.

"Daddy, are you at work?" Jade props her head in her hand and positions the phone.

"Yeah, it's only seven o'clock here," his deep voice answers with amusement in his tone. Like it's normal for people to work past seven when they started at six in the morning.

"You look tired," Jade says.

I pretend to wash the dishes and load the dishwasher while the two talk, glancing at the screen every once in a while. He can't see me over Jade's head taking up the entire camera area, thank goodness. Looking at Pete, I can't help but wonder what he'd think if I told him about my upcoming date with Reed. I'm sure he'd be surprised I ran into him, let alone that he's been actively pursuing me, but I don't think he'd care in a jealous sort of way.

"Guess what, Bug?"

"What Daddy?"

I clench the dish in my hand at hearing him use my term of affection toward her. Actually, my mom's that kind of stuck while she was growing up.

"I'm coming to Chicago," he announces.

"You are?"

"Well, I heard this special little girl was having a birthday."

"Me!" Jade points to herself.

I hate the way my intelligent daughter pretends to be a baby when she's speaking with her dad. Like he won't love her as much if she shows how smart and opinionated she is.

"Yeah, I wouldn't miss my little bug's birthday."

Gah. Bile rises up my throat but I manage to suppress my eye roll.

"I'm going to be eight." That was not an 'I'm proud to be eight,' that was a 'just in case you forgot, I'm turning eight.' On her fifth birthday, Pete thought she was four. Good times were had by all in the Keebler family that day, let me tell you.

"I know. I'm staying at Grandma and Grandpa's, how about you stay over there with us?"

He's kidding, right? On her birthday, he's going to try to take her away from me?

"Jade sweetie, let me talk to your dad after you're finished." I manage to keep my voice level when I really want to rip the phone from her grasp and unleash a series of vulgarities at my ex-husband.

"Okay."

"Is that your mom you're talking to?" I smile to myself, knowing his worst fear is it's my mom.

"Yep," she says, moving the phone to show me at the sink.

"Hey, Vic," he says.

I wave, my hand full of soap. "Hey."

"Can you bring the ocean with you?" Jade quickly hijacks the conversation. Not that I blame her. She waits weeks for his calls sometimes.

"I can bring you some sand and water."

Fat chance.

"Then I can take it to show and tell. My friend, Henry, has never seen the ocean."

"Never seen the ocean? What kind of sheltered life is this kid living?" He chuckles like that's actually funny.

"What does sheltered mean?"

"It means he hasn't seen everything yet." My mom walks by, tapping Jade's hip so she'll slide over and sit properly on the chair.

"I want to show Henry everything. Can he come with me to Los Angeles?" Jade bounces up and down on the chair and whines.

"Of course he can, but I'm not sure his parents would agree."

"Henry doesn't have parents." The sadness I hear in her voice every time she has to tell someone that is ever present.

"He doesn't. Who takes care of him?" Pete asks.

My mom joins me at the sink, and we share a look of mutual disgust that my ex-husband is rarely present in Jade's life but wants to play dad of the year when he is.

"His grandma and grandpa, oh and he's got a big brother."

"I'm glad he has his grandparents." I overhear the shuffling of paperwork. "Because I'm not sure a big brother would be much help."

Jade giggles. "No, Daddy, Henry's big brother is an adult. Mommy said it's a program to help make him a man."

"Make him a man?" Pete sounds skeptical and my mom laughs, patting my shoulder.

"Yeah, Re—"

"Time for bed, Jade." I cut her off and sit down next to her at the table before she says Reed's name. I'm not even sure why I care if she does. It'd be like a big middle finger to Pete, but it's not something I want to discuss with Pete in front of our daughter. Besides, I'm not ready to share something when I don't even know what that something it is yet.

Jade pouts and hugs the phone to her body. "That's a hug from me to you, Daddy."

He kisses his hand and blows it her way. "Do you see it, Jade, floating from L.A. to Chicago? I sent it express so it should be there at any moment."

I smile at the exchange. Pete's good at sweet-talking his daughter. She pretends to search the space between her and the ceiling. Runs out of the kitchen to the front door. "Got it!" she screams and runs back in with a clasped fist, sits down and flattens her palm to her cheek. "It couldn't get through the door."

Pete smiles the genuine smile that is rarely seen. It might only be reserved for his daughter. He wept the first time he saw Jade and it was the truest emotion I've ever witnessed him bear. Although she's out of sight and out of mind to him most of the time, she'll always be his number one.

"Good night, Bug," he says, his hand up in the air. "See you in a couple weeks."

"Night Daddy," She kisses the screen and I refrain from telling her how gross that is because she's way too cute and these rare phone calls light up her day.

Jade slides the phone my way and there I am in the little screen at the top right. My stomach revolts over the fact that I'm going to have to have a full-blown conversation with my ex. That, and the fact that I only have coffee and a bag of Doritos in my stomach.

Pete continues to concentrate on his paperwork.

"Go get ready and I'll tuck you in after I get off the phone with Daddy, okay?" She nods and hugs me, then kisses my cheek.

"Okay." She steps out of view and pauses. Her fingers in her mouth, nibbling on her nails.

"Jade," I sigh.

"You aren't going to yell, are you?" she asks.

Pete and I are more indifferent then argumentative, but the scars of our failed relationship are only a layer deep to our daughter. The one thing I wish I could take back is that. I should've never allowed us to fight in the next room. I'm sure she probably overheard things a little girl shouldn't.

"No, sweetie. Go."

She steps back, facing me until she has no choice but to turn around and head down the hall. Once the water in the bathroom is going, I focus my attention on Pete.

"You're coming for her birthday?"

"Yes, why wouldn't I? I should ask you to fly her back here." He closes a file folder, leans back in his seat and stares at me through the camera.

"Well, I'm throwing her a party here."

"Funny, I haven't gotten an invitation?" Like he'd know if he did. There's probably a month's worth of mail shoved in his new beach house mailbox.

"I haven't mailed them yet."

He smirks. "Still the organized one, I see."

My fist clenches under the table. "Well, raising your daughter, working and going back to school—"

He raises his hand effectively cutting me off. "Let's remember you chose that."

My jaw clenches so hard I fear my teeth could crack. But I need to play nice. I'm the one who gets to see our daughter each and every day. "Listen. Why don't I do the party on her actual birthday and then that way she can spend Saturday night with you and your family?"

"Fine?" he questions. "I haven't seen her in three months and you're making it sound like you're doing me a favor by allowing me one night. How cordial of you, Vic." He shakes his head. "I knew I should have fought you harder."

"We both know nothing would be different if I'd stayed in L.A."

"I would have been able to see my daughter more."

"What? Maybe twice more. Don't make me bring up how many times you were a no-show."

"You'd love that, wouldn't you? Any chance to portray me as a deadbeat dad. My checks are being cashed. She has health insurance. I'm doing my part." He lights up a cigarette and blows out a cloud of smoke. "The martyr bit is growing old, Victoria."

"When did you start smoking again?"

"Since you stressed me out so badly that I needed them to relax." A smile tips his lips. "I have a few big cases."

Pete has been an on-again, off-again smoker since he

first approached me at a bar with an unlit cigarette dangling from his lips and looking for a light. How foolish I was to think there was something sexy about him.

"Smoking isn't going to help." It'll flare up his asthma.

"Yeah, yeah, Mother." He exhales a drag and a cloud of white smoke covers the screen.

"Take care of yourself. All that stress and smoking—and if I had to guess there's a whiskey on the rocks to your right. Jade needs a father."

A chiding laugh escapes him. "She needs a father who cuts her mother big checks, you mean."

"No, that's not what I meant." My fingernails dig into my palm now.

He sits up straight and extinguishes the cigarette, grabs his drink to his right, and downs the rest of it.

"Let's remember, Vic, you giving me your holier-than-thou advice ended two years ago when you became a Clarke again."

He's always throwing it in my face that I took my maiden name back. Why does he care at this point?

"Okay, fine. I'll send you a carton of cigarettes and a bottle of whiskey. I wouldn't mind having Jade all to myself."

A laugh leaves his lips again, but it's a genuine one. Words that would've caused a knockdown, drag-out fight years ago, now halt our tempers because once we hang up, we're done with one another.

We don't have to sleep facing away from each other or go about our nightly routine in the same bathroom ignoring one another. We hang up and he goes back to what he loves—his work and on occasion barely legal women, and I get to tuck our daughter into bed. I definitely have the better end of this arrangement.

"I'll keep you posted once I book my ticket." He sits up straight, indicating he's ready to hang up.

"Fine. I'll let her know you'll be here for sure."

"Thanks. Get a good night's sleep, you look like shit." He smiles.

"Look in the mirror," I reply, and his smile grows even larger.

"Night, Vic."

"Night, Pete."

I click the button on the phone and bang my forehead against the kitchen table. He still has the capability to deplete every ounce of energy I have.

"Mom, I'm ready!" Jade screams and I push myself up using the edge of the table.

When I step away, my phone dings. Snatching it back up, I see that it's Reed.

Reed: *Raegan said she's on board to work pro bono for the foundation. Said she thinks it'll be pretty easy to get these people off Hannah's back. They have no case.*

Me: *Thank you! Hannah will be thrilled.*

Reed: *You can thank me properly on Friday.*

Me: *If you're expecting a blow job, you should know I bite.*

Reed: *I scoffed, did you hear me? What kind of guy do you think I am?*

Me: *I think you're exactly that—a guy!*

Reed: *I'll settle for a kiss.*

Me: *On the cheek.*

Reed: *How come when I'm making deals with you I feel like I got a shit poor education at law school?*

Me: *I'm a woman, Reed, negotiations are what we do best.*

Reed: *Wanna know what I do best? ;)*

My fingers stop moving and then start texting, only to

delete. I have a few guesses as to what he does best and the fact that my man-deprived body wants him to show me, is making me squirm. But I can't let that reflect in my response.

Me: *Typical man, can only master one tool.*
Reed: *One tool, huh? I have multiple tools—two hands, ten fingers, one tongue, one mouth, and one big long stick that finishes the job all the others start.*
Me: *Time for bed now. Good night, Reed.*
Reed: *Imagine me tonight? God knows, I'll be imagining you.*

I flush crimson red. I thought we were taking it slow, and now he's admitting to masturbating to thoughts of me?

"MOM!" Jade yells.

I stuff the phone in my pocket and head down the hall. It dings one last time.

Reed: *Just remember, you moved the conversation into sexting territory. :P*

Clicking my screen off, I walk into Jade's bedroom, praying the ache between my legs will dissipate enough that I don't actually need to do what he suggested before I can get to sleep.

Chapter Eighteen

riday comes with a bang and I don't know if that's good or bad. If the week would've dragged by, it would've been because I was anticipating my date. A good sign for sure. The fact that it was Monday and then, blink, Friday? What does that say?

I'm in the bathroom brushing my teeth one more time when the doorbell rings. A mixture of nausea and butterflies battle in my stomach. Not only do I have first date jitters, but I also had to sit Jade down last night and explain that Reed and I would be going out tonight on an adult-only outing.

"Reed!" Jade exclaims. "This is my grandma, Diane."

"Nice to meet you," my mom says and I'm sure she's shaking his hand. "What beautiful flowers."

Oh jeez, he brought me flowers. Roses I'm sure. Standard first date material. I watch the pinkness flush my cheeks and I spit into the sink. Turning on the faucet prohibits me from hearing anything further in their conversation. Which is probably a blessing.

Examining myself one more time in the mirror, I take a

deep breath. I don't look like a single mom, right? Another spray of perfume and I step through the fragrance and out the bathroom door. What's the worst that can happen? He doesn't like me and well, it will save a lot of time and energy.

"This is Moe," Jade says.

I round the corner to find Jade's hand in Reed's, sitting on the couch with Moe climbing over Jade to get to Reed. He snuggles into his thigh, leaving Reed's slacks covered with a thick layer of black fur. He hesitantly pets the animal.

"Mommy." Jade's soft voice announces my entry and Reed's attention shifts from the loving cat at his side to me in the doorway.

"Hey." He moves to stand and Jade releases his hand.

How does he keep getting more handsome? He's wearing a pair of charcoal grey slacks, a blue button-down shirt and a pair of black loafers that aren't shiny like the ones he wore Monday morning. His hair is gelled a tad differently, wilder but still put together.

"Hi." I lean my shoulder on the doorway and catch his gaze raking me over.

I worry my dress is too short, but from his heated gaze, I'm guessing he likes it. Long gone are the days I can wear anything tight and form fitting, but I show off my best asset that wasn't altered due to childbearing—my legs. My heels give the impression they're longer than they are which is great considering my petite stature.

"You're beautiful." This is why Reed won a date. I've never believed someone more in my life. That cocky persona he puts on has disappeared and when he says I'm beautiful, his voice shakes slightly, like that scares him a little.

"Thank you."

"Here." Jade holds up the flowers to him. "He brought flowers." She stands between us, smiling back and forth.

Reed takes the bouquet of tulips and holds them out for me.

"Thank you." Our fingers brush when we exchange them and a current blasts down to my toes and back up. "I'll put them in water."

I turn to head to the kitchen, but my mom is there. "I got it. You two go." She takes the flowers from my hands and I smile down at her since my heels have me towering over her.

"Thanks for watching Jade."

"Yes, Ms. Clarke, thank you for watching her so I can take out your daughter." Reed pokes his head into the kitchen.

My mom puts the flowers into the vase she already prepared. "I'm happy to do it. It was a pleasure seeing you again, Reed. Maybe you can come by for dinner sometime."

I crinkle my forehead at my mom who effectively ignores me.

"I'd love to." Reed side glances me and I shift my stance.

"Great, I'll talk with Vic and we'll let you know. Now, you two, go. Jade and I have a night of movies and popcorn."

Jade runs in, hugging my mom around her waist.

Reed holds out his fist to her. "Henry said this is unfair, so next time you guys come." He winks. Jade fist bumps him and then stops in front of me.

I bend down so I'm at her eye level. "Be good for Grandma. Go to bed on time. Don't fuss, okay?"

She peeks up at Reed and I shift her face back to me with a nudge of my finger on her chin.

"Promise."

I kiss her cheek and squeeze her to me. Once we're apart, she pushes me lightly, but since I'm mid crouch, I lose my footing and fall right into Reed's arms. I eye Reed like he planned it, but he shakes his head.

"Not my doing, but you smell amazing," he whispers, and I straighten, pretending he doesn't affect me.

"Sorry, Mommy." Jade has her am-I-in-trouble expression on.

"Let's go." I wave over to my mom who's leaning over the counter in front of a bowl of popcorn with a kernel between her fingers.

"After you." Reed steps back, allowing me to go first.

The chill of the spring night air settles around me. Reed shuts the door, walking in line with me down the walkway until we reach the sidewalk. I had expected to see Abe's blue sedan, but there's a sleek sports car parked along the curb. Its lights flash and it beeps when we approach.

I stop. "Is this yours?"

He opens the passenger door. "I hope so, or this date is going to get interesting when the police chase starts."

"Oh." I slide in as demurely as I can considering I have to bend so far down I'm practically sitting on the potholed street of Chicago.

He shuts the door, rounds the back of the car and before I can take in all the fancy controls and figure out what the wing trademark logo on the steering wheel stands for, the scent of his cologne surrounds me and blocks all working brain function.

"Is it okay if we head out of the city?" he asks.

"Sure."

"So, your mom's good if I fly you to Paris for the weekend?" His face is serious. No raised eyebrows or sarcastic tone.

"No, and you aren't."

He reaches over and squeezes my knee. "I'm kidding. I want to impress you, but I'm not that guy from Pretty Woman."

Embarrassment hits me hard and I immediately lose all my spunk. Of course, he wouldn't want to go to the trouble of doing anything like that for me. What a ridiculous thought.

"He only took her from L.A. to San Fran and operas aren't my thing."

He chuckles, shifting the stick around and then slowly eases away from the curb.

"Damn him. Who did he think he was going to impress with that?" Reed laughs as I fixate on his strong hand shifting the gears while his knee rocks back and forth with the clutch.

It's sexy as fuck.

"What kind of car is this?" I ask.

"Aston Martin. I keep it in the garage of my condo. Only take it out on special occasions." He glances over with a smile that says I'm special and embarrassment washes over me.

"I forget where you grew up sometimes."

"Good. I'm not what that upbringing usually implies." He signals and turns left.

"Do your parents still live there?"

We pull onto the highway, the engine purring away as he shifts and presses down the gas pedal speeding up on the on-ramp. Traffic is piled on the other side heading into the city and we're heading out.

"Yeah. They'll leave in coffins."

"They like it there?"

"They like the status of it. They like that my sister married our next-door neighbor growing up and they moved two streets over. The grandkids can ride their bikes over. They like that they can brag that my sister married a wealthy plastic surgeon. Never mind that he's never home. Never mind that she calls me once a week to say she's on the edge of a nervous breakdown and wants to divorce him." He glances over for a second. "Sorry, more than you asked."

"No, it's fine. I'm sorry for your sister. I've been there."

His shoulders slump when the car goes faster. Is that because I brought up Pete? Does it bother Reed to think about me being his ex-wife?

"Sorry," I mumble.

"Don't be." The car slows to a normal Chicago speed which is at least twenty over the limit. He finds his way over to the left lane and seems content to stay there for the moment. "I never want you to feel like you can't tell me something. There are no rules tonight, Victoria. You want to talk about Pete, go for it. You want to ramble on about Jade, I'm game. You want to complain to me about the egg salad sandwich you had for lunch this week that made you sick, cool."

I laugh. "I knew I should've just stuck with The Sandwich Place," I murmur.

Glancing over his shoulder, he changes lanes and catches my eyes on the way back briefly before they land on the road again. "I just want you to enjoy yourself. That's all."

"Okay."

"Okay?" he asks.

"Okay."

"So, I went on this date last weekend," he talks and my

body stiffens. He bursts out laughing, not finishing the story. "I'm kidding."

I laugh along with him.

"Henry told me a joke yesterday when I called to see how he was. Want to hear it?"

"Sure, but I have to warn you, I might put you to shame in the kid jokes arena."

"Are you challenging me?" he asks with amusement and pulls into the far-right lane, exiting one highway to hop on another one.

"I am." I shift in my seat, so I can look at him better.

"Okay, why are ghosts such bad liars?" he asks, finally relaxing in his seat.

"Um…because you can see right through them." I tilt my head in a fashion that says I know I'm right.

"You weren't lying. Okay, let me dig into my arsenal here." He thinks for a moment and I try to figure out where he's taking me, but since returning to Chicago I haven't ventured out of the city much. "Okay, what do you call a cow with no legs?"

"Oh." I think and replay all the jokes Jade and I have said back and forth. All the popsicle stick riddles and her stealing my phone to ask me. "Steak?"

"Is steak on your mind?" A flirtatious grin crosses his face.

"No. Is the answer steak?"

He pulls off the highway and turns right at the light.

"No, it's not. Another guess?"

"Roast?"

"You're so close." His fingers move up to show a little space between his thumb and forefinger. Turning left, he parks in front of a restaurant and we sit in the car for a moment.

"Just tell me."

"Ground beef."

My head falls back to the leather seat. "I should've gotten that."

"How about some steak though? I thought it was only fitting you get to taste a great steak on our first date."

I roll my eyes, though not in a bad way and push him gently toward the window. He turns off the car, climbs out all alpha and hot then rounds the front of the car so I get an eyeful of him. When he opens my door, I accept his hand.

"You're too much," I say.

"You have no idea."

He makes it sound like a promise. And suddenly I'm hoping with everything in me that Reed really is a man who keeps his promises.

Chapter Nineteen

To say that dinner with Reed was something out of a movie is probably an understatement. He was a gentleman the entire night. Pulling my chair out for me, suggesting a bottle of wine, discussing which steak on the menu was the best, sliding in a joke about how he's not on the menu tonight unless I ask for the special.

By my second glass of wine, the tension and anxiety that had been laced through my body had dissolved like salt in water. Sitting at a candlelit table tucked into the far corner of a restaurant I'd never be able to afford at this point in my life, Reed wooed me. It wasn't any one thing in particular. There were no grand declarations or heartfelt moments. It was just Reed being Reed.

We talked about anything and everything and I never once felt like I had to temper my responses for fear of judgment. He told me stories about him growing up—some of which involved Pete—and I confessed to some of my more embarrassing escapades as a teenager. I explained how much I enjoyed working with Chelsea and Hannah and about my job back in Los Angeles and he explained some of the inner workings of some of his cases.

By the time we stood up, I had to find my footing. With a full stomach and a contagious smile, I allowed Reed to take me by the hand and guide me to the coat room.

"Thank you," I murmur, sliding my arms into my coat.

"I'm the one who needs to say thank you. I'm glad you took that leap."

"Me too," I admit. I put myself out there and I couldn't know for sure if it was the alcohol talking or whether Reed had cast some sort of spell on me.

I CIRCLED AROUND, waiting for him to put on his own jacket. He hands the coat check some money and nods toward the door.

Leaving the warm atmosphere of the restaurant behind, I walk ahead, and he catches up, his hand molded to my hip rather than its usual spot on my lower back. His touch has my nipples tightening inside my bra.

Until tonight, I've kept my feelings for Reed in an iron box. Locked. Under my bed. Surrounded by other boxes I haven't wanted to dust off and examine the contents of. The fear that I'll turn into the old, naive Victoria Clarke before I lost myself to being Mrs. Victoria Keebler had waged a war inside and won.

It's been two years since the divorce and it took an entire year before I felt like the Clarke surname fit me again. My intuition assures me that Reed will handle me with gentle hands, but my intuition misjudged once before and although I received the best gift from my worst decision, I am still the one who picked Pete to share my life with.

All of that and yet here I sit, not wanting him to take

me home. Wanting a minute, even a second more with him...to see the crinkle around his eyes when he laughs at something I said, to have his gaze land on me like there's nothing he'd like more than to ravish me at that very moment.

My mind is so consumed with this internal debate I hadn't noticed we were pulling away from the restaurant. He's turned the radio on at a low volume and the silence between us isn't awkward, it's comfortable. His fingers tap along the stick shift, the lyrics low as they tumble out of his mouth.

For a moment, my mind flashes forward to what it would be like if we actually worked out. On our way home from a date night to find Jade and a set of twins still challenging my mom about their bedtime. Reed swooping them up in his arms when we walk in. Me sitting down on the sofa and talking with my mom about the night. Reed bringing us tea, snuggling up beside me on the couch as he fawns over my mother and me.

I smile thinking about what could be in the fantasy I've created for the two of us.

"You're quiet," he says, his hand finding my bare knee.

I swivel in my seat to face him. "I feel like all we've done tonight is talk about me. Tell me about your family."

His body tenses for a moment. "I've told you about them. They have expectations I don't quite live up to."

"Does being an ADA pay well?" I can't help but glance at the logo on the steering wheel.

He glances at me with a smirk on his lips. "Not enough for this, if that's what you're asking."

"Well, you wear three-piece suits, which by the way I still insist a personal shopper picks out for you, you drive this ridiculously priced car"—I pat the dash—"and I imagine you live in a nice condo with a parking space that costs more every year than my entire college education did."

He chuckles. "You know I'm a rich kid."

He says it as casually as you'd tell someone you love pizza.

"Am I to assume you have a trust fund?"

He glances at me again and that smirk hasn't left his face. "You assume correct."

I move to look straight ahead out the windshield, leaning back in the seat. This would be another difference between Pete and Reed. Pete's parents though rich, didn't save. They spent and continue to spend what his father makes. They were nouveau riche and my guess is that Reed comes from old money. Pete knew if he wanted to continue his lifestyle, he had to earn the money himself. Reed went the opposite route.

"From your grandfather?" I ask.

"Grandmother." He winks. "My mom's mom."

"So, your dad…"

"My dad is a successful businessman. A CEO of a major food industry company, but my mom's family money goes back generations."

"And your dad doesn't like you being an ADA either?"

He huffs. "Right? I guess money can change people. Here's a guy who worked his way up through the ranks and he thinks his money was wasted on my degree."

My mom would have been ecstatic if I'd become a lawyer.

"I wasn't brought up to do what makes me happy, Victoria. I was brought up to do something that had a lot of money and prestige attached to it so that my parents could brag."

"But being an assistant district attorney is a noble profession," I insist.

"Don't feel bad for me, I've had a good life. So, what if my parents don't like what I do? I learned a long time ago, that's their problem, not mine."

"You sound so sure. I mean parent's expectations have the capability of really messing up a kid."

He nods before checking his blind spot to change lanes. "Believe me, I think my dad hates the fact that I started mentoring at Big Brothers because that's when I found out the real world was far from the reality inside the tiny enclave I'd been raised in. On one hand, I was grateful for what I had growing up, but on the other hand, I wanted to help those who didn't have the same opportunities."

"You're like a noble prince." The sentence falls from my lips without filtering through my brain.

Shit. My filter must be soaked in red wine at the moment.

The car rolls to a stop and for a moment, I think he didn't hear me. His gaze is set forward, his hand wrapped around the gear shift, feet poised over the two pedals. Then he glances over, and his tongue is sliding over his bottom lip. "I love that you see me that way, but I don't want to set some unrealistic expectations for you. I have plenty of faults."

"I need details."

"Well, I don't cook. I order in every night. If you went to my condo right now, you'd only find a gallon of chocolate milk and a million takeout containers and condiments in my fridge. A cleaning lady comes twice a week because I am in no way domesticated. She washes my clothes, takes care of my dry cleaning, cleans the place. I stay up insanely late every night, usually crashing on my couch with a case file in my hand."

I smile, thankful that he's not perfect. Because perfect is an illusion. And I want the real thing.

"Sounds like you're a typical bachelor to me."

He shrugs, the light turns green and he accelerates back onto the highway.

"If I continue living this way, I'll be single forever."

"I wouldn't go that far."

He chuckles. "I'm kind of hoping I might be off the market soon." He glances over at me and winks.

I melt into the expensive leather seat. If it wasn't for my sweet Jade, I'd wish I would've met him before Pete. But taking Pete out of the equation takes my Jade away and there's no way I'd be me without her.

"Can I ask you a question?" His eyes focus back on the road.

"Sure."

"I know the rules of dating state not to talk about ex's, but what happened with Pete? If you don't want to answer just tell me to mind my own business."

My gaze veers out the window. "No, it's okay." I pause for a second. "I think Pete just wasn't ready to settle down. I think he *thought* he wanted it. His parents wanted it. I guess like your parents, they wanted to brag about him. But it just wasn't for him. He's a decent dad, I will say that. I mean he could be more involved and make more of an effort, yes. But when he does spend time with Jade, she's his whole world. If he had the time to see her a few times a week, then he probably would've fought for me to stay in L.A. I'm not sure what I would've done if that were the case."

"Why did you come back?"

"My mom." I sigh. "She was diagnosed with multiple sclerosis and I'm all she's got. Me and Jade. And I wanted to be here to help her if and when her disease progresses."

He reaches over, entwines his hand with mine, and says, "I'm sorry."

"Thanks." I shoot him a gentle smile, and when he

pulls his hand away, I realize I'm not as much of a fan of a stick shift as I thought. "She has good days and bad. She's still able to help me with Jade and at this point, she probably helps me more than we help her, but I realized when she made that call that I didn't want to be miles away from her. I needed to be here."

Reed nods. "Pete understood?"

I tip my head side to side. "For the most part."

"I'm glad." He winks suggesting he's happy because if I hadn't come back here, he wouldn't have met me again.

"Pete's not a horrible guy, just not a good husband."

I give him the clean version because if I gave him the dirty version, he'd probably drop me off at the curb and skid away. Nights when I went driving around looking for him, calling his phone relentlessly, finding numbers in his pocket, smelling perfume on his clothes. I shake off the memories.

"I like to think I'll make an excellent husband." Reed laughs, and I know he's joking, but he would make a wonderful husband to some lucky girl. I know he would.

He pulls up to the curb of my mom's house, parking and turning off the car.

"I had a great time," I say.

He shoots me his winning smile. "Me too. I hope you'll agree to another date?" His eyebrows raise.

"I think I can do that." I shift to face him, my voice lower and more sensual than usual.

He leans forward, his hand cupping my cheek. "I'm trying to go slow here, Victoria, but I really like you. Come to my condo this weekend for dinner?"

"Are we having chocolate milk?"

A smile tips his lips, but his eyes remain laser-focused on mine. "I'll hire a chef."

I shake my head. The scent of the mint he took when

leaving the restaurant reaches me as he leans even closer. "If you want me to come over, you make the dinner."

"I'll make dinner if you agree to kiss me right now."

"You can kiss me if you make dinner *and* dessert."

Our words are mere whispers as we inch closer and closer. My breaths grow shallow. I want nothing more than to feel his lips on mine.

"I'll make dinner and buy dessert if I can kiss you."

"Hmm…"

"Fuck it, a tube of cookie dough it is." His mouth slams to mine, not waiting for me to accept his offer.

His hand slides along my cheek, down and around to my neck. When he runs his tongue along the seam of my lips, I open for him and his tongue slides in, searching for my own. His lips soften, and his tongue slows. My body feels weightless, like I'm soaring with the clouds as we find our rhythm.

A moan escapes me, and he groans like he's tortured, his lips applying more pressure. Never have I felt such uncontrollable desire from a kiss. It's apparent that he's trying to maintain some composure, and I wonder if we were somewhere and he could strip me down, would he? If this was our tenth date instead of our first, would he pull me over his lap? Would I let him?

Our kiss slows, and my frenzied mind stops moving in overdrive, analyzing his kiss.

His hand stays where it is on my bare neck, and he rests his forehead on mine. "You have no idea how badly I want you right now." He's breathing heavily, his chest moving up and down as he works to control himself.

"I think I do."

He chuckles. "I'm glad it's mutual."

He undoes my seatbelt then he eases back, grabbing the keys and exiting the car.

"Holy shit," I mumble to myself.

The door opens, and his hand is outstretched in an offer to help me out of the car. I accept it, step out and he links his hand with mine, keeping them that way as we make our way to the front door. It's late, so Jade should be fast asleep.

The porch light above my head reminds me of my high school days when a boy would hesitantly kiss me goodnight and I feared my dad would open the door the entire time.

"Thank you again, I had a great time."

He steps forward. "So next Saturday then?"

"Can we do Friday?" I always spend Sundays with Jade.

"Friday it is. What's your preference in cookie dough?" He winks.

I jab him in the chest with my finger. "I'm not joking, Mr. Warner, you cook the meal."

He nods a few times. "Then get in the mood for pizza because more than likely whatever I come up with will be inedible."

"Thanks for a great night." He wraps an arm around my waist and pulls me closer so we're chest to chest.

I wrap my arms around his neck, enjoying the feeling of my fingers running through his short hair and the press of his hard body to mine.

"Drive home safely," I whisper.

He dips his head and I close my eyes in anticipation of the taste of peppermint in my mouth. Our lips collide again, and we're more frantic than we were in the car. Hungrier. Needier. He slides his hands down my back until they close around the globes of my ass. A whimper escapes me, and I press farther into him, fisting his longer strands of hair so he can't get away.

My back hits the brick of the house and the rigid bulge

in his pants pushes into my stomach. I want to lift my legs and wrap them around him so bad it hurts, but I'm outside my mom's house with a porch light broadcasting everything Reed and I are doing to the neighbors.

My hand falls between us and I push him away lightly. "Neighbors," I say, breathless and panting.

"Right." He steps back and grips the back of his neck, his face strained. "I better go before I beg."

I giggle and his gaze dips to my lips again.

"Good night, Victoria."

"Night."

He walks down the cement path to his car, stopping right before he slides in, nodding and signaling for me to go inside.

I wave and dig my keys out, my hands shaking as I try to unlock the door. I step into the house and collapse on the couch in the living room.

"That good, huh?" my mom asks.

Chapter Twenty

ade and I head out of the house Monday morning to find the Uber waiting. Henry's face peeks out the window like a Bassett Hound waiting for its owner to appear.

I shake my head as we head down the path. I told Reed last night that we were going to walk.

"We're walking," I say to Jade, loud enough for Henry and Reed to hear. "Henry, do you want to join us?"

Henry hops out of the car, all smiles, and Reed follows, stepping out from the other side. His tie clip is gripped between his teeth as his hands mindlessly work on knotting his tie.

I may look put together this morning, like my whole life is put together, but in reality, I've already argued with Jade over her hair, didn't have time to make myself a coffee, and the banana in Jade's hand is her only breakfast.

"Guess we all walk then," Reed says, joining us on the sidewalk.

Abe pulls away, no doubt meeting us at the school.

Henry and Jade run up ahead of us, lost in conversation about their weekend.

"Looks like someone raced out of the house again this morning," I joke.

"You just wish you'd seen me before I put on my suit." He winks.

I pretend to be annoyed while mentally creating a visual of a naked Reed in my head.

"A little early for the ego, no?"

I try not to glance at him as he knots his tie and then slides the clip into place. I fail miserably, but he lets me off with only a smirk.

"One day you'll find out, I wake up with it." His arms fall to his sides and he brushes my fingers with every swing of his arm.

I stuff them in the pocket of my jacket because what my daughter doesn't need is her mother showing up to school all hot and bothered.

"Tsk, tsk, I thought we were over this hard to get stuff?" he leans in and whispers.

My eyes instinctively close and shivers race up my neck.

"Watch it. I haven't really talked to Jade about us." I inhale a deep breath when his lips are so close that it would take no more than an inch to taste him.

"So, there is an us?" he asks.

"Maybe." I pretend to be playing hard to get, batting my eyelashes for extra effect.

"Just so you know, my lips will be on yours before I drop you off at work."

I stop, jut my head back. "Who said I'd be riding with you?"

He looks down at my empty hands. "Because I have a

tall coffee with a splash of skim milk and a shot of vanilla flavor waiting for you in the car."

His face morphs into a victorious expression, knowing my caffeine addiction has secured his victory.

"And you aren't going to give it to me until you give me a ride to work?"

He nods.

"That's kind of mean of you."

"I told you I wasn't the noble prince."

"Bye, Mom." Jade runs over, and I finally take in my surroundings, finding that we've broken the tree-lined path to the school courtyard. I liked it better before I realized that Darcie and Georgia's eyes were fixed on us.

"Oh Bug, I'm sorry."

She rests her chin on my stomach, her brown eyes that match my own, staring up at me.

"For what?"

I glance at Reed. "Nothing."

Her arms tighten around me. "Can I come to the office today?"

"Not today, but how about Friday?"

"Yay! Can we bring Henry one day?" I look to Henry who's standing next to Jade, already having said goodbye to Reed.

"I'll work something out soon."

She leaves me in a rush "Did you hear that, Henry? It's so much fun at my mom's office. There's candy and I can get on a computer and play games."

"Really? Reed bought me an iPad, but I don't have a computer."

I watch the two of them disappear into the school. My independent girl and the quiet boy, now the best of friends. Who would have thought?

"So, I need to know why you're asking Principal

Weddle to use the parking lot out back and why we need it roped off." Darcie's voice makes my entire body clench like the doctor's office just called to book my annual PAP smear.

She approaches, her arms crossed, Starbucks coffee in hand. Per usual, she wears flats and jeans, but today she's added a trench coat since rain is expected later today. Her auburn hair is long and curled, her makeup impeccable.

"It's a surprise, but believe me, people are going to love it," Reed says.

She fakes sincerity with a giggle and then her gaze lands back on me. "Vicki, I am the president of the PTA. *I* need to approve everything."

"It's Vic—"

I cut off Reed by placing my hand on his forearm. "First, it's Victoria. Second, Principal Weddle already approved it. He knows our plans and thought the fact that there will be a surprise at the event would increase attendance."

Let's just say, the principal was not easily convinced but eventually I argued enough valid points against his arguments and assured him all would cleaned up and that there'd be no trace of anything after we were done.

"Do you want to be the president, Vicki?" She spits out my name like it's poison on her tongue.

Now, I'm not totally opposed to being called Vicki. My dad used to call me by that name. But from this woman who doesn't know me? Absolutely not. The fact that she does it on purpose to annoy me makes me really want to put her in her place.

"No, I don't."

"Then—"

"I know where you're gonna go with this, Darcie, so let me just take care of it for you. No, I can't be president because I work. Yes, my husband and I are divorced. Yes, I moved here only recently and yes, I live with my mother. But all of that isn't really any of your concern. You assigned me a task—without asking, I might add—and I agreed to take it on. Now you want to place stipulations on it, but that's not really any of your business either." I pause long enough to take a breath and watch as her eyes grow even wider. "So, Darcie, why don't you drop your kid off and go do something productive rather than stand around here all morning judging the other parents like you have a doctorate in raising children."

She scoffs which I silently love because it means I've upset her, but I keep my cool, my expression blank. She's doing a terrible job in that department. Her cheeks are bright pink, and she clenches the cup in her hand so tight that it makes a sound of protest.

"Fine, do it your way. I only wanted to make sure you didn't have some sad booth that no one went to." She turns to Reed. "Nice of you to back me up, seeing as I gave you her phone number. It's called pay it forward, Reed, do you not understand the concept?" She doesn't wait for him to answer but instead stomps away. "Georgia!" she says and her sidekick who is way too old to be bullied follows obediently.

My heartbeat slows and the sweat under my arms feels cold as it starts to dry. I circle around to face Reed.

"Shit, just when I didn't think it was possible to want you more."

He shakes his head, then links our hands together, leading us to the car. When we reach the sedan, he opens the door.

I slide in to the vanilla scented car. "Good morning, Abe."

"Good morning, Victoria, or should I say Miss Bad Ass." His amused eyes find me in the rearview mirror.

"You saw that, huh?"

"Made my morning," he says with a chuckle.

"So, you witnessed the takedown, Abe?" Reed asks sliding in next to me.

I pick up my coffee from the beverage holder and sip the goodness I've been craving since my alarm went off.

"This definitely puts you in Prince Charming territory." I point to the cup.

"Hey now, I'm the one who stopped there," Abe jokes.

"Thanks, Abe." I wink at him in the mirror.

"Whoa, whoa, whoa, no taking credit. You tacked on another five dollars." Reed reaches for his own cup out of the holder and tentatively takes a sip.

Abe pulls away from the curb and we start our trek downtown.

"I was thinking maybe I'll go ahead and take Henry every day," Reed says.

"I never see who drops Henry off on the other days. A car pulls up to the curb, Henry jumps out and they pull away."

He nods. "An old silver Chrysler, right?"

"Yeah."

"His grandpa. He's not big on socializing. I think they're getting older and didn't really sign up for all this, you know?"

Pete always feigned caring about other people. He'd say all the right words, but it came off empty. With Reed, you see in his face how much he cares for Henry and how much he feels for what the family has had to endure.

"I can't imagine."

"Me either." He frowns for a moment, deep in thought.

We sit for a few seconds, trying to time our sips with

the stop and go Chicago traffic. Abe has the same morning radio show on as last time, but so far, the Second Date Update hasn't come on.

"No chance of seeing you until Friday, huh?" Reed asks.

Abe glances up to the mirror and then back to the road.

"I have school," I say, sticking my bottom lip out in a pout.

"Every night?"

"Tonight, Wednesday and Thursday."

"None of them are online?"

I shrug. "Some of the classes are, but I'm in my final year, graduating next December." I raise my crossed fingers. "Hopefully."

"I don't think I ever asked you for what?" He shifts so he's facing me more than straight ahead now.

"Business. General. Not even sure what I'm going to do."

His arms stretch out to reach for my hand, his fingers playing with mine between us. "You'll figure out what you love."

The warmth of his hand in mine feels good. The way his thumb and fingers glide along my skin. Not smooth but not callused, a mix.

"It's time," Abe turns up the volume of the radio.

"Second Date Update," Reed says, grinning like he's been waiting all week for another episode.

The rest of the ride in, we listen to a man who doesn't understand why he never got a call back, only to find out he had texted her asking for a hand job while they were watching a movie at the theater.

Reed looks over at me, waggling those thick but perfect eyebrows at me.

"No," I mouth with a smile and he threads his fingers through mine, giving them a squeeze.

By the time we pull up to the curb, I no longer want to climb out of the car, content to stay here in close proximity to Reed for a while longer.

"What's your views on PDA?" Reed asks, not opening the door.

"I'm a hard no."

"Even with me?"

"Especially with you." I give him a pointed look.

"Sorry, but it's Abe or the morning rush?" He points outside where people are walking past with rapid steps, trying to get to work on time.

"I have a text to return." Abe grabs his cell phone from the console and stares at it in his lap.

"How about a rain check on that kiss?" I say, trying not to laugh.

"Abe shut your eyes," Reed instructs, not taking his gaze off me.

"Um…"

"Just one," he says in a low voice that makes it hard to resist.

Then he slides forward, his strong thigh presses to mine, his hand moves to my neck and his lips land on mine. The kiss is brief but heart-stopping and by the time I'm opening the door to get out of the car, Abe's cheeks are as flushed as mine.

"Sorry," I mumble.

"No worries, I've heard worse." He salutes me as a goodbye and I exit the vehicle.

Reed and I both laugh as he walks me to the door of the office tower. I bet Abe has some stories that are better than the Second Date Update ones.

"Don't you have a job to get to?" I ask when he steps into the small foyer of the office building.

"I'm not sure I'm going to survive waiting until Friday." He wraps his arm around my waist and hugs me to his body.

"Well, you'll have to." I kiss his chin, the stubble from his neatly trimmed beard pricking my skin.

"Keep doing that and I *will* stalk you." He squeezes me tighter to his body.

I pull back. "Something tells me you know way more than you should about me."

I know he has connections to a database that probably shows my underage drinking ticket from high school.

He says nothing which I take to mean he *has* looked me up. I don't really mind though because in all honesty, I'd have done the same.

"Have a good day, counselor." I let my hand drift down his back and take a quick squeeze of his firm ass.

"You're playing dirty," he whispers in my ear, my earlobe finding its way into his mouth.

"Two can play that game." I kiss his lips, short and chaste. "Bye, Reed."

"Payback is a bitch," he says as he takes a step away, walking backward. "I'm going to open my door naked on Friday."

A woman who looks to be in her mid-fifties is approaching the elevator at that exact moment and glances over to him in disgust.

"Sorry, Ma'am."

She presses the elevator button as Reed and I stare at one another. I wave, and he steps back until the door is in his hand and he's gone with only a smile.

The woman and I step into the elevator, each pressing the buttons for our floors.

"If I was your age, I'd be showing up in a trench coat with nothing but my birthday suit on under it on Friday."

The elevator doors open on her floor and I'm too slack-jawed to respond.

I know that things with Reed will probably escalate into his bedroom, or more likely his kitchen table on Friday night and that has me mentally taking inventory of my body. My post-baby body. The one where nothing really went back to where it started.

I cup my breasts, lifting them then letting go, and watch as they fall back down like two sad sacks of flour.

I don't even turn on my computer after I walk through the office doors.

"CHELSEA!" I scream. "Divorcee dating meeting —stat!"

Chapter Twenty-One

Chelsea walks out of the break room with a coffee in one hand and a donut shoved in her mouth, powdered sugar sprinkled down the front of her blouse.

"What are you doing?" I ask, tossing my bag on the chair in front of my desk. "Those need to leave this office immediately."

I stomp past her and she follows me in.

"They're sooo good though. A gift from the new bakery around the corner." There's a whine in her voice as she watches me throw them in the trash.

"I need your help and I can't have donuts around at a time like this."

She sits down at the table, licking the sugar off her fingers. "What's up?"

"What's up is I'm going to be naked this weekend and this body has been consuming refined sugar and complex carbs for the past two years. The only way I've worked up a sweat is by eating spicy food or cleaning the bathroom."

"Naked?" Her eyes light up with mischief. "The steak?"

"Yes."

"So, the date went well?"

"The date did and now he's asked me over to his house on Friday."

"And the plot thickens." She leans back in the chair and crosses her legs in front of her with a smirk.

"This isn't some mystery. He's a man. I'm a woman. We're both old enough that we're not holding our V cards, so sex is absolutely on the table for Friday and—"

"Let's hope it's on the table. Table sex is all kinds of fun." She bites her lower lip and I'm sure she's remembering some escapade she's had in the past, but I do not want details.

"Can you focus for a second?" I can hear the panic creeping into my voice.

She gives her head a little shake and looks back in my direction. "Vic, when he unwraps you, he's going to be drooling over what he finds."

"No, he won't. I'm pretty sure he's never slept with a woman who has had a child before. I have five days to lose fifteen pounds."

Chelsea eyes my coffee and I follow her line of sight. "Shit." With one last sip to remember it by, I throw it in the trash.

"Only black coffee from this point forward." She sits up straight in her chair and leans forward, game face on.

I nod.

"We're going to cleanse." She stands and heads to her office.

I follow her. "But I shower every day?"

She stops walking and spins around to face me. "Not that kind of cleanse, woman. And you're heading to the gym with me after work. Tonight, is boot camp." She resumes walking to her office.

"But last time I went with you—"

She stands behind her desk, her fingers pressed to the hard surface, her gaze on me. "Okay, yes overdid it and had spaghetti legs for a few days, but—"

"Besides, I have class later."

"Ladies?" Hannah's voice rings through the office.

"In here," I say, peeking my head out of Chelsea's office.

"What's the scuttlebutt this morning? Chelsea's date?" She tosses her bag next to mine and takes off her designer coat, hanging it up on the coat hook.

"No date this weekend. It was my cousin's bridal shower."

"Oh, that must've been fun," I say.

She raises her eyebrows. "Have you ever been to a *fun* bridal shower?"

"Mine was fun." I shrug.

"Because you got all the gifts. Not to mention, my cousin insists on having a super-short engagement and so it was all just thrown together. And she let the guys crash it, so one of these things is not like the others." She points to herself.

My lips turn down.

"Add on the fact that my family already thinks there's something wrong with me since my marriage lasted all of two-point-two seconds and I get to re-live that whenever we're at something remotely wedding related." Her body shivers. "Hence my weakness to sugar donuts this morning. I'm an emotional eater."

Hannah glances my way, a huge smile on her face. "Donuts?"

"Don't waste your time, Vic threw them out."

Hannah pouts. "No donuts?"

"Nope, and we're going on a cleanse," Chelsea says.

"Oh, I want to join." Hannah sounds like we just said we're going to Vegas for a girl's weekend, not beginning a liquid funk. "I have just the person to help us. Wait, why are we doing this?"

Chelsea and I laugh at her train of thought.

"Victoria's getting naked this weekend."

Hannah's neck twists my way. "So, he's that good?"

"I don't know yet."

"Did you kiss?"

"Yes."

"And?" she asks and both their eyes zero in on me.

"It was phenomenal."

"Then he's gotta be good in bed. I've never had a bad kisser be good in bed or vice versa." She leaves the office. "Okay, I'm calling my guy. Clear our schedules for this afternoon."

And this, ladies and gentlemen, is why I love working for Hannah Crowley.

LATER THAT AFTERNOON, Chelsea and I follow Hannah into a storefront that looks nothing like a gym. And when I see that the guy who approaches us is wearing a unicorn hat on his head and purple leotard leggings, I'm wondering exactly what the hell I've gotten myself into.

"Um," Chelsea winds her arm through mine. "This is odd. Even for me."

"Tad." Hannah approaches him, and they kiss on the cheek and hug. Tad's gaze lands on us over Hannah's shoulder.

"These are them?" he asks, eyeing us top to bottom.

Hannah turns nodding at us with a big smile. "These

are my girls. Victoria and Chelsea." She points to each of us as she says our names.

"Pleasure," he approaches and does the double air kiss on each side of our cheeks, where you never actually make contact with the person. "Excuse the get-up, we're not your typical sweat center. I like things to be fun."

"Fun is good," Chelsea says.

"So…which of you is the desperate one?" He looks between us both.

"This one." Chelsea thumbs my way.

He winds his arm through mine. "Let's get started. That ass isn't gonna lift itself with us just standing here, sweetie."

I give Hannah my best wide-eyed help me look as I pass her, but she just chuckles under her breath. Traitor.

"So, who's the guy?" Tad asks, his other hand patting my forearm.

"Um…"

"He was the best man at her wedding," Chelsea calls out, walking with Hannah behind us.

"Oh!" He turns his head and his gaze finds Hannah for a second. "The body always wants what it shouldn't. Right, Han?" His eyebrows waggle.

"Quiet, Tad."

Chelsea moves her finger sideways between the two of them. "What are we missing?"

"Nothing." Hannah shoots Tad a look of warning. "We're here for Victoria."

"Right." He stops when we reach a long reception counter, takes my hands and pulls them out, taking in my body again. "First. You're gorgeous, honey and don't let anyone tell you otherwise."

"Thank you." I smile at him in appreciation.

"But anyone can use some cleansing and a detox. All

that bloating will disappear, and your skin will look ten years younger, fifteen in candlelight." He lets my arms drop and heads to a cabinet, taking out several bottles and placing them on the counter.

"Three, right Hannah Banana?" he asks, never turning around.

Chelsea and I laugh at his nickname for her, but she glances our way quickly and we rein ourselves in.

"Yes, we're doing this together," she says.

He looks over his shoulder. "I love the girl power thing, ladies. Which reminds me, did you secure that venue for the gala? I can't wait. Zak wanted to head to New York that weekend, but I said, nope, my girl is coming out in style and I need to be there to support her."

"Tell Zak I'll make it up to him," Hannah says, and the warmth and appreciation in her voice can't be missed.

"Come on now. I love when I get to make things up to my man." He winks at us while he positions all the pill bottles he's removed from the cabinet in three different piles in front of him. "'Kay, so here's the deal. We'll do a cleanse and you girls come here every night or at lunchtime, whichever you want. Shake and a probiotic for breakfast, sensible lunch and a shake for dinner. Actually, I'll bring you girls lunch to make it easier, so I know you're staying on track."

Chelsea grabs the box that says strawberry smoothie, reading over the ingredients. "I'm all for health, but—"

"It's good for the body." Tad winks and Chelsea shrugs.

"You're awesome, thank you," Hannah says as she watches him bag up the supplies.

"Well, don't thank me yet because you're going into the locker room and changing. I have a class in twenty minutes and you girls are going to be in it."

"What?" I ask, not prepared.

"Here." Tad steps around the counter and leads us to a shelving unit filled with workout gear. "Hannah," he says, throwing some clothes over his shoulder. "Chelsea." A pair of pants land on her head before she catches them. "Vic." I'm prepared and manage to catch my clothes. He turns, his finger padding his lips. "Shoes." His eyes light up immediately. "Sizes?"

"Can't we just start tomorrow?" Hannah asks.

"No, time is of the essence." He claps his hands in front of him twice. "We have until Friday, right?"

I nod.

"You get changed and I'll be right back." He walks toward the door of the supply room. "Go!" he says, and we scramble to find our way.

We follow the signs to the changing room and each set our clothes on a bench that runs down the center of the room.

"Tad's nice." Chelsea strips down in front of us. I don't know why I'm surprised to see she has zero inhibitions about nudity. "These are so soft." She touches the fabric.

"We've been besties since high school. Opened this gym a few years ago. His partner Zak is awesome, too. They make a great couple." Hannah folds up her clothes and places them in a nice pile in an empty locker.

I can't help but notice how pretty and feminine her lingerie is. Lace and satin. Probably La Perla. Trying to hide my cotton bra and panties, I hurry and get in the yoga pants and endorsement apparel Tad gave us.

Reed comes from the same type of upbringing that Hannah does. Is that what he's expecting of me? A woman who is always put together? God, I hope not.

My phone dings in the locker.

While Hannah and Chelsea talk about Tad and Zak

and how they met, I check to make sure the call isn't from my mom or something to do with Jade.

Reed: *Favorite dish?*

I fight the smile that wants to stretch across my face.

Me: *I'm half tempted to pick a hard dish like lamb.*
Reed: *Do you like lamb?*
Me: *Not particularly.*
Reed: *Ding. We're a match.*
Me: *Not many people like lamb, so…*
Reed: *Are you underestimating our fate?*
Me: *Um…I'm clearly stating that it's some sign that we both don't like lamb.*
Reed: *Fine. What about duck?*
Me: *Never had it.*
Reed. *What about sushi?*
Me: *Depends where from and please don't make that Friday.*
Reed: *Why? I could get all the supplies. We could do it together and then I can eat it off of you.*
Me: *Cliché alert.*
Reed: *Fine, you can eat it off me.*

I laugh and Chelsea slides along the bench until her hip checks mine.

Me: *As much as I like your body, I'm not sure about eating sushi off it.*
Reed: *Well I am VERY sure I'd enjoy eating anything off of you. Or just eating you in general. ;)*

What was a slight tingle between my thighs a second ago is now an incessant throbbing.

"Shit, this guy," Chelsea says.

I turn the phone away. "This is private."

"Fine, I'll leave your kinky ass to yourself." She stands and puts her hair in a ponytail.

Me: *Can we talk about this later?*
Reed: *We can test all this out on Friday.*
Me: *You really are relentless.*
Reed: *Only when it counts.*

My stomach flips a few times.

"Girls!" Tad screams into the locker room. "You have nothing I want to see, but if you don't get your butts out here now, I'm coming in."

"Let's go." Hannah and Chelsea leave the locker room and I sit on the bench staring down at his text, not knowing how to respond.

Me: *Gotta go. Have a great day.*
Reed: *I'll be thinking of you.*

I shove the phone into my locker, shut the door and lock it, feeling a little overwhelmed by the feelings taking over me. It all seems too quick, too early, too fast. It also seems as impossible to stop as a runaway train.

Chapter Twenty-Two

Thursday night, I arrive home from working out early enough to have dinner with Jade, so my mom could leave for a girl's night out with her friends.

I prepare my shake and watch Jade eat chicken nuggets as my stomach grumbles. The first day of the cleanse was brutal, but I'm getting used to the feeling of my stomach eating itself.

"How was school?" I ask.

"Good." She mumbles over her food. "I think I have a crush on Logan."

Oh boy. Is this stuff really starting already? "I think maybe you like him as a friend," I suggest.

"A lot of girls have crushes on the boys." She takes a drink of her milk.

"That doesn't mean you have to. There's plenty of time for that." I walk over and smooth out her hair, wondering if I could be the first mom to stop her kid from growing older. Her innocence is slipping away from me.

"It's not a big deal. He asked me to go to the carnival with him and his mom."

I sip my shake, my eyes closing while I try to pretend to myself that it's a real strawberry shake with whip cream. "What about Henry? He probably wants to go with you."

"That's what I told Logan. That Henry had to come with us."

"What did Logan say?"

"He said he's not into three-ways."

My shake spews out of my mouth all over the table.

"Mom!" Jade screeches and we both get up to grab the paper towels.

"Sorry," I say, taking them from her hands and cleaning up the mess while she sits back down to finish her dinner.

"I told Logan that we do four-ways all the time," she goes on to say while she watches me clean up.

Please, please hold it together, Vic.

"Four-ways?" I ask.

"Yeah, you, me, Henry and Reed," she says it in the tone of, like 'duh mom get a clue.'

"At your age, group outings are a good way to have fun." I walk over to the garbage under the counter and toss the paper towels in.

"Logan doesn't think so." She rolls her eyes.

"Well, then I guess he's going to miss out, huh?" I wink.

"You winked like Reed," she squeals.

"He must be wearing off on me."

I haven't dated over the past two years, so there's been no one I've had to talk to Jade about. No one that would penetrate our bubble, but Reed is slowly breaking past that hard, protective exterior I wrapped around us.

"Can we talk, Bug?" I ask, tears already threatening to spill.

"We are talking, Mommy," she says, literal as always.

"Yes, we are, but I want to talk to you about Reed."

"I like him." She bites one of her chicken nuggets.

"Me, too."

"I didn't like you going out with him just you two." Her lips tip down and she stares at me.

"You know adults sometimes do things on their own."

"Not you and Reed. You guys take us with you." She sips her milk and I press the remote to turn off the small television in the kitchen to stop her wandering eyes. "Mom," she pleads.

"We do take you and Henry with us, but things with Reed are…"

"I know, Mom." Her hand moves toward the remote, but I slide it away out of her grasp.

"You do?"

"Yeah, you and Reed need privacy. Jamie told me that her parents need privacy and so they lock the door on Saturday night and she can't get in until they open it on Sunday." My eyes widen, but she carries on. "Is he going to be my second daddy?"

"No, Bug. That's not what I'm saying. But I do like Reed and we like to spend time with you, but also just the two of us."

"You like a two-way?" she asks.

God help me.

"I want to get to know Reed better," I say.

"Like what his favorite game is?"

I shrug, a smile tugging on my lips. "Yeah and to see if I like spending time with him when it's just us two."

"Like play together. Logan likes basketball. I told him I like the monkey bars."

"Kind of like that, yes."

"Why don't you just ask him questions?"

I notice she's running out of ranch dip and needing

something to do other than listening to my seven-year-old give me dating advice, I busy myself with the task.

"I do, but the best way to get to know someone is by spending time with them."

"You keep saying spending time, Mommy, but you mean playing, right?"

I bite my lip. "Sure, if you want to call it that."

I work really hard not to let my mind drift off with all the playing we could do.

"I'm going to go out with him tomorrow night." I squirt more ranch dip on her plate and then return it to the fridge.

"What if he likes the same things as you?"

Maybe I'm doing this all wrong, but I've never done this before.

"Well, he doesn't have to like all the same stuff I do. It can be okay to like different things."

"So, I can have a crush on Logan even if he likes to play basketball and I like the monkey bars?" Her face is so serious it's hard not to laugh. Part of me wishes I would have recorded our conversation so I could replay it for her when she's older.

"Most of the time you'll find that it's your heart that tells you who you like."

She glances down to where her heart is. "My heart doesn't speak to me."

Yep, I'm lost. No GPS, lost in the middle of nowhere making a bunch of left turns with not a soul in sight. *Damn it.*

"Your heart doesn't speak, it feels, Bug."

Again, her head falls down, staring at her heart. "I feel nothing."

Trying to lead us back to the main road I try a different route. "You say you love me."

She shrugs. "You're my mom."

"You love Grandma?"

"Yeah."

"Daddy?"

"Yeah."

"Henry?"

"Ew. No. I like Henry."

"You've only known Henry for a few weeks, but what if you remain friends for years? Then you might love him."

She shrugs and from the lost look in her eyes, I see this conversation is going nowhere.

"Forget all that. I wanted to let you know that I'm going to Reed's tomorrow night and Grandma is watching you. You can pick what you want to do together on Sunday."

I take her dish since she's done.

"Can I watch television now?"

"Yeah, sure."

She runs into the other room and I rinse her plate, placing it in the dishwasher. My stomach is empty, and my craving for chocolate is in high gear over the conversation with Jade and the fact that in twenty-four hours I could be naked in front of—or under—Reed Warner.

Chapter Twenty-Three

The next day after a long day at work, I walk through the rotating glass doors of Reed's condo building. I realize now, that his condo is right downtown which means it's so far out of his way to take Henry to school it's ridiculous.

"Ms. Clarke?" a man behind the desk asks me, standing up in what I assume is a doorman uniform.

"Victoria."

His crooked teeth emerge with a smile. "Mr. Warner informed us of your visit." He rounds the corner and presses the up button on the elevator.

Does everyone get this treatment?

"Thank you for the warm welcome." I'm not sure what else to say since I'm unused to this kind of thing.

He chuckles quietly like we're in a library.

"We've always got an eye on what's going on around here," he says and motions to the ceiling behind me.

I glance around to find cameras in every corner. Seconds later the elevator arrives and the doorman steps in, scans a card, and presses the button.

"When the doors open, step out and then knock three times, click your heels together and use one hand to pat your head while the other rubs your tummy."

He laughs at his own joke and I lean in to check out his badge. Connor.

The elevator dings as we reach Reed's floor and the doors slide open.

"I'm only kidding," he says. "Mr. Warner will be waiting for you. Enjoy your evening."

I step out and the door shuts behind me. Suddenly, fear washes over me as I think of what this night could bring.

The elevator didn't take nearly as long as I needed it to and I slowly proceed down the hall, the plush carpet absorbing the sound of my heels. Soon I'm face to face with apartment number 1801. A gold plaque is secured to the outside of the door and it reminds me more of something you'd see in an office tower rather than a residential condo.

Pulling out my phone before I knock, I check out my teeth for the millionth time, finger my hair into position after the beating it took from the Chicago wind and pink my cheeks to give them a little color.

I've just finished taking inventory of myself when the door springs open and a mouth-watering Reed stands in the doorway.

"Hi," I say, turning off my phone and tucking it inside my purse.

"Hey, glad you found me." He steps to the side, his arm extended inviting me in.

"It's like breaking into a bank." I accept his invitation and try to keep my mouth from falling open in appreciation of the marble floors in the foyer.

From his address, I knew he was in the gold coast and when the taxi pulled up outside, I knew the condo would be on a level I was not familiar with. But marble floors, windows that span from one corner to the next and overlook Lake Michigan?

"Sorry, they take security pretty seriously here."

The click of the lock has me turning to see him strolling toward me. He slides my purse from my shoulder and drops it on the big round table in the foyer.

"Jeez, Reed, you couldn't afford the penthouse?" I joke following him into the apartment and to the kitchen.

"There's a retired basketball player up there." His voice doesn't hold the sarcasm mine did.

"I was kidding."

He glances up at me through his long eyelashes. "This was in my family. It's convenient to the courthouse and the office." He shrugs and goes back to the meal prep he must have been doing before I arrived.

"You must dread Mondays." I toe out of my heels and meet him in the kitchen.

His knife pauses mid-cucumber and he waits for me to focus on him. "It's the best day of the week."

I blush, wanting to hip check him out of the way so I can have something to do with my hands, keep me busy and prevent me from making a fool of myself.

"So, there's chicken and potatoes in the oven, and I'm just finishing with the salad."

"I'm impressed." I open the oven door and bend down to inspect his skills.

The room spins and fades in and out, my head feels heavy on my shoulders. I feel myself pitch forward, everything in my sight coming in flashes before I feel my hip hit the floor and blackness overtakes me.

"Victoria." Soft knuckles drag down my face. "Vic."

My eyes flutter open with some effort and Reed's face hovers over mine.

Oh my God, I didn't, did I?

"What happened?" I ask, already cringing because I think I know what he's going to say.

"You passed out."

Oh my God. How mortifying.

"Do you feel sick? Are you diabetic? Heart problems?" he asks in rapid-fire succession.

I giggle from embarrassment because it's my go-to mechanism to hide what I really don't want to tell him.

I sit up on his comfortable gray couch. How did I get all the way over here? "No. I just…"

He sits on the coffee table in front of me, his eyes concerned, his hands on my thighs as he waits for me to finish.

"I was on a detox cleanse this week." My voice is soft and purposely low in the hopes he hears anything else and whatever it might be, I'll go with it.

He sits back, one corner of his lips tipping down. "Why?"

I draw my legs up to my chest and wrap my arms around them. Reed stands and heads over to the kitchen.

I hear the oven open and a dish pulled from the cupboard. A plate put on the counter. Silverware scraping, and I don't have it in me to turn around and see what he's doing or get up to help him. I'll just sit on his couch and act like I didn't completely ruin our date by passing out on his kitchen floor.

"You didn't hit your head, thank goodness," he says from the kitchen. "I was able to slide catch you before that happened. When's the last time you ate?"

"I had a salad for lunch."

"And?"

His voice grows closer and I loosen my legs, crossing them on the couch, still not ready to get up.

"A smoothie for breakfast."

He sits back down on the coffee table holding a plate with chicken, potatoes, and some salad on it, a bottle of water tucked under his arm.

"How many days have you been doing this?"

I peek up. "Five." My voice is so timid it reminds me of when my dad would hover over me as a teenager and ask me why I snuck out. There was no good answer other than I thought it was a brilliant plan until I slid in through my window to find him on my bed expecting me.

Now it's Reed waiting for my answer to another brilliant plan that left me dead weight on his kitchen floor.

I watch his hands maneuver the fork and knife like the well-groomed man he was trained to be as a boy. Moments later a fork with chicken on it rests before my lips. "Eat."

Not about to fight him on this, I open my mouth and take the piece of chicken from the fork, letting him feed me like a child.

"I'm really okay. Let's eat at the table."

"You're not getting off that couch until this entire plate is gone." He raises his eyebrows daring me to challenge him.

And have a little just-ate belly when I get naked? No thanks. My stomach growls in protest.

I take a few more mouthfuls and say, "Only a few more. Really I'm good."

"No, I need you to have energy." He holds a fork full of salad in front of my lips.

Before I can open and accept his offering a drop of salad dressing drips on my blouse. The new expensive blouse I just bought from a boutique I can't really afford.

"Uh," the sound escapes me.

"Sorry." He looks it over. "Let me get something to clean that."

He stands from the coffee table and I follow him into the kitchen where he has a dishrag ready with the tip wet. I hold my hands out for him to give it to me at the same time his finger moves toward the stain.

Ignoring me, his finger gently touches my shirt, but in order to clean the stain, he needs something to press against. Unless I want his hand under my shirt, which I do, but not necessarily to work out a stain, I need to take the dishtowel from him.

He allows me, and I dab the stain even though I know that the salad dressing will have oil in it and more than likely I'll never wear this blouse again.

"I'm sorry." He bites his lower lip and the sight has heat building between my legs.

"It's okay." I put the dishtowel on the kitchen counter, giving up hope.

"Can we start over?" he asks, his arms sliding down on either side of my hips.

"Please." I stare up at him, loving the transformation from timid, unsure eyes to his lust-filled gaze.

"I've been wanting you alone for so long, I'm nervous." His body inches forward and I draw in a breath.

"Are we being honest?" I ask.

"Yes. Nothing you tell me will change the way I feel."

"I went on the detox cleanse because I'm scared of you seeing me naked," I say the words fast and in succession as if somehow, they won't be as embarrassing that way.

Confusion transforms his features and then a tentative smile reaches his lips. "You're gorgeous, why would you worry about that?" He moves another inch closer and I close my eyes to find my equilibrium.

"Have you ever been with a woman who had a baby?" My head tilts and his smirk grows wider.

"I haven't."

I nod. "See, the body does all these things to prepare a woman for motherhood and they're not sexy, Reed. Not by a long shot."

He grabs my hips, hoisting me up onto the counter. "You're sexy as hell, Vic, and I want to show you *exactly* how sexy you are to me." His hands run along my inner thighs, parting them for him.

I lick my lips in anticipation.

His fingers unbutton the top button of my blouse. "We should probably get this dry cleaned." He undoes another button and the back of his knuckles brush against my skin, making me draw in a ragged breath. More buttons come undone and he leans forward pressing his soft lips to my chest while his hands finish their handy work and he pulls the blouse open for his viewing pleasure.

"Reed," I sigh, sliding my hand across my stomach— the part of me I'm most insecure about.

The stretch marks Jade left me are now thin and white. Not horribly noticeable but evidence that my body once held a child and that I'm not an unmarred twenty-year-old.

"Please, Victoria, you're beautiful and I want to cherish you." His lips cast kisses along the swell of one breast slowly moving to my other. Just as my eyes are closing and my mind empties of all the doubts about me being enough for him, his hands slide me forward and I'm wrapped around him like a koala bear. "I'll feed you the rest after."

He carries me down the hall and I can't help but sprinkle kisses along his defined jawline and suck his earlobe into my mouth. The bulge in his pants teases me as he stops in the middle of the hallway and presses my back to the wall, his lips claiming mine.

Our kiss is ravenous and urgent, our mouths colliding, fighting for dominance. All the worries that consumed my mind the entire week, disappear with his demanding kiss. I'm not thinking about the stretch marks. I'm not thinking about my wider hips or my breasts that aren't as perky as they were pre-pregnancy. I just want more. More of Reed Warner.

"Never diet again," he says through noisy kisses. "Especially for me."

I say nothing, taking his cheeks in my hands and bringing his face to mine so our lips can crash together again.

Stepping back from the wall, he continues down the hall. When he steps us into his bedroom, it's obvious a bachelor lives here with its dark wood and grey linens. There's another set of windows that look out over the Chicago skyline.

For the first time in a long time, hope blooms inside me and I wonder if happily ever afters really can come true.

Chapter Twenty-Four

Reed didn't toss me on the bed as his hungry eyes suggested he might but laid me gently down as he stared at me while stripping off his t-shirt.

His love arrow might as well have blinked in neon, pointing me to what was mine to explore tonight. His muscles weren't bulging out, but they were defined and flexed with every movement he made.

I sat up on the edge of the bed before he had a chance to cover me with his body. My body yearned to feel us skin to skin. To roll around in his high-thread-count sheets, exploring and teasing one another.

My fingers tremble as I take the button of his jeans in hand. I watch him watch me with smoldering eyes as I free the button. He sucks in a small breath through his already taut smile as I lower the zipper, and a low groan rumbles out of his mouth. I kiss the skin right above the waistband of his boxers as I slide his jeans down to a puddle on the floor.

His turgid erection presses against my chin, making me eager to taste him. I slide my hand up his thigh, over the top of his boxers, taking his length in my palm and pressing against his hardness.

"You're playing with fire," he says and when I rest my chin on his stomach, staring up at him with hooded eyes, he takes my face in his hands. "I'm going to explode if you continue."

At a painfully slow pace, his hands slide down my shoulders, grabbing my own hands and pulling me up to my feet. "I need to see you."

All those fears rush forward again, and Reed must notice because he takes my spot on the bed, bringing me close, kissing the exact area where Jade left her mark. Circling my belly button with his tongue, his hands graze over my shoulders until my blouse cascades behind us onto the floor. Not stopping, his lips, his hands continue their mission, unclasping my bra.

His eyes are closed and he's yet to see me while he blindly strips the bra from my body. The delicate lace joins the pile of our clothes on the floor. A thrill rushes through my veins when his thumbs brush across my nipples only to continue on their path of exploration, resting at the top of my jeans. Flicking the button open with ease, he smirks, his confidence shining through.

I run my hands along his scalp, his hair soft and soothing to my frenzied nerves. The sound of the zipper going down echoes through the room and the fact we're seconds away from each being in our underwear is both exhilarating and frightening.

It reminds me of being strapped into a roller coaster as it leaves the starting gate. This ride is moving and the pit of my stomach is anticipating climbing that first hill.

Hooking his thumbs in the belt loops on either side, he drags the jeans down my legs and I step out of them. His hands mold to my hips, his thumbs sneaking under the sides of my silk panties and he urges me to take step out of my jeans.

He opens his eyes and his appreciative gaze moves over my body, stirring another wave of passion for this man. When his gaze finally meets mine, I see the burning in his eyes is a carnal, hedonistic need. Just like in the hallway, all my fear crumbles and he pulls me forward, his hands sliding to my ass.

He sits on the edge of the bed and I lower my weight, straddling him on the bed, my nipples hardening from rubbing against his bare chest.

His hand brushes the strands of my hair from my forehead. "You're beautiful and every time you doubt that, remember how rock hard I am in this moment." He captures my hand in his, guiding it down to the bulge in his boxers. "This is the truth stick."

I smile and shake my head at his absurd thinking.

"What?"

He rolls me over and hovers above me the humor fading, and he grinds into me. "If you weren't beautiful and sexy and tempting I wouldn't be so rock hard."

"You're a man. A strong breeze can make you hard."

"I'm not a thirteen-year-old boy, Victoria." He circles into my center once again and I suck in a breath. "This is all because of you."

"So, what you're saying is that you have a peter meter?" I giggle through a gasp as he rocks into me again and hits me in a particularly sensitive spot.

"Call it whatever you want. Just know that it wants you to the point of desperation."

I don't want our sex life to be him having to convince me of my sexual attractiveness. I want to ride him like I own him. I want to say dirty things and not care about being judged.

"Condom?" I ask him.

He leans across the bed and my pussy clenches, missing the feel of him immediately. I move to shimmy my panties off.

"That's my job." He grabs my wrist to still my movements.

I hold my hands up in the air. He returns a second later, pulling down his boxers and his dick springs out. I lick my lips in a subconscious reaction.

Taking in his hard length, I become even wetter. He uses his fingers to roll the latex down his length, and saliva pools in my mouth with the urge to wrap my lips around him.

As soon as he has the condom on, he finishes sliding my panties down my legs and flings them over his shoulder.

Falling on top of me, his lips take mine and he slowly enters me as we enjoy a languid kiss. Once he's fully seated inside of me, I raise my hips to meet him.

It's not awkward like I assumed it would be. I thought we'd fumble to find the same groove. But I should have known things were different with Reed. That we'd connect in the bedroom the same way we do outside of it.

Somewhere between the moans and groans, the exploring hands, and found erogenous zones, Reed Warner showed me what it's like to be a woman. To feel beautiful, wanted, sexy and treasured while in his arms as he moved in and out of me.

He takes his time, a slow dance until my body heats to levels that demand more. Knowing me well, his thrusts turn more eager, more demanding and soon our soft moans are replaced with grunts, groans, and dirty words. His gliding hands turned gripping and strong. Both our muscles tense and contract, desperate for a release.

My toes curl against the bed sheets, my insides

contracting as I kiss his shoulders. Reed takes me to the edge and my teeth emerge like a vampire desperate for blood. Each cry from my lungs is louder than the one before until I clamp onto his shoulder and my body trembles with release.

His own pleasure-filled groans intensify before he stills inside me and comes with a sound I know I'll never tire of hearing. Spent, he collapses on top of me after finding his own nirvana.

Our bodies are covered in a slick sheen of sweat, and I'm sure my hair must be a tangled mess. Reed grabs the top of the comforter, urging me to slide under, which I do. Once I'm tucked in, he kisses me briefly on the lips. "Now I feed you."

He disappears from the room and I take the moment alone to flail my legs and arms on the cushy mattress. He's just as great in bed as he is out of it. That hope for a happily ever after that was planted when we walked into the bedroom, now sprouts.

REED RETURNS to the bedroom empty-handed and goes to his drawers, pulling out a pair of track pants to cover his lower half. He grabs a t-shirt out of another drawer and walks over to the bed, passing it to me.

"Come." He holds his hand out for me to take while I slip the shirt over my head.

Leading me down the hallway, I catch a glimpse of another bedroom and a bathroom as we pass by them. We reach the kitchen and he pats the counter. I climb up with his help and notice a plate waiting there for me. He grabs another plate and slides up to join me on the counter. We both waste no time digging in.

"You feeling okay?" he asks a second later, hopping down and moving to the fridge.

"Yeah." I eat a few of the roasted potatoes. "I thought you said you couldn't cook?"

"Turns out I can follow a recipe." He shrugs, pulling out a bottle of wine and stepping to a cabinet to pull out two wine glasses.

His mannerisms are effortless as he opens the wine bottle and holds it just right, so the wine doesn't splatter out of the glass. Handing me mine, he slides back up on the counter.

"It's delicious." I sip the wine and place the glass beside me.

"Not exactly how I expected tonight to go, but I have no complaints." He leans over to kiss my cheek then gets to work eating his own meal.

"I'm sorry I ruined it."

"I'm the one who spilled salad dressing on your blouse, which I'll replace, by the way." His eyes glance at my legs as I cross them.

"No, you won't. If I didn't do that detox cleanse I wouldn't have passed out which means you wouldn't have been feeding me in the first place."

He leans forward and presses his lips to mine. "I'm having a great time."

"Me, too."

"I know you're scared, Victoria. I know taking a chance and putting your trust in someone isn't easy for you."

My eyes want to fill with tears. How right he is.

"You're the best chance I've taken in a long time." I mean it. Reed has given me no reason to doubt his intentions or the type of man he is. My head falls to his shoulder. His strong shoulder that I know would try to carry the weight of my messy life. "You scare me," I admit with a whisper.

"You scare me, too. Believe me." He almost sounds defeated, but then he pulls away, setting his plate to the side and takes my head in his hands. His lips meet mine again—confident and sure. "For you, I'll try," he whispers. "I can't sit here and promise this will end in a castle with fireworks bursting in the sky. We could both end up hurt, but I know you're worth it. You're worth the heartache that's possible. All I'm asking is that you try with me."

"Sounds so easy."

"I'll start. I've never had a long-term relationship. Never really found anyone I wanted to try it out with. I tend to work a lot. Some cases are so consuming I forget to have a life. For you, I want to try to change that."

"My turn now, huh?" He nods. "My experience with Pete stole my belief in marriage. He buried the little girl who thought fairy tales came true. You've somehow managed to get her to poke her head above ground, but I don't see it as an easy feat. For you, I want to try."

He smiles at me using the same phrase as him.

"I guess I'm asking you for patience. There's a big case coming to a head this week and it's a make or break for my career. I've never been with a woman during a time where my focus needs to be solely on work. For you, I want to try." He picks up his wine glass.

I pull my legs up to my chest and pull his shirt over my legs. "I promised myself after Pete that I would never put someone above myself again. My schooling and Jade come first. A man wasn't part of that plan, but for you, I want to try."

His finger tucks a loose strand of hair behind my ear. "I've never wanted to win something more than I do your heart."

"I've never wanted a man to hold on to it as much as I want you to."

"So, it's done. The terms are laid out. We're both agreeing to try?"

"Do you ever stop being a lawyer?" I chuckle.

He leans in to place a chaste kiss on my lips. "No." He slides down from the counter, opens the fridge and grabs a container. "Dessert and a movie?" he asks.

"Definitely."

His arm circles my waist and he assists me in finding my footing on the floor. Then his strong hand is in mine as we round the counter and sit on his couch. He places a blanket over us and his big screen comes to life with the click of a remote.

"Reserve your energy because I'm not even close to being done with you yet." He kisses my forehead, hands me a fork and we Netflix and Chill for the rest of the night.

Chapter Twenty-Five

Somehow, Reed swindled me into a four-way date on Saturday. As he dropped me off at home at six in the morning, he used his charm to convince me to go to the zoo with him and Henry, and to bring Jade along of course.

Now, as they run ahead of us to see the dolphins, Reed's fingers search for mine, brushing against them before pulling away again.

"This is torture," he says.

I laugh, laying my head on his shoulder, keeping my eye on Jade and Henry. If she looks up, I can straighten fast.

"I need a whole night. How else can I show off my breakfast skills?" His fingers continue playing with mine and my stomach flutters with every touch of his hand.

"Well… Pete is coming in next week and he'll be taking Jade for the weekend."

"Pete's coming?" he asks, and instead of being happy I can sleep over at his house for two nights, instead of one, his voice is clipped.

"Not the reaction I was expecting."

He leads us to a bench where we sit down while the kids watch the dolphins swim around.

"Sorry, I guess I'm a little insecure when it comes to you."

I take a chance and kiss his cheek. "I've been divorced for two years."

"Yeah, but he might want you again once he knows you're taken."

His arm is swung behind me on the bench, but his expression says he's not here in the moment, that his mind is far away.

I use my finger to turn his chin my way. "Taken, I am." I eye him hard and he nods. Not convincingly though. "Reed?"

"I know, I know. I don't doubt that, trust me." He reaches out and squeezes my hand. "But I also know Pete. He's not going to be happy about us."

Jade and Henry run to the next window, following a dolphin. Jade tells Henry how dolphins can tell a woman when she's pregnant and how a dolphin told her mommy she was pregnant with her. Pete likes the story much more than I do, but Reed definitely doesn't need to hear that story right now.

"Maybe we should concentrate on the fact we can be naked in your condo for an entire weekend," I lean to my side and whisper.

His gaze falls to my lips and I lick them. He shifts in the seat, adjusting himself. "Don't tempt me."

"What?" I ask, standing up to head toward Jade and Henry before the mob of people swallows them up and I lose sight of them.

"You know exactly what you're doing." He joins me, his hand finding my ass and squeezing.

"That's highly inappropriate behavior for a zoo," I say over my shoulder.

He inches closer. "You do realize this torture you're inflicting will be returned tenfold in the form of me denying you orgasms, right?"

I laugh so hard people around glance over.

"What's so funny, Mommy?" Jade asks.

"Oh, Reed just told a joke."

The two small faces look to him. "Tell us!"

"Well…" he pauses to think of one. "Why did the dinosaur cross the road?"

They look at one another, their mouths transforming to different shapes as they try to think.

"Give up?" he asks.

Jade looks at me eagerly waiting for the punchline, so she can laugh as hard as I did.

"What? What?" Henry pleads.

"Because the chicken wasn't born yet."

The kids giggle, look at each other, and shrug before turning back around.

"Tough crowd." Reed shakes his head and then leads us out of the dolphin area with his hand on the small of my back.

For the rest of the day, we sneak touches and manage to get in one chaste kiss while the kids were enthralled with watching the chimpanzees fly from tree to rope and back.

We stop to drop off Henry, and Reed asks if we want to go in and meet Henry's grandparents.

"I want to see your room." Jade opens the door of the taxi before I can object.

"That's what I get for letting her sit by the door."

Reed pays the taxi driver and waits patiently at the car door until I get out.

Henry and Jade walk right into the house.

"Jade!" I softly scream because I'm sure Henry's grandparents won't appreciate them storming in so noisily.

"Ned is quiet, but Helen will keep you here until tomorrow if you let her, so you might want to plan your exit now," Reed says as we walk up the path to the front door.

Again, his hand lands on the small of my back and those butterflies slap their wings in my stomach.

Reed knocks on the door. "Helen? Ned?"

"Reed." A woman emerges out of the kitchen drying her hands on a waist apron.

She's cute, with short, curly dark hair and a small frame. I'm not sure I'd even think she was a grandparent.

"Helen, this is Victoria Clarke, Jade's mom," he introduces me.

She holds out her hand. "What a pleasure. We've heard so much about Jade and you. You guys have had a lot of joint outings it seems." She smiles and her petite hand fits in mine.

"It's great to meet you as well. Yes"—my eyes search Reed out—"we have been doing a lot. The kids have fun together."

"Henry just adores Jade. Talks about her all the time."

A huge boom rocks the floor, a few glass knickknacks wobble in the curio cabinet to my left.

"HENRY!" a man sitting in a recliner yells, who I assume is Ned.

"Sorry!" Henry screams down. It's the loudest I've ever heard him speak.

Helen glances over to the bald head, shakes her head and waves him off. "Grumpy," she whispers.

"I hear you," he says.

"Then get up and introduce yourself. Reed is here with

Jade's mother." All the while she's lecturing him, she's eyeing us with an apology.

"Who's Jade?" he asks.

"Listen to your grandson every now and then and you'd know."

The recliner rocks, creaks and then it's not only a bald head in my view but the rest of his imposing figure. A tall man and if Henry gets his grandfather's height, basketball might be in his future.

"Evening, Ned." Reed approaches the man, hand out, straight back.

"Reed," he says, but his eyes are on me.

Immediately, I want to shrink into a ball and roll back down the porch.

Reed returns to my side. "This is Victoria. Henry's friend Jade's mother."

Ned's big hand swallows mine up. Callused palms scrape against my skin while we shake.

"Hi," I say in my meet-the-parents sweet voice. They aren't Reed's parents, but they are important to him.

"Pleasure." He eyes Reed. "Is this what you do when you take Henry out? Use him as bait?"

I swallow deeply and Reed laughs, though it's not his usual one. This one is forced, and I can tell he's uneasy.

"No. We met during a drop-off at school. Henry and Jade were already friends and I know Victoria from way back."

"Well, if I'd known you can catch something like this, I'd take him out more often." He laughs, but Reed and I stay quiet, unsure how to react.

Helen swats him over the head and joins in laughing.

"Please excuse my husband. He's joking." She eyes him, and he moves fast, tickling her ribcage.

"I had them going, didn't I?" He looks over at us,

yellow stained teeth emerging, but a genuine smile none-theless.

"Would you like some pie? I just made blueberry, Henry's favorite."

Without waiting for an answer, she turns and heads to where I assume the kitchen is.

"What do you have, half a brain? Go," Ned says.

Reed and I step forward. I can't speak for Reed, but I do so out of fear. Someone failed to mention that Ned is scary.

The smell of baking hijacks all my senses when I step into the kitchen. "It smells delicious, Helen."

She busies herself with cutting the pie and getting some ice cream out of the freezer. A woman after my own heart.

"I like to make one of Henry's favorites at least once a week. After Trevor and Katie's accident, I like to see him smile."

She turns around with a sad smile on her face and points to the fridge where a much younger Henry is wedged between the smiling faces of a man and a woman. He's the spitting image of his dad.

"I'm sorry," I say, and Reed slides a chair out for me.

"Thank you. It's been three years now. If God would've allowed us, we would've had more children. Then Henry would be having fun with his aunt or uncle rather than learning how to play pinochle." She glances over her shoulder.

"He's a great card player." Reed's hand finds my thigh under the table.

"Let's hope I can raise him decent enough not to be a card shark in Vegas when he's older." She brings two plates over.

"I'll never allow it to happen," Reed says, removing his hand from my leg and digging into the pie with his fork.

"I know you wouldn't." She pats his hand and stares over at me. "Reed is our savior. Treats Henry like he's his son, not just a Big Brother mentor."

I smile over at the man who's stolen my heart. I imagine he's collected Henry's too. And Helen's. Not sure about Ned.

"Well, we live just over on Monroe, Henry is welcome anytime."

"Thank you. Henry said Jade is new. When did you move?" Helen asks.

"Reed!" Ned's bolstering voice booms from the other room. "Come here!"

Reed wipes his mouth with the napkin Helen gave him and stands up to exit the room.

Once Reed leaves, Helen's eyes rest on me to answer the question she asked. Is it wrong to be scared for Reed?

"We moved here a few months ago from Los Angeles."

"Los Angeles? Oh, I was there once. A long time ago. Ned was stationed in San Diego right before he shipped out to Vietnam. We spent the last free weekend he had exploring southern California." Her eyes glaze over and I assume she's reliving some memory. "We'd thought that after Trevor left the house, we'd be able to do some traveling, but… God had other plans." She pats the table and stands, exiting the room. "Henry! Jade! Come have some pie."

Footsteps sound overhead to the sound of cheers.

"Never take time for granted, dear." She presses her hand to my shoulder, stopping at the counter and cutting two more pieces of pie.

Jade's never had blueberry pie. I hope she doesn't offend Helen. I can't help but take Helen's words to heart.

She probably never envisioned her elder years to involve raising her grandchild.

"Blueberry? YAY!" Henry jumps around and then his small arms cling around his grandma's waist. "Thank you."

She pats his blond hair and straightens his glasses. "It's your favorite."

He clings to her harder.

Jade stays by my side looking down at her small piece of pie and then back to me.

"Just try it," I whisper.

"It's so good, Jade." Henry sits down, piling forkfuls into his mouth, leaving a purple stain around his lips.

Jade sits down next to him and only takes bites of the vanilla ice cream at first. Helen watches her intently.

"She's never had blueberry pie before," I say.

"You know Trevor and Katie were friends at their age." She moves her attention from them to me. "Katie would sit right where Jade is. One of those next-door neighbors turn friends and fall in love things. It was such a romantic story. I'm glad I got to witness it."

"My mom had dark hair too." Henry points to the fridge at the picture I just admired. "Those are my parents."

Jade looks over and then buries her head in her pie and ice cream. I have a feeling I'll be playing a game of twenty questions later tonight.

"May I use your bathroom?" I slide out from the chair.

"Of course, it's right near the front door."

I walk through the dining room to find Reed and Ned's heads bent over a set of papers, each with a glass of whiskey or scotch next to them. Reed glances up, the pen he's using to keep his place as he reads through the papers pausing. His expression looks like he just saw the worst car crash. You know the one where you see the paramedics pulling someone out and goose bumps travel up your spine.

"I'm just going to the bathroom," I say, not sure what else to say at our awkward exchange.

He forces a smile and then stares back down at the paperwork.

By the time I'm out of the bathroom, Jade has her coat back on and Reed is standing at the door with her. Helen, Ned, and Henry stand there to say goodbye.

"Oh, we're leaving?"

"I told them how you need to study for that test," Reed says.

Reed holds out my coat for me. I slide my arms through the sleeves. "It was great meeting you. Thank you for the pie."

Ned shakes my hand. Helen hugs me and Henry high fives us, but hugs Jade close to his body.

I smile as widely as I can, baffled as to why Reed is pushing us to leave so quickly.

"Walk?" I ask.

"Yeah." Reed's hand smooths down his cheek and he blows out a breath.

Jade skips along in front of us, stopping to admire some tulips and flowers that are starting to bloom.

"So, are you going to tell me why we rushed out so fast?" I ask.

"They want me to be his guardian should anything happen to one of them." There's no tremor in his voice and he's not fidgety. Does nothing get to this man?

"Oh boy," I say.

"Yeah."

"What did you say?"

We round the corner and Jade stops to pet a dog that probably just wants to do his business.

"I told him I had to think about it." Reed seems lost in his own head.

I definitely don't want to weigh in on the subject. I'm just a girlfriend, a recent one at that. Still, I can't help but wonder what Reed will do. It's not like when you agree to be a guardian for a young and healthy married couple where the chances are slim you'll ever actually have to step-up. In this case, there's a strong possibility that in the next eleven years, something could happen to Ned or Helen, and Reed will become solely responsible for him. Even for a saint like Reed, a request like that is enough to test anyone's level of commitment.

Chapter Twenty-Six

"Thank goodness that asshole isn't here." Hannah slides into the booth at Torrio's Table the following Tuesday, taking in the other patrons.

"Yeah, thankfully," Chelsea agrees as her eyes sweep over the bar.

I have a feeling she may have had an appreciation for the silver fox that Hannah loves to hate.

"Why do you hate him so much?" she asks. "I mean I get the fact that he was your ex's divorce attorney, but—"

"He's a pompous ass who tried to take everything from me. Believe me, he has a reputation and my ex hired him because of that reputation. A surgeon's salary and the house in North Shore wasn't enough for my ex. He wanted my money and my trust fund, too. Thought he was entitled to it. After all the shit he pulled." Hannah's body tenses and I glance to Chelsea to with a look of warning.

Lucky for us the same waiter from last week comes by and places three vespers down on the table.

"Thank you," Chelsea coos, her eyes taking him in.

He eye fucks her for a minute and then turns back around like he's playing hard to get.

"Do not screw the wait staff here, Chels." Hannah's perfectly arched eyebrows raise.

"Never," Chelsea says but fights the laugh that's trying to escape.

"Let's chat about Victoria," Hannah says picking up her drink. Both sets of eyes shift to me.

"What?" I sip my vesper. The citrus taste is refreshing on my tongue and welcome with the inquisition I know is coming my way.

"You must be exhausted from dodging our questions for two days," Chelsea deadpans.

"Fine. We agreed to try to be together."

"Sounds romantic," Chelsea says with an eye roll.

"Try?" Hannah asks.

"It *was* romantic, actually. And yes, we're going to try the dating thing." I take another sip to fortify myself.

"I'm proud of you," Hannah says, her perfectly manicured hand running up and down my shoulder. "That takes guts. What did your ex say about it?"

"My ex?" I place the drink on the table.

"About the steak?" Chelsea adds.

"I haven't mentioned it yet. It's none of his business. Reed doesn't even talk to Pete anymore."

The two of them share a look across the table and return their attention back to me.

"You need to tell him," Hannah says what I know they're both thinking.

"What are you going to do say, 'surprise, I'm screwing your best man?'" Chelsea's overdramatic display causes some heads to turn in our direction.

"He's coming for Jade's birthday, right?" Hannah lowers her voice.

"Yeah."

"Do you think he'll see Reed?" she continues her questioning.

"I hadn't really thought about it." My fingers knot in my lap.

Chelsea knocks on my head. "Hello? McFly!" She does a spitting image of the asshole in the Back to the Future movies. "Plan ahead because this is going to crash and burn if you leave it to fate."

"We're all adults. Pete doesn't care who I date. It's not like I get any say in who he sees. We've been divorced for two years."

They both shake their heads.

"Do I have to knock on your head again?" Chelsea asks, sipping her own drink.

"No." My hand covers my head. "Leave me alone."

"Sweetie, your ex, Pete…" Hannah says softly and slowly like she's speaking to a child. "Pete is not going to be okay with this. Especially because you have a daughter, which means his best man is going to be seeing more of his daughter than he is. I think you should tell him and nip this in the ass right away."

"Otherwise, he shows up and gets a surprise and you'll be breaking apart a brawl. But," Chelsea says, leaning in. "If that happens, call me first. I love a good fight over a woman."

I roll my eyes then sit and think for a minute. Maybe they're right. "Okay. I guess I should tell Reed I'm telling Pete first, right?"

"If you want to keep 'trying,'" Chelsea puts the word in quotation marks. "Definitely."

I glance to Hannah's whose head is bobbing up and down in agreement.

"In the meantime, let's celebrate you getting laid on a

regular basis." Hannah raises her hand and then puts up three fingers.

The waiter spots her, and I down the rest of my drink. Telling Pete about Reed? How come this never crossed my mind before? Chelsea should be tapping my head to figure out if there's anything else in there besides air and googly eyes for Reed.

SOMEHOW HOURS later I end up at Reed's condo. Connor stands from behind the desk when I manage to get my half-drunk body through the revolving doors after whizzing around two times and realizing I was back on the street.

"Ms. Clarke." He rounds the desk and studies me. "I don't have you on the list for tonight."

"Do I need to be on the list?" I ask, using his desk to prop myself up.

"Well, Mr. Warner has a permanent list. Let me see if you're on there."

"A permanent list?" My gaze blurs to follow him walk back around the desk. He types into the computer and I inch over the edge of the tall desk. "Tell me Connor, just between us, are there any other women on that list?"

He glances up, his non-verbal scolding telling me my answer. He's not at liberty to say. "Ms. Clarke," he sighs. I'm not sure if he's upset with my intoxication or my curiosity. "You are on the list but let me ring him just to make sure he's home. I haven't seen him this evening."

Spotting the chairs in the lobby, I make my way over on unsteady feet and sit down. "Whatever you say, Connor."

I hear Connor talking for a moment, then his voice

turns hushed and I know he's probably telling Reed what bad shape I'm in. I should've listened to Chelsea and Hannah, but they over-served me and I'm horny and on edge about telling Pete.

My eyes close and what feels like a second later my body is lifted like an angel has me in his arms.

"Thanks, Connor. I got it from here."

Reed.

I release a contented sigh. My eyes flutter open and I see that he's carrying me into the elevator. My hand runs along his stubble and I can't fight the smile on my face. "It's you."

He chuckles. "Is this what girl's night entails? Getting shitfaced?"

I rest my head on his strong shoulder and then somewhere between staring at his beautiful blue eyes and luscious lips, we're in his condo, where he lays me down on the couch.

"Is this where I'm sleeping?"

"I need your phone, Victoria." He places my purse on the table.

"Do you have another woman in your bedroom?" My eyes finally focus in on his shirtless self, pajama pants hanging way too low on his hips to be appropriate.

"What?" he asks with a crease in his forehead.

"Who's on your permanent list?"

"My permanent list?"

I sit up and the room spins for a second.

Ooooooooooogggghhhhhhhhofofofofofofofffff

A huge burp escapes and my hand flies up to my mouth. "Excuse me." Even with how drunk I am, I feel the heat rushing up my neck to my cheeks.

He chuckles. "I need to call your mom, babe."

I pick up my purse and then put it in his lap. "It's in there."

My head falls back to the cushion and the weight of my eyelids wins. I feel him pick up my arm and use my thumb to open my phone and I'm suddenly too tired to protest or think of how ridiculous that is.

"Hi, Mrs. Clarke. This is Reed Warner, Victoria's boyfriend." There's a pause. "She's here, but she's had a few too many drinks with the girls. Are you okay if she stays here tonight?" Another pause. A laugh because my mom is oh so funny. "You can handle Jade, too? Great. I'll bring her home in the morning." Another chuckle on his part. "Have a good night."

He rounds the couch and I attempt to pick up my head, but it falls back down to the couch. "Good news, babe, your mom said you can spend the night." He laughs, his two arms sliding under me again and picking me up.

"I thought I was sleeping here."

"You sleep in my bed." He carries me down the hall, sets me on the bed. He gently takes off my shoes, strips off my clothes, and places a t-shirt over my head before tucking me into bed.

"You're sweet," I say, my hand running along his cheek, my thumb pressing into the cute dimple on is left cheek.

"You're drunk." His smile says he's not mad. "I just have to finish up some work. I'll check on you in a few." He walks to the door, turning off the light.

"Reed?"

"Yeah?"

"You won't listen to Pete, right? You won't let him bully you into not dating me?"

The light flicks back on and his footsteps on the hardwood floor grow closer. The mattress indents and he takes my hand in his, kissing my knuckles.

"Is that what you're worried about?"

"That and your permanent list."

He laughs. "You don't need to worry about either. Pete can't bully me into giving up the best thing I've ever had. Just because he's an idiot and fucked it up, doesn't mean I'm going to do the same." He kisses my knuckles. "And, so we're clear—you're the only woman on my permanent list. Not even my mother is on there. I added you and Jade after last Friday." He bends down and kisses my forehead. "Now, go to sleep."

The mattress rises without his weight on it anymore and I slip into sleep at peace with his answer because I believe him.

WHEN MY EYES open next there's still darkness filling the sky and I'm in bed by myself. Pulling the sheets back, I sit up and stay in that position for a second assessing how I feel. When I notice the bottle of water placed on the nightstand, I crack it open and down half the contents, feeling my hangover setting in already.

The echo of papers rustling, and buttons being punched on a computer comes from outside the bedroom and so I follow the noises to Reed's dining room table. He sits there bare-chested in his pajama pants, a beer in his left hand, a pen in his right, looking over some papers sitting beside his computer.

"Hey," I announce my arrival into the room.

He slowly glances over, and his smile warms my insides. Raising his hand, he holds it out for me and I walk over.

"I'm sorry," I say.

"Don't be. I quite enjoyed working out here knowing you were in the other room."

My fingers entwine with his and he slides the chair back, pulling me onto his lap.

"Still, you saw me at my worst."

He buries his face in my neck, kissing the delicate skin. "I liked taking care of you. I guess I'm kind of a caveman." His free hand slides up my thigh, his fingers bypassing the edge of my panties. "Not to mention, I'm due for a break."

"Oh yeah?"

He stands, holding me to him and I swear his muscles don't even flex. We only venture to the other side of the table, where it's not filled with paperwork. He lowers my body until my feet find the floor. Once I find my footing, he swivels me around, so I face the expansive window and the dark waters of Lake Michigan.

His hand slides down the edge of my panties and his chest presses to my back, his hot and wet mouth at my ear. He doesn't say anything, but his rapid breathing is enough to tell me he's as ready as I am.

Fisting my panties, he slides them down my legs, his mouth following on the back of my thighs. I can't see what he's doing, but from the shuffling of clothes, I'm assuming he's taken off his pajama pants.

When he stands back up, his chest presses against my back, his cock poised between my ass cheeks.

"Tell me I don't have to leave you to get a condom?" he whispers.

"You're clean?" I ask, sounding needier than I thought I would.

"Yes."

"Then no, we don't need anything."

He exerts some pressure between my shoulder blades,

forcing me to bend forward more. His dick slides farther down my ass cheeks, teasing my slit. He doesn't ask me any more questions, trusting that I wouldn't trick him into a pregnancy, and me trusting the fact that he's clean.

Slowly, he enters me from behind and my back arches, but he flattens his palm on my lower spine to keep me in place.

The pace is painfully slow and gentle until he's coated in my wetness. He gains speed quickly and it's different than the other night. Tonight is all about primal need and releasing tension, not soothing words and building trust. Pulling my arms back, he grips them in place on my back and takes control of the rhythm.

In and out, my ass slapping against his pelvis, his balls swinging and hitting my clit with each thrust. I'm not sure if it's waking up in his bed, or the alcohol in my system that makes me hornier, but it takes no time at all for me to hit that edge.

Knowing it, he releases my hands and they land on the window with a slap of my palms. His large hands cup my breasts, pinching my nipples, his mouth wet on the back of my neck.

"Harder," I pant, and he increases his speed. "I'm going to come." My mouth clamps down, and I bite down on my lip.

"Come," he says, his thumb sliding between my lips. "Come, baby."

I bit down on his thumb and release the exquisite tension only Reed can make me feel.

Right after I come, he pumps into me a few more times, one hand pulling up the back of my t-shirt and gripping my shoulder to keep me in place.

He pulls out and I feel his cum spray all over my back

with his contented groan. I moan, too, loving the feeling that he's somehow claiming me.

When we've both caught our breath, he eases off the shirt I borrowed and uses it to clean off my skin.

Leaving everything in a pile on the floor, he picks me up and I wrap my legs around his waist.

"Time for us to get some sleep." He kisses me, his tongue exploring my mouth the entire way to his bed.

Then as he already did hours before, he tucks me in, but this time he slides in next to me. My eyes lose the fight, but he whispers in my ear. "Don't worry, babe, I'll take care of Pete."

I head to dreamland knowing Reed would slay any dragon that came my way, but Pete is my problem and I'm the one who needs to warn him before he conquers the castle I'm currently living in.

Chapter Twenty-Seven

Thankfully, Hannah lets me off early on Friday so I have time to run home and meet Pete before we go together to pick up Jade from school. This will be the first weekend that I won't be with her and as much as I can't wait to spend it with Reed being an adult and doing only adult things, I'm going to miss her.

"I don't want to see him," my mom says as I run around the house, trying to clean it up.

"You don't have a choice. I wasn't going to drop her off at his parents."

I pick up all the handicap bathroom stuff I bought to have installed and throw it into my room. Another day.

"Your aunt wants to meet Reed," she changes the topic again.

"She will when things are a little farther down the road."

She sits in her chair, People magazine half opened, her reading glasses on the tip of her nose. "She lives in Montana, and she's coming to visit this weekend. She won't see Jade until Sunday. The least you can do is have Reed come to dinner, too."

"Mom," I sigh. "Can we talk about this after?" I straighten all her magazines and books into neat piles on the bookcase. The woman refuses to read on a digital device. Claims it's not the same as holding the words in your hands.

"Sure, but I'm not sure I want Pete to set foot in this house."

"Do it for Jade."

"Jade should know what an ass her father is. She's going to find out when she's older and it's going to break her heart." She flips the page of her magazine.

"So, your advice is for me to break her heart now?"

She peeks over the edge of her magazine and blows out a breath. "I suppose you're right, I just hate all the pain he's caused you. It's going to be all I can do not to kick him in the nuts."

"Mom!"

She closes the magazine and throws it on the table I just organized. "I hope Reed kicks his ass."

"No one's kicking anyone's ass."

The doorbell rings and my mom slides to the edge of the recliner, ready to answer it.

"I got it." I wave her off.

She rolls her eyes, grabs the magazine again and buries her head behind it. Great, this should be wonderful.

I open the door to find Pete in his relaxed look. Gray jeans, white t-shirt with a black coat slung over the top and open. For a second, I remember how excited I used to be when he'd show up at my parents' house to pick me up. How I thought he was the best guy ever and I'd love him forever.

"Pete," I say, trying to keep the disdain from my tone.

"Vic." He steps over the threshold before I actually invite him in. Typical. "Where's Jade?" He looks around and spots my mom in the recliner. "Diane, nice to see you."

She peels back the corner of her magazine. "Jackass," she regards him, and he glances at me, annoyed.

I shrug.

"It's been two years, Diane."

"Not long enough," she singsongs, hiding once again behind the magazine.

I move to put on my coat. "I figured we'd walk down there to pick her up together. I have something I want to talk to you about."

"If you changed your mind about this weekend, I don't want to hear it. I haven't seen her in months. My family is expecting her—"

I cut him off with my hand. "That's not it."

"Cool your jets, Rico Suave," my mom chimes in from behind her magazine.

Pete sets those brown eyes my way, asking what the fuck?

"Okay, Mom, you've made your point," I say.

She shuts the magazine a second time. "I'm not sure I have. If Pete has a few hours, I'm sure we can rehash all the reasons why I think he's a piece of shit."

"Mom," I sigh.

"I'm not sure what you want from me, Diane." Pete has his hands splayed out at his sides.

"I could send you an email detailing all your faults and suggestions on how to fix them."

"Great, can I do the same?" he snips.

I swivel Pete's shoulders so he's facing the door and ease him toward it. "We're going to get Jade."

"Uh-huh. Be careful, Chicago drivers aren't so great. If

Pete stumbles off the sidewalk, don't go being a hero, Victoria."

My shoulders fall, and I stare at my mom from behind Pete's back with a look that suggests she lose the attitude.

"Always a pleasure, Diane." Pete nods and opens the door.

"How very polite of you. Winnetka can teach you how to talk to people but seems to have failed on teaching you how to treat people."

I shut the door and turn to find Pete already lighting a cigarette.

"Nope, not around Jade."

He inhales. "After dealing with your mother, I deserve one."

"Just don't when you're around her, okay?"

He exhales, and a puff of white smoke follows. "Sure. Whatever." He shrugs.

He's probably lying, but it's not like he has her all the time.

"How far to school?" he asks.

"Just down the road. A couple blocks."

We step inline, him taking the street side of the sidewalk.

"So, what do you have to talk to me about? Not enough money to cover expenses?" He takes another drag of his cigarette and gestures to the neighborhood as if asking how that would even be possible.

"Don't be like that."

He swings his arm around my shoulder and squeezes me closer to him. "Oh, Vic, that's our relationship. We go back and forth. Married or divorced, that won't change."

I roll my eyes and push him off of me.

"Besides, I'm kidding. You know I don't mind paying for Jade."

I half smile, not sure where this man emerged from.

"I wanted to let you know that… I met an old friend of ours recently." I hear the hesitation in my voice and I'm sure he must pick up on it because he stops walking and turns to look at me.

"Who?" He takes another drag of his cigarette and exhales smoke in my direction. My stomach rolls from the smell.

"Reed Warner," I say his name like I'm not even sure if that's his name, which of course I am. I may have actually written Mrs. Warner on a scrap paper like a teenage girl this week, ripped it up and threw it away.

Looking nonplussed Pete starts walking again. "Reed? I think he's more an old friend of *mine* than yours, right?" The way he asks the question is almost accusatory.

"Yeah, but he stood up in *our* wedding."

He purses his lips staring up at the sky like he didn't remember. "Oh yeah."

"He was your best man," I remind him.

"Yeah, yeah, I know."

He so didn't remember. This is Pete, somewhere after 'I do' and 'It's a girl,' I lost him. I lost him to success.

"Well, it turns out he's a Big Brother to a boy that Jade is friends with."

"Wait." He holds his hand up. "The boy trying to be a man thing?"

"Yes…No… I mean, yeah, Reed is Henry's big brother. You know the program."

"He still does that? Why?"

"I don't know, Pete, maybe because he's a nice human being?"

His face is laced with confusion. "Did he lose his license to practice law or something?"

"No, he's the assistant district attorney. He's doing it

because he wants to." I stop us because we're nearing the school and I need to get this out before we get there.

"He's an ADA? What a pussy. He makes dimes when he could be making dollars. What the hell is wrong with him?"

"Okay, let's forget the whole Big Brother thing and what path he's gone down to practice law. There's more."

He eases his stance, his eyes narrowing on me. "You're not one to beat around the bush, Vic, what is it?"

Finally, a light bulb went off.

"We're dating." The words rush out of my mouth like the Colorado Rapids.

"You're dating Reed Warner? Our best man?"

"According to you, he was just your best man."

"Don't be snide. You're dating Reed?"

I nod.

He huffs and tosses his cigarette butt on the sidewalk.

"I thought you swore off lawyers?" He digs into his jacket for another cigarette.

I pull out my phone to check the time. We still have five minutes before Jade gets out.

"Turns out not the good ones." I smile, hoping to ease some of the sting.

He cups his hand over the cigarette and lights it, blowing a stream of smoke out of the corner of his mouth. "Shit. You just ran me over with a dump truck. I thought you were gonna ride my ass about her routine or some shit. Not the fact that you're dating…my best friend."

"He's not your best friend. When's the last time you talked to him?"

He thinks again, his eyes staring up at the dreary gray sky. "I don't know. Maybe six years ago? You're happy?" he asks, looking back down at me.

I nod and smile, thinking this is going to be fine. That I worried for nothing.

"I am."

"You look like you lost a few pounds." He smiles, looking me over.

"Gee thanks." I pat his flat stomach. "Cool it on the beer, yeah?"

He laughs. "You and Reed, huh?"

"Yeah."

"Sneaky bastard." He inhales and exhales the smoke. The cigarette hangs from his fingers. "That's it though? Just dating? No wedding on the horizon? You're not knocked up or anything?"

"No, I practice safe sex after I ended up stuck with you for seven years." I give him a saccharine smile.

His eyes crinkle at the edges. "She's the best thing we did." He glances over to the school.

"That's the truth."

He swings his arm around me, flicks the cigarette into the street and walks us the rest of the way to the school. "She was worth all the fighting and screaming and losing my youth."

I hip check him. "Um, I'm the one who lost my youth."

He doesn't say anything and eventually his arm falls off my shoulders, but the silence between us is content and easy.

Why did I worry so much?

The minute we break the tree-line and the courtyard opens up, all eyes are on Pete. Darcie and Georgia's mouths hang open and a few others whisper to each other as they wait for their kids.

"Mean moms?" He nods at Darcie, able to pick the head viper out of the pack.

Back in Los Angeles, Jade went to a private school and he was familiar with their kind.

"Yep."

"Wanna fuck with them?"

"How so?"

"Do they know you're with Reed?"

I glance away from Pete and see Darcie approaching. Of course. She's like the fucking police of a small town. No one enters without being questioned.

"Yes, they do." I shrug.

"Vicki," she says.

Pete's hand slides into mine. I feel none of the warmth I do when Reed holds my hand.

"Darcie. Georgia," I say each name with the annoyance I feel toward them.

"Who's this?" she asks, her eyes rolling over Pete's body.

"This is Jade's father, Pete."

He puts his hand out to shake without ever letting go of mine. "Hi. I'm in from Los Angeles." They shake hands.

"Vicki, I thought you were with Reed?" Darcie asks with a glance at our joined hands, trying her best to stir up trouble.

Pete stares over at me for a moment, I think he's going to act like we're not divorced and he's just found out I'm cheating on him. "They know about Reed?" he whispers to me, loud enough for them to hear.

I nod, still not understanding where he's going with all this.

"Are you two still married?" Georgia asks.

Pete leans forward. "Who said we were ever married in the beginning? She's a Clarke. I'm a Keebler. Jade's a Keebler."

They look at one another, trying to figure out the puzzle he's presented them with. Are they dense enough to not realize I took back my maiden name?

"Oh, so you," Darcie's eyes drop to our entwined hands. "Are together?"

Pete closes the gap between us and the bell rings to say school's out. The principal opens the doors, waiting for the kids to pack up their backpacks and get out. Jade's expecting my mom, which will make Pete being here that much more special to her.

"We're all together, if you know what I mean." Pete winks.

"Oh," Darcie's hand covers her chest. "Like?"

Georgia's eyes crinkle, her head flipping from Darcie to Pete then me.

"Open relationship." He winks again, and she steps back like she could catch whatever we have.

"Open?" Georgia stares around all of us trying to figure out what the hell we're talking about.

I bite my lip to keep from laughing.

The kids are running out of the school and racing down the stairs.

"Please though, keep it on the down low. You know how some people judge." He cringes.

Jade runs down the stairs, spotting Pete.

"DADDY!"

He releases my hand, bends down and scoops his little girl up in his arms. They swing around, and I almost feel like I'm in a movie as I watch on. The pit of my stomach burns over the fact that I took her away from him.

"Hi, Henry," I say, patting his head as he stares at Jade with her dad.

The entire courtyard seems enamored by the scene.

When Pete places her back down, Jade wipes tears

from her eyes and Pete stares down at her with water in his own. "I missed you," Pete says, and Jade wraps her arms tight around his neck.

"I missed you," she murmurs into his jacket.

A horn honks and Henry looks up. "My grandpa is here. Bye, Jade, have fun this weekend."

"Wait," Jade says, halting Henry in his tracks. "Daddy, this is my friend, Henry."

Pete puts out his fist and Henry bumps it. "Nice to meet you," Pete says. "I heard you've never seen the ocean?"

He shakes his head.

"Never, Daddy," Jade confirms.

Pete digs into his pocket. "Here." He pulls out a bottle of sand with ocean water floating at the top. "It's sand and water from the Pacific Ocean."

Henry takes it and stares at it for a long moment. "Thanks," he says, with wide, awestruck eyes.

The horn honks again and Henry turns. "I gotta go."

"Bye, Henry," Jade says.

"Bye." He glances back to me and I wave.

"Where's mine?" Jade asks.

Pete pretends to forget her and Jade pouts. "Would I ever forget my girl?" he asks, pulling another bottle out of his jacket.

In that moment, Pete has won every person in that courtyard over. Here, he's the charming dad who loves his daughter so much it brings him to tears. Hell, for a second, I was right there with them. There's a reason why he's the best defense attorney in Los Angeles.

Chapter Twenty-Eight

On the taxi ride over to Reed's, the melancholy of not having Jade all weekend while she visits Pete's parents with him sets in. Not knowing where she is, or what those poisoned people Pete calls family will say to her. I try to push it out of my mind. Pete only wants the best for his daughter so I have to trust he won't let them say anything disparaging about me in front of her. The same way I won't let my mom talk shit about Pete when Jade's around.

The taxi stops, and I climb out, this time able to get through the revolving door the first time through. #winning

"Hi, Connor," I say.

He stands, waves and digs through his drawer, holding an envelope in his hand.

"I have something for Mr. Warner, do you mind taking it up with you?" He meets me at the elevator. Pressing the up button and then scanning his card to allow me up to the floor.

"Sure." We exchange the envelope.

"Nice to see you again, Ms. Clarke." He tips his head as the doors shut.

"Nice to see me not stumbling and shit-faced," I say to myself in the silence of the elevator. My face reddens just thinking of the spectacle I made of myself the last time he saw me. Not my finest hour.

Reed's already leaning against his doorframe when the elevator doors slide open. He's biting an apple with a grin on his face.

"Hey," I walk up to him, dropping my overnight bag at our feet.

The sweetness of the apple has me craving more of him as our lips meet and his tongue slides into my mouth.

"Hey," he says after he ends the kiss. Bending down he picks up the bag. "How are you?"

I nod. "I'm okay."

On the counter in the kitchen, there's a bottle of wine with a glass already poured. "Figured you might—"

I glance over.

"Yeah, well, I didn't know what shape you'd be in." He chuckles, and sets his apple on the counter then places my bag against the wall in the hallway that leads to his bedroom.

"I'm fine. Really." I retrieve the glass, toe out of my shoes and sit down on the couch.

He sits down next to me, his arm slung across the back of the couch, wrapping my hair around his fingers. "How's Pete?"

My head falls back, and I turn his way. "Surprisingly, good."

He raises his eyebrows. "You told him?"

"I did."

He leans forward and kisses my lips. "I would've handled it."

"I know." I kiss him this time, sliding closer into the nook of his arm. "I had to do it."

"How excited was Jade?"

I lean forward to set the wine glass on the coffee table and then lean back into Reed. My arm stretches across his stomach, his thin sweater smelling of his cologne.

"So excited she cried."

His lips dip because he's so aligned with my feelings.

"Am I horrible for moving her here?" My knees come up to my chest and I nuzzle into him more.

His arms tighten around me. "If you hadn't moved, we wouldn't have reconnected, so my answer is no."

I giggle and kiss his jaw, the stubble pricking my skin.

"You're biased."

"You did what you had to do. Pete could move here. You don't have to always be the one to make the sacrifice." I stare at him with love in my eyes, my hand landing on his cheek and inching up as he inches down until our lips meet.

For a moment, I'm lost in Reed. In his sweetness, his capability to take on my problems with ease, in his feelings for me.

"Okay!" I stand up suddenly with enough enthusiasm to startle Reed. "I am not ruining our first kid-free weekend."

He chuckles, kissing my stomach. His hands move up the back of my legs until each hand has a chunk of my ass in them.

Using all his force, he pulls me down onto the couch, rolling me to my back. Climbing on top of me, I widen my legs to make room for him. "I have a great idea." His lips travel up my neck to my jaw until he claims my mouth.

I don't object to his hands finding their way under my shirt or when they explore down the front of my yoga pants, and I definitely don't stop him when he reminds me how good we are together on his couch.

He always has the best ideas.

THE NEXT NIGHT, Reed and I go to dinner and to a late show. We're standing by the bar, me drinking wine and him a whiskey on the rocks waiting for the Broadway show to begin when someone calls out his name.

Lost in our own world, Reed doesn't hear it right away, so I tap him on the arm. "That guy," I say, pointing to a man in a suit approaching us.

He's probably Reed's age, dressed in a nice suit with a woman trailing along behind him.

"Reed," he says, putting his hand out.

"Hey, George." Reed shakes his hand.

The woman smiles at me and I smile back. Reed pulls me into his side, his hand protectively on my hip.

George drops the woman's hand and since they're both wearing wedding rings, my guess is it's his wife. She looks around at the people surrounding us like she'd rather be talking to one of them, apparently not at all interested in the conversation that's about to commence.

"I haven't seen you since you were handed the Weinstein case. Is it still expected to go to jury next week?" George looks like an eager puppy whose master just said treat.

Reed stands straighter, but still, his hand hasn't left my hip. "It is."

"You know what'll happen if you win, right?"

Reed shrugs and takes a big gulp of his drink. "There's no if. I have to win. That slimeball deserves what's coming to him."

"You will. That's why they picked you." George's excited voice has a few people turning their heads.

"George MacIlroy, this is Victoria Clarke. George used to work with me until he went on his own in the defense sector."

I hold my hand out. "Nice to meet you."

He shakes my hand, staring at me and a moment of fear grips me, wondering if he knew Pete. Then he turns around. "This is my wife, Cassie."

The blonde smiles, shaking our hands with no real enthusiasm.

"Nice to meet you," I say, and she smiles, continuing to look anywhere but at us.

"Back to Weinstein. I know you've gotten some dirt, right? I mean you're Reed Warner." George apparently has propped Reed up on some imaginary prosecutor pedestal.

Reed shrugs. "You know I can't talk about it."

George nods. "I know, I know. But damn, I was talking to someone the other day about you and when they said you were the ADA assigned to the case I thought to myself, he's going places."

Reed glances down at me, and then to George. "I have to win it," repeating himself once more.

The lights blink, and Reed's hand tightens on my hip, leading me forward.

"Good to see you." He nods to George. "Nice to meet you." He directs his attention to Cassie. "Enjoy the show."

"Yeah, maybe we'll see you during the intermission."

God, I hope not. That was weird.

I smile, and Reed guides us to the entrance to our seats, but before we can make our get-away, George snaps his fingers.

"That's where I know you from."

"Just go," Reed whispers, but I look over my shoulder to see him approaching.

"You're Pete Keebler's wife."

Reed circles around, his hand leaving my body for the first time all night. "Ex-wife." The word comes out sharp enough to cut glass.

George covers his mouth with his fist. "You're dating Keebler's ex? I knew you were ballsy, Reed, but—"

"Mind your own business." Reed turns us back around and we're ready to enter the doors to the theater, leaving overzealous George and his neglected wife behind.

"Can I be there when he finds out?" George says to our backs.

Okay Reed, don't hate me after this.

I circle around.

"I'm not sure where I met you before, George, but I can tell you I don't remember you. It was most likely at some boring work-related function where you were probably so busy ignoring your wife that you happened to notice me. Tell me, were you as far up Pete's ass that night as you are up Reed's tonight? Let's make one thing clear. We're not in high school anymore." I talk to him in a tone like he can't comprehend what I'm saying. "The gossip mill doesn't exist. Pete knows I'm dating Reed, not that it's really any of your business. Go get your wife and show her some affection and then maybe you'll get lucky tonight and you can stop bitching to all your friends down at the club about how you never get any."

George stands in front of me, eyes wide, but doesn't respond. Then his gaze shifts to Reed almost asking, 'seriously?' I'm about to turn back around when George laughs. Bent over, uncontrolled bellowing.

"Shit. No wonder you and Keebler didn't make it. Tell me, how many times were the police called?"

Before I can respond, Reed's brushing past me. "Mac-Ilroy," he warns.

I push him back by the chest before we get kicked out.

As George is still bent over, I lean down to speak into his ear. "You can find humor in whatever you want but know this. Reed is the one who's going to get his cock sucked by me tonight. He's going to fuck me in every room of his condo and probably a few times tomorrow morning. So, while you're beating off to porn in your basement while your wife sleeps upstairs, please remember it's because you're an asshole."

George's fake laughter stops.

I wind my arm through Reed's and lead him through the doors into the theater.

"Shit, I'm so turned on right now," Reed says with a groan.

"Good thing we're in a box and I'm wearing a dress." I waggle my eyebrows and his hand slides from my hip to my ass, grabbing it and sliding close to me.

"God, you're one in a million." He kisses my cheek as the guy leads us upstairs to our own private viewing section where Reed definitely got his money's worth.

<h1 style="text-align:center">Chapter Twenty-Nine</h1>

"I'm so fucking tense." Reed balls his fists as he leans against the desk in his office. "I swear if the jury doesn't find him guilty and sets him free I might go ballistic."

I've never seen this side of Reed. He's ready to rage, to fight and something carnal inside of me wants to be the one he unleashes on so that I can tame him.

I sit in the chair in front of him—my legs crossed, my arms folded—trying to appear as if seeing him in court and how he is here doesn't turn me on.

"I'm sure you'll win them over just like you did my aunt on Sunday."

A smile tips his lips for a second. "Aunts are easy. Convincing twelve people to all agree on the same verdict. Not so easy."

Reed just performed his closing argument in the case an hour ago and now, though he says it could be days before they have an answer, here we are in his office, waiting for the jury's verdict.

I stand, unable to see him like this and not do something any longer. Wrapping my arms around his neck, I pull my body flush against his. "You need to get your mind off of it."

"I do, huh?" he asks, his hands landing on my ass and squeezing.

Some men are breast men or leg men. Reed is all ass. He admits his favorite position is doggie because he loves watching my ass while he plunges into me.

I press my lips to his. "Why don't you sit in your chair and let me get to work." I wink, and he licks his lips, his mouth opening a sliver.

I take his hand, leading him to the opposite side of his desk and push him down into his chair. He falls with a pft to the leather chair and I drop to my knees in front of him.

"Vic," he says in practically a moan.

His dick already tents his slacks. I love the effect I have on him. Keeping my eyes on him, I unbuckle his belt, unbutton his pants and slowly lower the zipper until his black boxer briefs appear, a welcoming bulge front and center.

I lift the waistband of his boxers, peeking in to see the head of his cock pulsing and ready for my mouth.

Reed's arm stretches toward his desk and I hear him hit something that causes a beep to sound.

"Yes, Mr. Warner," his assistant asks through the intercom.

"No interruptions unless it's the" —I take him in my mouth—"verdict."

"Yes, Sir."

The octave change in his voice probably clued her in to why he's asking for no interruptions with his girlfriend in the room. Do I care? Nope.

Pushing him as far down my throat as possible, his hands tighten in my hair. Wrapping the strands through his fingers, he bucks up. I dig my hand down to play with his balls and his head falls back against his chair, his eyes unable to stay open.

I work him, slowly, to allow him the most pleasure he can get before we have to return to reality. Twisting and swallowing, licking and twirling, Reed groans when I pump him at the base.

"Victoria," my name a plea on his lips. "Don't stop. You're so fucking good at it."

His words only spur me on more and I move faster, wanting him to experience the ecstasy he gives me.

He bucks again and stills, his cum squirting into my mouth and I wait patiently until he's completely spent. Licking him clean, I pull up his boxers and stare up at him.

"I'll never wait for another jury without you again."

I smile and rise to my feet.

Not bothering to zip up his pants, he swivels his chair and positions me on the edge of his desk.

"My turn," he says, licking his lips.

I shake my head. "No, that was my gift to you."

He hoists me up on the desk, directing one leg to the armrest on one side of him and the other to the armrest on the opposite side. His head slides up under the fabric of my dress. "Your panties are already soaked," he observes, and I laugh.

"Wouldn't you be hard if roles were reversed?"

"Baby, I'm already hard again."

I giggle leaning back on my elbows.

He slides one finger up the inside of my thigh and I open my legs wider. Just as he slides it underneath my panties, a buzzing sound shakes the desk underneath me.

"Please tell me that's a vibrator?"

"Afraid not, babe." He sits up and grabs his phone.

"Warner," he answers, holding his hand out to help me up. "Be right there."

He stands, tucks himself completely in, zips, buttons, and buckles himself back into the GQ man I'm used to seeing.

"Relax," I say, pressing my lips to his.

He smiles, but I know he's worried.

"They came back in record time, which means they were sure about their decision. Let's hope I did my job well enough." He pushes a hand through his hair and blows out a long breath. "Listen." He helps me off the desk and I slip on my heels. "You're to leave this office and go downstairs. Talk on your phone or pretend you are. When you see me walking down the hall, you are to ignore me. Act like you have no idea who I am."

"Why?" I smooth the front of my skirt to try to work out a wrinkle that's formed from our shenanigans.

"Because no one else needs to know who you are."

"Okay," I say offended, but whatever. I ignored the fact that he told me not to wait for him after closing arguments and that his assistant would let me into his office. Now I can't even walk downstairs with him?

"It's for your own safety." He kisses my forehead. "I put away bad people. People who have friends who might want revenge. I'd feel better if no one outside of this office knew you were my girlfriend."

I smack a smile on my face like I'm not freaked out.

"Afterward, just head back to your office and I'll call you when things calm down."

"Okay."

"Thanks." He winks. "I'm glad you're here."

He puts me at ease as I leave his office, his secretary's knowing eyes on me.

I head to the elevator bank, go down and I'm about to

call Chelsea when I walk toward the courtroom, but I tuck my phone back in my purse finding Pete leaning against the wall.

"What are you doing here?"

He smirks. "I wanted to see our boy. See if he wins. It's a big case."

"I thought you were headed back to Los Angeles?"

"I decided to stay the week. Jade can't stop talking about this carnival thing on Saturday. She invited me over to your house for cake tomorrow since it's her actual birthday."

"That's not part of the deal."

"What deal?"

"You need to okay these things with me." I cross my arms over my chest.

"You always were cute when you were mad." He laughs at me.

The press lingers around the doors probably waiting for Reed or the defender to make a statement about which way they expect things to go.

"I'm not joking this time, Pete."

"Neither am I. I disappoint her enough with not being around. One more week isn't going to kill you." He tucks his phone into his pants pocket.

"Aren't you itching with not being in a suit at a court-house?" I ask.

"No, but I forgot how much I love Chicago."

The heels of the press descend down the hallway. Reporters with microphones out and cameras already zoomed in.

Reed exits the elevator and you'd never guess he just received a blow job upstairs. His briefcase is in his hands, his lips straight, expression intense as he nods a few times at the people yelling out questions to him. He answers a few but never slows his pace on the way to the courtroom.

He passes by me, a fleeting glance in my direction and I question if he even saw me. If it wasn't for the quick scowl I saw cross his face I'd say no.

"Your boy isn't happy." Pete pushes himself off the wall to follow the group in.

"Why do you say that?" I rush to keep up with him.

"You really are piss-poor at reading non-verbal clues." He shakes his head like this is a disappointment to him.

"What did I miss?" I ask while I push past the heavy courtroom doors.

"His hand tightened on his briefcase. His eyes stayed on yours a beat longer than they should have. His one look to me had the threat of physical harm in it."

"You got all that in the split second he walked by us?"

He laughs and stands outside one of the rows, motioning for me to go in first. Following behind, he sits next to me, thigh to thigh.

"He told you not to act like you knew him?" Pete whispers.

"It's none of your business." I wish Pete would stop asking questions about Reed and me.

"Good boy. Glad to know that all his bullshit about being on the good side of things, didn't make him naive."

"Okay, you can stop talking now." I roll my eyes.

"If he's going to be a permanent fixture in your life, I have to make sure he can protect you both."

"*I* can protect us. *Me.* I've done a good job of it for the last seven years."

His hand pats my knee and I slide it over, so it drops off. "Relax, you're drawing attention to yourself."

I scowl in his direction just as the judge enters the courtroom. Everyone stands, Reed glancing over his shoulder to spot Pete and me. There's no recognition or emotion in his gaze.

"You may be seated," the judge says and we all sit down.

"Your boy is threatened by me. Funny. *You* divorced *me*," Pete continues to talk even though I ignore him.

The head juror hands a piece of paper to the sheriff who hands it to the judge. She reads it and my focus is on Reed. He's sitting straight, his arms resting on the table, waiting for the verdict. The defendant stands.

"Here's the big moment," Pete whispers and I elbow him in the ribcage.

"We the jury find the defendant…guilty."

The juror continues talking but I watch as the tension leaves Reed's shoulders. He glances to his partner who helped him, and they share a satisfied look.

A few people on the defendant's side cry out and the judge bangs his gavel to get everyone under control. The defendant's head falls into his hands as he weeps. It's all very dramatic and it isn't until a woman on the other side tries to jump the separation to stop them from taking the defendant away that I understand why Reed was so adamant about not letting anyone here know we're together.

Once it's all said and done, Pete and I stand.

"Well, now your boy has his pick of DA offices in the country."

I glance back to see Reed's gaze on me as I leave the courtroom with Pete. I want to raise my hand, but I follow his instructions and tuck my head down, leaving without acknowledging him.

"What are you talking about? And would you please call him by his name instead of 'my boy,' it's getting old."

Pete follows me outside. Like Mother Earth knew it'd

be a day to celebrate, the sun is shining, the birds are chirping, and people are littered across the courtyard enjoying the weather, ignorant to what just happened in that courtroom.

"You think after winning this case, he's going to stay an assistant district attorney, emphasis on 'assistant?'"

"He doesn't want to go into the private sector. Not everyone is a money grubber."

"That money grubber supports our daughter. Well, I may add." He lights up a cigarette.

"Fifteen feet rule," I singsong and he takes a few giant steps away from the front doors.

That's the difference. Reed follows the rules while Pete disregards them.

"People are going to want him, Vic, he won't be in Chicago long." He pats me on my back, smoking his cigarette and heads to a taxi. "See you tomorrow night."

He flicks the cigarette to his side and a woman screams at him since it almost hit her. He ignores her and gets into the cab probably instructing the driver to run her over.

Why is Pete always like the cloud on an otherwise beautiful day?

Chapter Thirty

*H*annah has been so understanding. Needing a day to regroup, I took off Jade's birthday because not only do I have to make her the grumpy cat cake she requested, but I'm just not in the mood to deal with people. Especially after Pete's comment about Reed not staying in Chicago. It's been eating at me since the words left his lips.

"This is cute." My mom comes in and sits on the breakfast stool, turning the picture and directions toward her.

"I'm pretty sure Moe is her inspiration."

"He is a grump."

"You think?"

She watches me for a few minutes, as I add the eggs and oil into the box mix and whisk it together.

"How are things with Reed?" she asks.

The doorbell rings and I crinkle my eyebrows at my mom. Neither of us are expecting anyone and I swear if it's Pete, my mom might drop kick him on the spot.

She walks to the door and opens it.

"You must be Mama Clarke."

Chelsea.

"Chelsea, right?" My mom laughs knowing she got it right from the way I've described my co-worker.

I wipe my hands on a dishcloth and walk to the doorway between the rooms, spotting Hannah there, too. They each hold colorful gift bags stuffed with tissue paper.

"I'm Hannah." She puts out her hand for my mom, but my mom pulls her into a hug.

"This is an unexpected surprise," she says to both of them. "Are those for Jade?"

"We're crashing the birthday shindig and just note, we're highly offended we weren't invited." Chelsea points to me.

"I didn't think—"

"You thought wrong. We love that girl, too." Hannah comes to my side. "And we love you. Since when do you need a personal day?" She tilts her head. "You can't come to us, we come to you."

She holds out her arms and I step into them hugging her body to mine.

"Don't forget me." Chelsea runs over and the three of us are in a huddle.

"I feel left out," my mom jokes.

"Come on, Mama Clarke." Chelsea waves her hand and my mom comes over.

By the time we all part, they look at me like they're waiting for instructions.

"You want to help with her cake?" I ask.

"Not really. Do you have any wine?" Hannah asks. "Sorry, but you don't want my help. Trust me."

"I've got wine."

They follow me into the kitchen, my mom playing

hostess and me finishing the cakes by putting them in the oven to bake.

"So, why the personal day?" Chelsea asks, sipping her wine.

"I was just asking her about Reed," my mom chimes in.

"Something happen?" Hannah asks like she'd be heart-broken if it did.

I wipe down the counter where I was working. "No, we're good. It's just that big case he won."

"I saw him on the news. The camera doesn't add ten pounds to him that's for sure." Chelsea waggles her eyebrows my way over the rim of her wine glass.

"Isn't it a good thing that he won? He gets to keep his job," Hannah jokes.

"Or move to a different city. He's the assistant district attorney and Pete seems to think he'll get offers to be a district attorney and probably not in Chicago."

"Fuck what Pete thinks," Chelsea says, immediately covering her mouth after and looking toward my mom. "Sorry."

My mom waves her off. "My sentiments exactly, Chelsea."

Hannah falls back to her seat. "Oh. Well, that's not good."

"Have you talked to him?" my mom asks.

I mix the frosting because I want to do anything but think of this thing between us ending before it really gets started.

"No."

"Then why are you so upset? Ask the man." My mom talks like she's one of the girls and inside I smirk. It's good to see her vibrant.

My phone buzzes with a text and Chelsea slides it my way.

"I'll finish that." She comes behind the mixer. "Relax, I grew up with a big family who doesn't eat store-bought anything."

I smile and head down the hall for some privacy.

Reed: *What time did you want us tonight?*
Me: *Whenever. I'm just making her cake and I'm going to order pizza.*
Reed: *Want some help? I'm about to leave work for the day.*

I look at the time. It's only one.

Me: *Chelsea, Hannah and my mom are here.*
Reed: *So, I'd be invading girl time?*
Me: *No, you can come. I have some manly stuff I need done.*
Reed: *I do like when you make use of my manly skills.*
Me: *I need some grab bars installed in the bath.*
Reed: *Not what I had in mind, but I'll be over soon.*
Me: *Okay and I'm kidding about the grab bars.*

I head back into the kitchen, stuffing my phone in my back pocket. "I feel like the party is about to start without Jade."

Chelsea already has one batch of cream frosting done and she's on to the chocolate.

"Um, who are you? Betty Crocker?" I ask.

She shrugs. "I told you, big family."

"Well then, I'll work on the fondant face." I sip my wine. "Reed's coming over."

All six eyes land on me.

"Talk to him." Hannah pats my hand. "No need getting upset over nothing."

"You're a sensible woman," my mom says.

"Not when it comes to the silver fox," Chelsea adds, and I almost spit out my wine.

Hannah picks up a crumpled napkin and throws it at Chelsea.

"You know it and we know it. It's only a matter of time before you sleep with him."

Hannah balks, but it doesn't escape my notice that she doesn't argue against Chelsea's claim.

A BIT later the doorbell rings. We've got the frosting made and Chelsea's demanding she spread it, but the cakes are still cooling.

I open the door to find him in a light sweater and dark jeans. Casual and edible.

"Good afternoon." He grabs my hand and pulls me out onto the porch then shuts the door. "They're all in there, right?"

He pushes me against the side of the house, his hands already on my cheeks, his lips millimeters away from mine.

"Yeah."

"That's why we're out here."

His lips crash onto mine, his tongue sliding in through my parted lips. His knee wedges between my legs and grinds into my center. If we weren't on the porch and I didn't have a household of friends inside, I'd suggest a heavy make-out session in his car. Then again, Abe probably dropped him off.

Closing the kiss, I drag oxygen back into my lungs. Luckily, he continues to hold me up before I crumble to the ground.

"Sorry, I missed you." He leans in and kisses my forehead.

"Don't be."

He keeps me in his arms, staring down at me with the loving look I'm slowly becoming addicted to.

"Can we talk?" I ask.

"I knew something was wrong." He leads me over to the bench on my mom's porch, my hand in his. "What's up?"

"The case you won. Biggest case you've ever had?"

Just the mention of the case, a look of exhaustion crosses his face. "Not the hardest, but the biggest spectacle, yes. The most televised one for sure." His hand fiddles with mine. "Why?"

"Is there a chance you might become district attorney in Chicago?"

He huffs. "No. The DA spot isn't going to be up for a while here."

"Like how long?"

"Why all the questions?" He leans forward to look into my eyes, as if the answer lies there.

I shrug. "Just curious."

"Remember, I like how forthcoming you are. Just spit it out, Vic."

"Is there a chance that you'll be offered a higher position somewhere else and you'll leave Chicago?"

His head falls down and his hand grips mine even tighter. Looking up from the corner of his eye, he nods.

He fucking nods.

I want to scream NO and run down my street refusing to believe that he'll be gone.

"There's a chance, but I might not. I mean no one's reached out yet."

"The case just ended yesterday."

He nods again. "Yeah, but all I can say is that at this point, I haven't been asked to go anywhere."

"And if you are?"

He blows out a breath. "Honestly?"

I pull my hand from his grasp and tilt my head in a what-the-fuck-do-you-think, mannerism.

"I don't want to think about it. I can't stay assistant forever, there are things I want to achieve in my career but leaving Henry and you wouldn't be easy."

I can tell he's thought about it which makes me think the possibility of him getting an offer is much higher than he's implying.

"Did you sign those guardian papers for Henry?"

He shakes his head. "Not yet. I have a friend looking over them first. I told Ned I'd let him know next week."

"And if you move?"

He turns directly to me, gripping both my hands. "I don't want to discuss this, Vic. If the time comes, we'll talk about it of course, but that time is not now, and I feel like this is all wasted breath. You're getting upset when nothing's happened and here's me trying to figure out how to keep everything I love together. When in reality, the call might never come."

I stare down at our joined hands in my lap. Sensible Reed has made his appearance and talked me off the ledge.

"It's Jade's birthday. Let's enjoy it. Worry about this shit later."

I smile, and he wraps his arm around my shoulder, pulling me into his chest. Calm quickly replaces the tension with just the scent of his cologne.

"One more thing." I stare up at him, shooting him my best innocent eyes. "Pete's coming to dinner."

He rolls his eyes. "Great."

He stands, takes my hands and pulls me up. "Now, let's enjoy the day."

"Okay. I should get in there before Chelsea decorates Jade's cake all by herself." I head to the door, his hand in mine.

"That's a bad thing because?"

"Because I make her cake. I'm her mom."

He nods, but I can tell he clearly doesn't understand a mother's right to complain about having to do something while insisting on doing it herself at the same time. It's a mom thing.

Chapter Thirty-One

"Do you want me to grab Henry?" I ask Reed, staring at his ass bent over in the bathtub.

"No, I'm almost done. It wasn't that hard." He stands up, pulling on the bar. Then he pretends to sit down in the tub and pull himself up.

"I never would have thought you could do that."

He narrows his eyes at me. "You thought I was too white-collar, did you?"

He steps out secure in the fact the grab bar will hold my mom's weight if she needs it and stalks toward me.

"A lawyer. Winnetka. Rich boy." I flip up my fingers counting the reasons off.

He reaches me, tickling my ribcage until he gets me right where he wants me, in his arms.

"Maybe I should have worn my tool belt?"

I wiggle to get free. "That and no shirt. You'd look much manlier. Maybe Ned can help you out."

His fingers dig deeper until he's got my hands over my head and his body has me pressed against the wall. He trails his nose along my neck and up to my ear—back and forth, a painful arousal building deep inside me.

"I think you know how manly I am," he whispers sliding his other hand up my shirt, cupping my breast over my bra.

"Someone could come," I whisper.

"Tell me how manly I am."

"You're manly."

"You don't sound convincing." His fingers pinch my nipple and I push into his touch, unable to stop myself.

"Your manhood is so manly I'm sore for days."

He hems and haws. "I need more information."

"Well, counselor, I'm not sure what you're looking for."

Another tweak of my nipple and I moan.

"Shh… you're going to get us caught. Now, where were we?" His fingers pull down the cup of my bra. "Tell me."

"You're so manly that I bet you can fix my bed."

"What's wrong with your bed?" he asks while he rolls my nipple between his thumb and forefinger, like he's playing a game.

"It doesn't squeak." I pretend to pout.

"I do believe I can fix that for you, ma'am." His lips land on mine.

"Ew, keep your kinky shit to yourself."

At the sound of Chelsea's voice, Reed doesn't let go of my hands, but he does pull his other one out of my shirt.

"Way to kill the mood," he says over his shoulder to her.

Chelsea laughs. "I like you. Now get out of the bathroom. I gotta go."

Reed lets go of my hands. "We're going to get the kids anyway." He walks out of the room and down the hall.

"Well, aren't you guys just like June and Ward Cleaver?" she yells down the hall at us.

"I don't think June bites Ward," Reed says without even turning around.

"HA! She said she was a biter."

"And I have the scars to prove it," Reed and Chelsea continue their banter until we reach the kitchen.

"We'll be right back. Getting the kids." I wave to my mom and Hannah who are admiring the job Chelsea and I did on the cake. I let her help a little, but she's going to need to have her own kids if she wants to do it again.

Reed and I head down the sidewalk, holding hands, the crap from earlier pushed to the back of my mind, as I choose to focus on Jade's birthday.

"So, Pete's coming tonight?" Reed asks, which I knew was coming.

"He's her dad."

"I know and if this is going to work, we'd have to face him together. The bubble was nice for a while though."

I nod. "The bubble was indeed very nice."

We round the trees and the courtyard is packed full of parents. Darcie and Georgia along with all the other moms stare over at us with judgment in their eyes.

"Why does it seem like everyone's staring more than usual?" Reed asks.

"Because Pete told them last Friday that we have an open relationship and pretty much eluded to the fact that we all sleep together."

"All?"

"The three of us. You, me, and him."

"Pete's totally not my type," he jokes and I'm thankful he doesn't take it seriously.

"Mean Moms were being nosy, and he thought it was funny. But he would since he gets to go back to L.A. and we'll be here."

He looks around. "I'm surprised people believe it. Then again, most people will believe anything."

We wait patiently while Darcie gives us the stink eye and a few moms look Reed and I up and down like we're in the market to open our bedroom and taking resume's.

What feels like a lifetime later, the bell rings, the doors open, and Jade and Henry run out.

Jade's got a birthday crown on her head.

"YAY!" She runs right into me and I pick her up. "Happy birthday!"

I saw her this morning, made her pancakes with sprinkles, but now she really gets to celebrate.

"Happy birthday, Jade." Reed holds up his hand in a high five.

"Thanks."

The four of us walk down the street and it strikes me how much we must resemble a family. One girl, one boy both of whom are fighting for dominance over which one gets to tell us about their day first, Reed and I sharing a look every so often.

The warm sensation in my chest crystallizes to ice the moment I catch sight of the car outside my mom's house—Pete's sports car that he couldn't bear to part with when we moved to L.A. He's been storing it at his parent's place since. It's expensive and tends to stand out like a quarter in a sea of pennies in this neighborhood.

"Look at that car!" Henry says and points to it.

"That's my dad's car," Jade says proudly.

"Is that my birthday girl?" Pete stands from where he was sitting on my mom's porch and holds out his arms.

My sweet Jade abandons us and runs into Pete's awaiting embrace.

Henry follows, and I initiate the hand hold with Reed, needing the support.

Pete spins her around in a circle and she squeals. Same old, same old.

"Hey, Henry," he says in a louder than normal voice. "You enjoying that sand?"

"I showed my grandpa."

"I bet he thought it was pretty cool," Pete continues to gloat, glancing our way to see my hand in Reed's.

"He said it probably came from Lake Michigan."

I laugh because I envision Ned telling Henry it's no different than the sand right down the street.

"That's pure California sand." Pete looks to Jade whose head is already nodding in agreement.

Henry looks to Reed and shrugs.

The conversation stalls once Reed and Pete's eyes meet.

"Bug, go inside," I say. "Chelsea and Hannah are in there and I think they have gifts."

She squeals and wiggles until Pete lets her down and then she grabs Henry's hand, pulling him into the house.

"Reed," Pete puts his hand up in the air. "How the hell are you?"

Reed's hand stays firmly in mine as he reaches out and shakes Pete's. "I'm great. You?"

A huff leaks out of Pete, but no one acknowledges it. "I saw your performance in court the other day. Hell of a case."

"Thanks." They drop hands and we stand. Reed and I a united front with Pete on the other side.

"I was telling Vic, Chicago won't be able to afford you."

Reed squeezes my hand. "So, I heard."

"Just want her to be prepared for when you leave."

Pete's smile says he's toeing the line and hoping Reed's the first one to cross.

"I'm not leaving."

"Okay, well, let's go have pizza and cake," I say, wanting out of this awkward encounter.

"Sounds good. Remember eight years ago, when you were screaming like a hyena." Pete chuckles and follows us into the house.

"I was squeezing a walnut out of a pinhole," I say between clenched teeth.

I hadn't thought about the fact that not everyone else knew Pete until we walked in and Chelsea and Hannah's eyes zeroed in on him.

"Oh, shit, he's back," my mom grumbles.

"Jade," I mouth, and she glances around.

"Jade's showing Henry her room. Would you like a drink, Reed?" she asks, purposely not asking Pete.

"I'd love one, thanks, Ms. Clarke." Reed follows my mom.

"Please, call me Diane."

"Thank you, Diane." Reed winks at me and then heads into the kitchen.

"That woman might hire a hitman one day," Pete says and then steps forward into the room, his arm extended. "I'm Pete Keebler."

Hannah shakes his hand. "Hannah Crowley."

"Crowley?"

She smiles. "The one and only."

I'm surprised he doesn't perch a seat right next to her. Everyone knows the Crowley name in the Chicago area, but Pete steps to the side to shake Chelsea's hand.

"The cookie elf?" She shakes his hand briefly and then wipes her hand on her slacks.

"Funny," Pete deadpans.

"I'm glad to be done with those jokes." I laugh, heading into the kitchen. "Do you want something to drink?"

"Just a water," Pete says, and I disappear to find Reed and my mom talking at the kitchen table.

"So, you're not coming back in?" I ask.

He leans back, holding out his hand which I easily accept, and he pulls me to his side.

"Your mom and I have declared this the Pete-free zone."

I shake my head. "You have to get along with him. He's Jade's father."

"I'll always be cordial, but it doesn't mean I have to be in the same room as him." His hand grips my hip and he pulls me into his lap.

We laugh, and my mom is staring over at us with happiness gleaming from her own eyes.

"I'm not sure I'm cool with the PDA while Jade is in the next room," Pete's voice sounds from behind me.

I stay planted on Reed's lap and lock my arms around his neck, planting a kiss on his cheek.

"Oh, yes, because you hiding in a hotel room with your mistress was great for your little girl. It destroyed her parents' marriage." My mom stands and leaves the room without another word.

"You'd think I cheated on *her*." Pete shakes his head, pointing to the fridge. "Water?"

"Oh yeah, sorry, I got distracted."

I can't deny it feels good to see Pete walk on eggshells around my house after I walked on them for years.

"I see." He heads to the fridge. "Your friend Chelsea should try stand-up."

Reed and I share a look to say she's probably nailed him with a few zingers already. With Chelsea, it's any ex, not necessarily her own. She hates them all.

"She is funny," I say.

He grabs a water out of the fridge. "Cute cake. Remember when we baked the turtle one that year."

Reed's muscles stiffen underneath me.

I'm sure Pete's remembering the lovemaking on the kitchen floor covered in flour, but I remember him not coming home until ten that night. Me yelling, him screaming and then fighting until we make out. Pete always forgets the bad.

"The pizza should be here soon." I stand up so when Jade comes out she won't see me on Reed's lap.

Pete sits down across from Reed and there's enough tension in the room you'd think they were mob leaders having a sit-down.

"I gotta know, I mean I know you're rich, but why choose the DA's office? You could be a defense lawyer," Pete asks. "Still trying to act like you're holier-than-thou?"

"I enjoy putting the bad people away." Reed spins his own water bottle on the table.

I busy myself getting the paper plates and napkins out. If they're both going to be a part of our lives, then they have to get along.

"Lucky you're rich, because the job pays shit."

Reed stares blankly at him. "Money doesn't buy everything."

Pete huffs and leans back in his chair. "It's funny that you have the whole golden boy act down pat, but you think it's okay to steal my wife and daughter."

My hand slaps the counter. "I'm not your wife."

"Fine, my ex-wife," Pete counters, but he's still posing the question to Reed.

"I guess I'm not all that good then."

I smile at Reed for keeping his composure.

"What if I was here to get her back?" Pete asks.

I freeze and every muscle in my body tightens.

Reed sits up straighter. "Are you?"

"Maybe." He shrugs.

"Then I'd say you missed your chance. She's with me now."

"Hello, the choice is mine." They each turn their attention to me. "Pete, cut the shit. We're over and if you're jealous over Reed it'll disappear as soon as you're back in L.A. Reed, you know what we have."

He smiles.

"Last warning." I hate that I sound like a mother delivering an ultimatum, but it's the only way to do this. "Get along because it's Jade's birthday and if either one of you ruin her day, you'll be asked to leave."

They each glance at one another and then lean back in their chairs.

How many hours before Pete's on a plane back to L.A.?

Chapter Thirty-Two

"You have got to be kidding me!" Darcie's steps pound on the pavement, her bullhorn clutched tightly in her hands.

The tow truck lowers the car in the roped off area while Reed's positions the various sledgehammers, hammers, gloves, baseball bats and other tools we picked up to do some serious damage to this car.

I might even have to buy a handful of tickets myself. Pete hops on a plane tomorrow and let's just say my patience has worn thin. There's a reason we're divorced.

"Oh, hey, Darcie. Georgia," I say, acknowledging Mean Mom number one and her constant shadow.

"This is your idea of fun?" Darcie asks in a screechy voice.

"Yep."

"The kids can't do it, they could get hurt. Do you want that on your conscious? Maybe your boyfriends can afford the lawsuits, but I know you can't."

She thinks she's going to bully me to breaking down. Not happening. I laugh a little that she still believes Pete,

Reed, and I are in some kind of relationship. What an idiot.

"It's a parents-only event."

"You'll get no one. I'll make sure of it." She stomps away, but she can't do anything about it because Principal Weddle already okay'd it.

Reed walks over to me. "How angry is she?" he asked with a chuckle.

"Pretty pissed off."

"Good."

I step into him, wrapping my arms around his neck and lifting up on my tiptoes to kiss him. We have a little time before the carnival starts. Pete is bringing Jade after she slept over at his parents' last night.

"Let's go grab some coffee?"

He checks out his watch behind my back. "We have an hour."

"Perfect."

We choose to walk the two blocks to the nearest Starbucks since the weather is nice today. His hand swings in mine on the way back and I think of how I could really get used to this.

"Since we have some time before everything starts, we need to discuss something. I was going to wait until tonight, but I can't," he says.

The pit that's been in my belly since the topic of him relocating elsewhere came up, morphs into a crevice.

"You got an offer?" I ask, hoping I'm wrong. It's not that I don't want him to succeed in his career, but we need more time to see what this is before we make big decisions about our future together.

He nods toward the park a block away from the school and leads me over to a bench where we sit.

"Tell me, Reed."

He sets our coffees down behind him on the bench, both of his hands taking mine in his. "I got an offer."

My eyes burn, and my nose crinkles and that crevice turns into a gorge. "Of course you did."

"It's in New York," he says.

"City?" I clarify although I already know. Of course, he could be the DA in New York City. How could I ever compete with that?

"Take it," I tell him. I have to force the words out of my mouth. I know what it's like to put your dreams on hold for a relationship and I can't ask him to do that for me.

"Will you come?" he asks, with hope in his eyes.

"So, you're going for sure? You've already made the decision?" My heart shatters, cracks and then splits into two.

"I don't know. It's a huge opportunity that will probably never come again. But this"—he motions between us —"I know is the real thing."

I stand, and his hands drop to his lap. "You don't know that. We've haven't been together that long."

He stands, too, and wraps his arms around me, his stubble pricking my cheeks. I lean in to his security. "Time isn't an indicator of love."

I rest my hands on his chest. It feels so safe in his arms, but the urge not to repeat past mistakes shouts its mantra in my head.

Protect yourself. Look out for yourself. You can do it on your own.

"Reed, I just got here and besides, I have my mom, Jade, and my schooling to consider. I gave up everything I was working toward for a man before and look where I ended up."

He steps back, and my hands fall between us.

"I'm not Pete." His eyes fill with an anger I've never seen from him before.

"I know, but you've got to see where I'm coming from."

He steps forward again, taking my hands in his. "I know you're scared. I know you've been hurt, but I'm not him. I'll take care of you and Jade and your mom can come with us."

I shake my head. "She won't want to leave everybody and everything here. She's spent a lifetime here. Otherwise, she would have just moved to L.A. in the first place."

"Okay. Let's just leave it on the table. They don't need an answer until Wednesday. Just think about it." Hope shines brightly in his eyes now and I have to glance away.

I don't want to tell him, but no matter what, nothing will change. It's either a long-distance relationship—which the thought of makes me want to throw up because I'll never see him—or nothing. And a long-distance relationship would be even more difficult given the fact that my daughter is already having one of those with her father.

He wraps me in his arms and I close my eyes wondering how much longer I'll have him here with me.

"Let's get this carnival over with and we can discuss it more tonight when you're at my house."

I nod. I know it wasn't Reed's intention to put a dark cloud over today, but his news as wonderful as it is for him, makes me want to put on my pajamas, play sappy eighties love songs and cry over a tub of ice cream.

Because sooner or later, he'll have to make a decision. And if he makes the right one, it means leaving me behind.

***

"YOU HAVE every divorcee buying the tickets, so they can imagine it's their ex's car?" Pete comes up with Jade on his shoulders.

"Maybe you have aggression you'd like to get out," I say, taking the tickets from a mom and handing her some protective eyewear. I set the clock for five minutes once she picks up her object of choice.

"Not on a car." He glances at Reed, who's talking to Helen.

"Give it a rest."

"I heard a little rumor." Pete lowers Jade off his shoulders and she runs over to Henry.

I follow her progress and Reed signals if it's okay for Helen to take Jade and Henry inside the school. I nod.

"Don't." I hold my hand up, but Pete doesn't listen, as per usual.

"Your boy is going to New York, huh?"

I shake my head, ignoring him, eyeing the clock and watching the woman go to town on the hood of the car with a hammer.

"You going to follow? Because you'll need my permission to take Jade even farther away from me." He crosses his arms with a smug look on his face.

"It's none of your business."

"That's where you're wrong, Vic, Jade is my business. Where you go, Jade goes."

He's right. We both know it. I would need his permission to move Jade to New York. Tears well up in my eyes as the emotions I've been suppressing all afternoon rise to the surface, hitting me like a hurricane-force wind.

"Oh my God, just let it go right now! I will tell you if anything changes."

"Hey." Reed comes to my side, quickly appraising the situation—me about to break down in tears and Pete's smug face. "Can't you just give it a fucking rest?" he says to Pete. "You had your chance. You treated her like shit. She divorced you two years ago."

They both take a step closer to one another.

"You're going to have her uproot her entire life, so you can say you won?" Pete grinds out.

"What are you even talking about?" Reed asks, looking at him like he's an idiot.

They're chest to chest and I wiggle my hands in, trying to push on both of their chests to separate them. A crowd is forming around the perimeter of our little group.

"You're pissed because you always wanted to compete with me. I got the girl, I got the family, and I make a shit-ton more money than you." Pete laughs like Reed's a joke.

"What are you talking about?" I ask Pete as I push on his chest.

"You think I'm playing a game?" Reed asks, cold fury in his voice.

"I think you threw yourself at her because you want to be able to hold it over me. Guess what? It worked. I want her back."

The buzzer goes off and the woman comes over with a huge smile on her face and sweat beading down her forehead, handing me back the eyewear protection.

"Next," I call out to keep things going, but Pete's words ring in my ear. He wants me back?

No one comes up to take a turn because they're all enthralled in Reed and Pete's argument.

"I told you, three is a crowd," one woman says to another and they laugh.

I roll my eyes.

"We were always in competition. Who got a better grade? That night, I stole Vic out from under your nose and you've never forgotten it." Pete crosses his arms, a smug look on his face like he's won the argument.

"I saw her first," Reed fires back. "You may have spent the better part of a decade with her, but she was always mine. And you know it."

The buzzer drops from my hands and they both look over at me.

"What?" I ask quietly.

Reed steps toward me, reaching out but I back step until I hit the metal barrier.

"No." I shake my head, putting the eyewear in my hand on my face. "I'm some sort of prize in a sick game between you two?"

"No. That's not it." Reed fights for me to listen to him, but Pete stays in place, happy with what he's accomplished.

I hit the timer, grab the baseball bat and a can of spray paint and push past the barrier toward the car.

Jumping on the roof, I swing the baseball bat down on the windshield, hitting it over and over again until it shatters. For the next five minutes, I stomp, hit, pound and generally go ballistic on the scrap of metal. My shitty marriage to Pete *wham*, Reed only being with me to get back at Pete *wham*, my feelings for Reed *wham*, the fact he's leaving me *wham*...all the tension and emotion that's been whirling around inside of me unleashes.

The buzzer goes off and I wipe the sweat from my brow before I pull out the can of spray paint. In big pink letters on the hood, I spell out what must come first. ME.

I drop the bat on the pavement and walk past Reed without a word. Everyone else is standing around like I'm Negan from *The Walking Dead*.

Haven't they ever seen a woman let off a little steam before?

Chapter Thirty-Three

I'm not even to the street before Reed's hand is clasping my arm.

"Hold up. Let me explain."

I stop and turn, showing him my tear-stricken cheeks. There's no more hiding how much this man means to me. How much what was said hurt me.

"Come here." His arms tighten around me and I bury my head in his chest. "He's making it sound bad, but it's not. I promise."

I look up at him, waiting for an explanation.

"Come." He leads me to that same park again, sitting me on a swing this time. "He's right on one thing. I saw you first. That night you met Pete, I was there."

I try to remember him being there, but I was enamored with Pete immediately and I was in college and drinking, so the details are fuzzy.

He sits down in the swing next to me. His large body and the small swing gives him the illusion of a giant.

"I pointed you out, but you were having so much fun with your friends I didn't want to be that douche who approached you and took you away from them. My eyes were on you the entire night. The more attention I drew to you, the more Pete was intrigued. I went to the bathroom and by the time I came back, you were talking to him and laughing at something he said. I paid my share of the tab to my other buddies and left."

"Why didn't you say any of this before?"

He looks at his feet digging a hole into the wood chips. "How does it sound?"

"Sounds like you had a reason to chase me."

He raises his eyebrows. "That's not why I'm dating you."

A small smile creases my lips. "I know." I do. Deep down I know Reed and he wouldn't use someone to seek revenge on Pete.

"You do?" The chains creek as he turns the swing so he's facing my direction. "Have I always been attracted you? Yes. Even when I shouldn't have been? Yes. I like to think fate interceded and gave us a second chance. If I'd barged my way in there that night, Jade might never have been and she's the true light in your eyes. As much as I was pissed at Pete and hated him asking me to stand up there to watch you marry him, it wasn't for naught. It was for Jade. I'd never wish things were different."

I lean forward and place my hands on his cheeks and plant a kiss on his lips. "You truly are a prince."

"I only want to be your prince."

I sit back, twisting the swing.

"Vic?"

I have to do what's right. "You have to go to New York."

He shakes his head and I nod mine.

"You do. You have to do it for yourself. You're right, I have Jade. Reed, you're something out of a fairy tale. As selfishly as I want to keep you in Chicago with me or pack up Jade and move to New York...I can't. I know you're not Pete, I do. But I can't give up on myself. This time around I have to pick *me*. I choose me."

He exhales a long, ragged breath.

"I'll support you. We'll do long distance until your graduate. We'll spend the summer getting Jade acquainted. You can search for a job. It won't be like it was with Pete. I'm your biggest supporter. You can have your independence *and* me. I promise."

Tears burn in the corner of my eyes and I do my best to keep the tears from falling. "I can't."

He stops fighting for a moment though I know the lawyer in him is thinking up his next argument and it's only a matter of time. He wants to win this case and I wish he could, too, but he needs to go to New York and I need to stay here. There's no way around it.

"We could do long distance. I can fly back every weekend," he says, desperation in his voice.

"That's not a relationship, you know that. Even when you do come back, I'll have Jade with me every weekend."

"Why are you fighting this?" he stands up, pacing in front of me, threading his hands through his hair.

"I told you, I need to choose myself and you should do the same."

He falls to his knees in front of me, wood chips flying, his hands resting on my thighs. "I've fallen in love with you, Victoria. Can't you see that? I love you and I want you in my life."

My hand runs down his cheek. "You want me in your life on your terms."

His head drops to my lap and my fingers thread through his hair one more time, attempting to memorize the sensation since it may be the last time I get to do this. He stands up again without warning, the adoring expression he usually bears while around me gone. "I'm constantly being punished because of him."

"That's not it."

"It is. You can't open up and let happiness in, even when it's the real thing because of everything he put you through." He's back to pacing, with each step taken farther from me.

"I can't go to New York and leave my entire life behind." My eyes burn as the tears finally escape and roll like a river down my face.

"That's just an excuse. New York is your way of pushing me away again. Fine"—his hands fly up in the air —"you win. I fold." His expression slices me open, flays me and opens all my wounds for his inspection. "Bye, Victoria."

His back hunches as he walks away in the direction of where his car is parked. I watch him climb in and drive off. He doesn't squeal his tires, or stick up his middle finger, but just as easily as he walked back into my life, he leaves it yet again.

Chapter Thirty-Four

The next day, I'm in a taxi with Pete and Jade. Jade wanted to spend as much time with her dad as possible, so I agreed that we'd go with him to the airport. Ok, so it was partly so I could make sure he actually got on the plane.

"I'm going to miss you, Daddy." Jade nuzzles into her dad.

He kisses her head. "I'm going to miss you too, but I'll be back soon. Promise." His eyes glance over her head to me. "Maybe you can come out this summer."

"And play at the beach?"

"Yeah." He raises his eyebrows.

I look out the window not answering him. He'll fight me if he really wants her, but as soon as he's back in his office, his attention will be consumed, so there's a chance it won't happen anyway.

The taxi pulls up to the curb at the airport and we all climb out, Pete paying.

"This is where we say goodbye, Bug." My hands slide down her long hair, fisting it in a ponytail and releasing it.

"Can't we go in with him?" she whines.

"They won't let us past security."

She pouts. Pete grabs his bag out of the trunk and sets it on the curb, then crouches down with his arms out. "I'll miss you, Bug," he says, holding her tight.

I have no idea how he does it. How he's able to leave her for months at a time. Our situation sucks, but how can he not have a more active role?

His eyes close and then open. "Be good for Mommy," he says, his voice quivering.

"I will." He stands up and Jade comes to my side.

"Get your hair done or something," he says to me, a crack of a smirk on his face. He's testing the waters.

"Use that gym membership," I say back.

We hug, patting each other's backs and keeping at least five inches between our lower regions. It makes Jade happy to see us gracious to one another.

"I'm sorry," he whispers.

Pulling back, I nod, tears pooling in my eyes. It's the second time he's apologized since everything went down. Not only for arguing with Reed, but for saying he still wanted me. Apparently two minutes after it flew out of his mouth he realized how ridiculous that was. So, he's not a complete idiot.

Jade and I watch Pete go through the sliding doors, one last wave in our direction before the crowd swallows him up from sight.

Jade hugs my leg, tears free falling down her cheeks.

"Oh, Bug," I say, the tears I was holding back, finding their release.

As we get back in the taxi, we each cry for two very different men who mean the world to us.

THE NEXT MONDAY, my heart is my throat until I drop off Jade and see Ned walking Henry up to the door.

Darcie and Georgia side-eye me but don't approach. It doesn't escape me that in their minds I went from two men to none. Not that what they think of me is high on my list of things to get me down.

I hug Jade, tighter than I usually do and head toward the train. By the time I get to work, I'm ten minutes late because of a train delay.

"You're late," Chelsea says, placing a coffee on my desk with a muffin.

I take off my coat, hanging it up and taking my bags to my desk.

"You didn't have to." I motion to the coffee and muffin.

"You're my girl and I know you're hurting. Carbs make people happy." She smiles sitting down in front of my desk. "I hate to ask, but the steak…"

"Packing his stuff for New York is my guess."

She nods, biting her lip. "Do you not want to talk about it?"

I shake my head and pray I don't cry at my desk.

"Okay." She stands and disappears into her office.

I type in my password and a lone tear slips because I stupidly put hottiereed as my password. I lift my notepad to write down the messages from the weekend to see a folded-up Post-it note stuck to my desk.

You're a very dirty girl, but I'll totally lick you clean.
~ R

My head falls to the desk with a thump. He must've left it there the last time he was in here, but I've only just noticed.

"What's this?" the door opens and Hannah waltzes toward my desk, concern in her dark eyes. "Are you sick?"

"She's heartbroken," Chelsea answers from her office.

"Why? What happened?" Hannah sits down in the chair in front of me.

"I'm a horrible person." I rub my forehead.

She leans forward. "No, you're not. Talk to me."

"Reed got offered the DA position in New York City, he asked her to go, she declined. Hence the defeated head on the desk position." Chelsea joins Hannah by sitting in the chair next to her. "I brought her a muffin. I'll totally fill in until he's out of your system."

I sit up, grab a Kleenex and pat under my eyes. "What if I never get him out of my system?"

"You will." She reaches forward and pats my hand. "Men are like that killer pair of heels in the shop window. They look so good, but you just know in the end, they're going to hurt like a bitch."

"That's helpful, thank you." Hannah looks at Chelsea with a what-the-fuck expression.

"She just needs to find another pair. How could he think you'd just drop your life and follow him?" Chelsea asks.

Hannah's questioning gaze lands on mine. "Did he?"

I nod.

"What are you thinking right now?" she asks.

"That I want to run down to his work and tell him I'll follow him to Africa if he wants me to."

She laughs. "Thought so." She stands. "My advice is to give it some time."

My heart splinters thinking about more time away from him. I know it was the right thing to do for everyone involved, but that doesn't make it hurt any less.

"You're taking the rest of the day off." Hannah walks to the coat rack, holding out my jacket for me.

"No, Hannah, I can work."

She shakes her head. "Nope. You're going home."

I stand, my shoulders slumped as I slide my arms into my coat and Chelsea hands me my bags. They each pull me into a big hug. "You'll get through this," Hannah whispers.

"He wasn't that hot," Chelsea offers, and we all laugh a little because we know Reed actually was *that hot.*

"Now, you go." Hannah opens the door and motions for me to leave.

I walk out, and when I reach the sidewalk, my mind wanders, wondering if Reed is in that building down the street. Is he packing a brown box to take with him? What could have been between us if the timing was right?

I shake my head. Weeks from now he'll be gone, and I won't have to worry about running into him. That should help me. Yeah, right.

Chapter Thirty-Five

wo weeks later…

TO SAY I'm finding my footing again would be a complete lie. I go through the routine of my life. I drop Jade off, I go to work, I attend school, I take care of what I need to. None of it with a zest for life. None of it with a smile.

"Mommy," Jade says interrupting my internal thoughts. She skips along the sidewalk, more chipper than usual for a Monday morning.

"Yeah?"

"Henry said Reed went to New York City?"

Jade hasn't asked me much about Reed and I see she's been getting a lot of her information from Henry.

"Yeah."

"When's he coming back? He's been gone for a long time." She doesn't look at me and I know she doesn't understand what's going on. She thinks he went for a vacation, not to live there permanently.

"I don't know, Bug. He moved there for a job. He lives there now."

Her feet halt on the cement and she twirls around, her hands landing on her hips. "What?"

"He got offered a job there, so he moved."

"Why would he do that?"

I tighten her ponytail, easing her forward with my hand on her back. "You'll understand when you're older."

"Why would he leave you?"

Talk about a question that's like throwing a boulder at me, but in the weeks since Reed left, I've learned to compartmentalize. "He didn't leave me."

I pushed him to leave.

"It was a really great opportunity," I add.

Her hand weasels into mine and she leans into me. "I'm sorry, Mommy."

I squeeze her hand. "Thanks, Bug."

I smile down at her and Reed's words come back to me. She truly is my light. But he was a close second.

We break the tree line and even though he hasn't dropped Henry off in three Mondays, my throat still tightens on the ridiculous chance Abe will pull up to the curb and Reed will walk Henry up to the school.

Jade circles around me, waving and saying hello to friends.

"Bug, you gotta go to school."

She continues circling. Darcie and Georgia have moved on to someone else to pick on now. Most of the drop-off and pickup parents now ignore my existence which is fine by me.

"In a second. I'm waiting for Henry." She continues circling me, her hands running along my shirt as she rounds each side of me.

I glance at my phone. "It's getting late, maybe he's not coming."

"He's coming," she singsongs, not stopping.

"One minute, Jade then you have to go into school."

"He'll be here." She skips around me.

I roll my eyes, waiting for the minute to be up.

"Jade doesn't want to go to school today?" Darcie asks, and I glance her way.

"You know Mondays." I'm polite instead of telling her to piss off and mind her own business which is what I really want to do.

"I knew it," Jade murmurs.

I turn, and the familiar sight of Abe's car unleashes the butterflies in my stomach.

Henry runs out, heading right toward Jade and my breath is stuck in my throat waiting to see who else is in the backseat.

"Ready, Jade?" Henry asks.

Jade hugs my legs. "Bye, Mom."

"Bye, Bug." I pat her back, my attention solely focused on the car.

The back door opens on the street side. A few cars passing by honk and then *he* circles around—a silver tie clip gripped between his teeth as he ties his tie. Just like the first time I saw him again, his blue suit is pressed and tailored to his body, his hair gelled to messy perfection. I refuse to take my eyes off him in case I really have lost it and my imagination has conjured him up.

He holds up his finger in my direction, walking past me and up the stairs to the school. "Henry," he says, holding his fist out.

They fist bump and then he descends the steps, his eyes never leaving mine. I'm still in a state of shock as he comes to stand in front of me.

"Ready?" He holds his hand out.

"For?"

"The rest of your life."

I smile, fitting my hand in his. He pulls me into his chest and we couldn't get closer if we tried.

"I'm sorry," he murmurs. Pulling back, he holds my head in his hands.

"I'm sorry, too. I love you, Reed. I should have never made you choose. We can do long distance. We'll figure it out."

He shakes his head. "No, you were right about that. If we're going to give this a chance, we can't be seven-hundred miles away from one another."

"Then what are we going to do?" I ask and press my lips together, waiting for his answer.

"When I first saw you again, my heart skipped a beat. I never believed in that shit. I mean I knew I'd eventually fall in love, but for your body to have a physical reaction? That stuffs for fairy tales and TV. With you though, I've never been surer of anything. You were meant for me." He tucks my hair behind my ear and leans in close. "Victoria Clarke, I choose *you*. I'm not taking the job in New York."

His lips fall to mine and I close my eyes basking in all the love and adoration of his kiss. We break apart and I glance at the faces around us. Jade's giggling at the top of the stairs, her hand over her mouth and she smiles at me before heading into the building.

"Are you sure?" I whisper.

"One hundred percent positive."

He holds his hand out for me and I take it. And I'll never let it go again.

Epilogue

One month later...

"Ready?" Reed walks into the office as I finish typing my email.

"Almost," I say.

He sits down in front of my desk looking gorgeous in a navy blue suit. He props one foot up and rests it on his knee.

"Did you win?" I ask.

I would watch Reed in court every day if I could, but after the last case, I've kept my distance. He's absurdly paranoid and it's hard for him if I'm there.

"I did." A huge smile crosses his face.

"I'll have to make sure to give you a congratulatory kiss."

"Just a kiss?" He sits up, grabs a Post-it note and a pen.

"Is that for me?" I ask, eyeing the note in his hand. With my hand on the mouse, I close out everything and log off.

"It's not always about you." He winks, scribbling something in his lawyer handwriting which reminds me of a doctor's.

"I'll be right back." I pretend to say goodbye to Chelsea, so he has an opportunity to hide the note for me to find on Monday.

"Hurry. Abe's waiting."

"Only you can get an Uber to act like your own personal chauffeur." Hannah comes out of her office, leaning her shoulder on the doorframe with a manila folder in her hand.

"Hi, Hannah," he says.

"Where are you taking our girl tonight?" she asks.

The two talk and I peek my head into Chelsea's office.

"I'm leaving."

"Thanks for the update, I'll be sure to call NBC and let them know," she jokes, standing and following me out. "Reed 'The Steak' Warner, how the hell are you?" She acts like she didn't just see him yesterday.

I've been granted with a pickup and a drop-off every day for a month. I can't complain. There's something about almost losing something that makes you hold it tighter.

"Chelsea," he says and smiles, tossing the pen into my holder and standing to his feet.

"Would you guys mind dropping this off at the tax attorney's office? His office isn't too far." Hannah holds out the envelope and I snatch it up.

"Sure." Then I look to Reed. "We have time, right?"

He nods.

The envelope is snatched out of my hands. "I'll do it. You two go." She shoos me with her hand.

"Thanks, Chels."

"I'm going that way anyway. I'm on a search for penis paraphernalia and I might just grab myself one of those

Unicorn Cock vibrators. My cousin's bachelorette party is coming up."

She rolls her eyes like having to go into a sex store is such an inconvenience for her would upset her. Having to go into a sex store. This is Chelsea we're talking about.

"Want to join me?" she asks Hannah.

"Me and you in a sex shop?" Hannah shoots her an expression that says never. "I'd rather not get arrested tonight."

"Fine. Leave it to me to be the curator of cock on my own then." Chelsea shrugs like she doesn't really care, which she probably doesn't.

"Okay, have a great weekend, girls." I wave goodbye and Reed pats my lower back to get me going.

Once we're down on the sidewalk, I spot Abe leaning against his car, reading a book while he waits.

"The Realtor is meeting us there?" I ask.

"Yeah."

Reed has decided he doesn't want to live downtown anymore, so he's house hunting closer to us. He says he's found one he really likes and wants my opinion.

"Hey, Abe." I smile and wave at him.

"Victoria," he says, rounding the car to get back in.

Reed opens the door and I slide inside. Reed's hand plays with mine as we pull away from the curb.

"I firmed up some plans last night with Pete."

"Yeah?" he asks.

"I'm going to fly out there with Jade to drop her off and then fly back to pick her up. She'll stay for a month this summer." I take in a deep breath. It's going to be horrible, but she deserves to spend some time with her dad and he promises he won't work the whole time.

"A month?" he asks.

"Well, he's going to hire a nanny and take two of the weeks as vacation."

Reed nods. "Nice of you."

"I was wondering though, would you want to come with us and maybe if it's okay with Ned and Helen, Henry could come when we go to pick her up? We could stay—"

"I'll go both ways. You're going to need me after the drop-off." He smiles, his fingers tightening in mine. He knows me well.

"Thank you."

"You're welcome." He smiles. "I'm pretty sure since I'm his guardian if anything should happen, Ned and Helen will be fine with us taking Henry."

I slide closer, laying my head on his shoulder. My eyes close briefly from the late nights studying for exams. Three more weeks until I graduate, and I can cross off one thing off my list.

"We're here," Reed whispers in my ear.

"Sorry," I mumble, lifting my head to see my mom's house. "What are we doing here?"

Reed says nothing and steps out, holding his hand out for me to take. "Have a good weekend, Abe. See you Monday."

"Bye, guys." He waves and once Reed shuts the door, he pulls away.

"So…I wasn't exactly telling the truth when I said we were going to look at a house I was interested in. And I hope you're not mad, but…" He takes my hands in his. "I bought the house next door to your mom's. My plan is to renovate it, make it large enough to fit all of us. You don't have to move in with me, but I want to be close to you."

He guides me up the walkway, pulls out a key and inserts it in the lock.

"This is not me asking you to choose. This is me wanting to be as close to you as possible. I'd love for you and Jade and your mom to move in here. Or just you and Jade and she can stay next door on her own as long as she's able. I knew you'd want to be by your mom, so…" He trails off, opening the door and waiting for me to take the lead.

The thing about Chicago housing is that next to one bungalow is a three-story flat and next to that is a renovated single family. It's a hodgepodge of housing types. Reed's bought the single-family home that needs some updating, but nothing major.

"It's beautiful." The light that streams in through the front windows highlights the hardwood floors and moldings. The place has good energy and being close to my mom makes it perfect. We can get out from under her and she can maintain her independence. But we can still help out around the house and with meals since we're so close.

I walk farther into the house to take it all in.

"The kitchen needs some work, but I have some ideas."

Warmth blooms in my chest the more I see, but Reed takes my silence the wrong way.

"I don't want to pressure you, Vic. If you completely hate the idea, I can renovate it and turn it for a profit."

I shake my head. "I'm not feeling pressured." Turning back around to him, tears fill the corners of my eyes, but they aren't the sad kind this time. "It's perfect."

"I'm so happy you think so." He erases the distance between us and lifts me into his arms. "What does that mean exactly?" A nervous chuckle escapes his lips.

"It means," I close my eyes for a moment and then let them slowly open to the man who has stolen my heart and soul. "We're moving in together."

His arms tighten, and he swings me around. "Thank

you," he mumbles and I'm not sure if he's talking to me or fate itself.

My phone rings and Reed lets me go to grab it out of my purse in case it's the school or my mom.

He ventures down the hall while I press accept on Chelsea's call.

"What's up, Chelsea?" I ask. "Did you know he bought the house next to my mom?" I say, unable to contain my excitement.

"Did he? I didn't know." Her voice is flat and doesn't hold any of the humor I'm used to.

"What's wrong?" I ask.

Reed comes back into the room, his eyebrows furrowed wondering what he's missing. He wraps his arms around my stomach from behind, kissing my neck.

"I saw the tax attorney."

"Is he hot? You've been into good guys lately and what tax attorney isn't a good guy, right?" I giggle when Reed nips at my neck.

"Hey now," he whispers.

"He's not a good guy, Vic." She sounds near hysteria as she sucks air in and out of her lungs. "He's my ex-husband!" she screams.

Oh, shit.

The End

Cockamamie Unicorn Ramblings

The Charity Case Series was born from an idea for a book Elisabeth (Piper) had before we decided to form Piper Rayne. It was going to be called Divorcee Dating (did you catch the term in the book?) and she'd written the blurb and everything.

So, in order to turn her idea of one book into three, we had to find two more women. After writing The Manny and introducing you to Hannah Crowley, we knew she was born from Elisabeth's idea and her book, Happy Hour (Book #3) would be the story Elisabeth had in mind originally. Not that it was Happy Hour at the time, we just knew she was our woman to take on the task.

The only thing we did want was three women who had been introduced in previous books to get their own. It's easy to write snarky and quick witted secondary characters. We're not in their heads. They can say a funny line and disappear into the darkness. Add on the fact, we needed them to be divorced. It was tricky to figure out who the other two women would be.

Let's talk Victoria, since Manic Monday is her book.

You'll have to wait for Chelsea until Afternoon Delight. Sorry, but we can't give you all the intel.

When Victoria was written in The Manny originally, you were given a short glimpse of her character as Jagger's assistant. We didn't know then that she would get her own book. The fact that she had a kid was just kind of thrown in there when Payne spilled his drink on her desk. Actually, the fact she was hiding having a kid was supposed to say more about Jagger than it was about Victoria.

By Jagger's book, Chore Play, we thought Victoria might get her own book at some point. Her and Jagger sparring was just so fun to write. I think we didn't want to say good-bye. We added an ex-husband and the decided the kid would be a seven-year-old daughter. All we had to do was get her to relocate from L.A. to Chicago. And that's when we decided that she'd only do that if it were to help out someone she loved dearly.

Some of you are probably saying, yeah, yeah, we like Victoria, but give us the skinny on Reed.

Reed sure is dreamy, right? In our plotting, we knew we wanted the guys in Charity Case to be different than others we've written. We wanted to do another series with only the heroines POV (sorry dual POV lovers, but we'll be writing some extra scenes in Reed's POV as bonus material). We agreed he needed to be a good guy—not a player or a bad boy. Someone who would pull Victoria out of her self-imposed dating hibernation and make her realize how beautiful and strong she is.

Fun fact on how fast our stories can change. Reed was just going to be an attorney, but he was never going to be their best man until we were writing the blurb and realized what's the conflict again? Since we'd never done an ex best friend storyline before it was a winner.

That's about all the 411 on Manic Monday.

. . .

OUR USUAL DREAM team plus a few new additions who need a round of applause.

Letitia from **RBA** Designs for the amazing covers. From the first Manic Monday she sent, we were in love. This series is actually Piper's favorite of all of ours. So far anyway! ;)

Ellie from Love N Books for line editing. Thank you for dealing with our usual question, "we'll have it next week, how fast can you turn it around?"

Shawna from Behind the Writer for her eagle eye proofreading skills and making sure everything flows.

Sarah Ferguson and Social Butterfly PR for their organization, patience and help on not only Charity Case Series but on a daily basis.

All the bloggers who carve out time to read and review our books. For the teasers you make, the word you spread, the messages you sent. It only spurs our excitement for the next book.

Our first readers of a really shitty, unedited copy—Heather, Angela and newbie, Tina.

This is the first time we reached out to some of our readers for help. Neither one us knew much about Multiple Sclerosis and we didn't want to write something we knew nothing about. Thank you to Tina Morgan, Melissa Godwin Lane, Anna Fay and Heather Fueger. We are sorry that this disease has touched your life in either yourself being diagnosed or a close friend or family member. Your information was invaluable. Though it wasn't the basis of the story itself, we did want to make sure we portrayed Victoria's mother accurately.

All our early ARC readers, first for wanting to read our stuff early and for posting their reviews.

And of course, all our unicorns. <3 Your excitement and enthusiasm for our characters keep our inspiration on overdrive. We are thankful each day to have every one of you Unicorns in our corner.

Next up is Chelsea! It's no surprise that according to the poll in our Unicorn Facebook group that Lennon and Jasper have to make an appearance. Now to weave that in…huh? We cannot wait for you to get Chelsea's book because Dean might be the complete opposite of Reed except for the fact, he's going to win her over whether she believes him or not.

XO,
Piper & Rayne

BTW – There was just something about Pete. Yeah, he wasn't the best husband the first time around, but we think there's something endearing about him. Should we straighten him out and make him deserving of his own book? We kinda want to write one…

About Piper & Rayne

Piper Rayne is a USA Today Bestselling Author duo who write "heartwarming humor with a side of sizzle" about families, whether that be blood or found. They both have e-readers full of one-clickable books, they're married to husbands who drive them to drink, and they're both chauffeurs to their kids. Most of all, they love hot heroes and quirky heroines who make them laugh, and they hope you do, too!

My Almost Ex

My Vegas Groom

The Greene Family Summer Bash

My Sister's Flirty Friend

My Unexpected Surprise

My Famous Frenemy

The Greene Family Vacation

My Scorned Best Friend

My Fake Fiancé

My Brother's Forbidden Friend

Hockey Hotties

My Lucky #13

The Trouble with #9

Faking it with #41

Sneaking around with #34

Second Shot with #76

Offside with #55

Kingsmen Football Stars

You had your chance, Lee Burrows

You can't kiss the Nanny, Brady Banks

Over my Brother's Dead Body, Chase Andrews

The Baileys

Lessons from a One-Night Stand

Advice from a Jilted Bride

Birth of a Baby Daddy

Operation Bailey Wedding (Novella)

Falling for My Brother's Best Friend

Demise of a Self-Centered Playboy

Confessions of a Naughty Nanny

Operation Bailey Babies (Novella)

Secrets of the World's Worst Matchmaker

Winning My Best Friend's Girl

Rules for Dating your Ex

Operation Bailey Birthday (Novella)

The Modern Love World

Charmed by the Bartender

Hooked by the Boxer

Mad about the Banker

The Single Dad's Club

Real Deal

Dirty Talker

Sexy Beast

Hollywood Hearts

Mister Mom

Animal Attraction

Domestic Bliss

Bedroom Games

Cold as Ice

On Thin Ice

Break the Ice

Box Set